RUNNING WITH WOLVES

CYNTHIA COOKE

Published in Great Britain 2014
by Mills & Boon, an imprint of Harlequin (UK) Limited,
Eton House, 18-24 Paradise Road, Richmond, Surrey, TW9 1SR

© 2014 Cynthia D. Cooke

ISBN: 978 0 263 91387 3

89-0314

Harlequin (UK) Limited's policy is to use papers that are natural, renewable and recyclable products and made from wood grown in sustainable forests. The logging and manufacturing processes conform to the legal environmental regulations of the country of origin.

Printed and bound in Spain
by Blackprint CPI, Barcelona

Many years ago, **Cynthia Cooke** lived a quiet, idyllic life caring for her beautiful eighteen-month-old daughter. Then peace gave way to chaos with the birth of her boy/girl twins. She kept her sanity by reading romance novels and dreaming of someday writing one. With the help of Romance Writers of America and wonderfully supportive friends, she fulfilled her dreams. Now, many moons later, Cynthia is an award-winning author who has published books with Mills & Boon and Steeple Hill Books.

This book is dedicated to my good friend
and critique partner, Kelly Keaton!

Chapter 1

Shay Mallory felt the sensation of being watched as she walked down her long driveway, her tennis shoes crunching on the sparse gravel. Late morning fog hovered in the branches of the tall redwoods forming a canopy above her. She breathed deep the briny scent of ocean air and willed herself to relax. Not an easy task.

A twig snapped behind her. Tensing, she peered over her shoulder at the deep shadows lengthened by the soaring trees, but saw no one. She was being jumpy. There was no one there. Nothing to be afraid of, and yet she was. Fear clung to her back, digging its long sharp claws into her shoulders, a constant reminder of its needling presence.

She'd spent her whole life jumping at imaginary threats, constantly moving until one town blurred into the next. But her paranoid father had been dead a long time now. For years, there had been just her and Grams in these woods, and no reason to be afraid. No reason to jump.

A whimpering sounded behind her. Smiling, she stopped and turned.

"Hey, Buddy." She squatted next to the large husky that had been shadowing her and rubbed the thick brown fur on his cheeks. He looked more like a wolf than a dog and had been her only companion since Grams died last year. If it weren't for him, she'd be completely alone. She brushed off the thought and the sense of deep sadness that came with it. Until she figured out what was going on with her, spending less time around people would be better anyway.

Buddy sat and she patted his head. "You can't come with me, Buddy. You know that. You scare people."

The dog whined and, lying down, dropped its head onto its outstretched paws, looking absolutely adorable. "I know. They're idiots. Stay here. I'll be right back. Promise." She stood and, with a lighter step and a pat to her pocket to make sure she had her iPod, she hurried down the road.

She knew she should move closer to the city and try to find a job in a design firm. Home-based graphic design businesses could be tough to get off the ground since it seemed as if everyone and their brother could design a website these days. But there weren't too many places she would be able to live with Buddy. He needed room to run, to stretch his legs, to be free where some gun-happy yahoo wouldn't mistake him for a wolf and shoot him. She'd find a way to make the money to fix up the old house and stay right where she was.

In her home.

As Shay considered her options, she crossed Highway 1, and headed toward picturesque Main Street. Thank goodness, with the onset of school and the cooler weather, most of the summer tourists were gone and she encountered no one on her way. She passed through an alley between two buildings and walked into the hardware store.

"Good morning, Shay," Mr. Henderson said from behind the counter. "You know, it's not sunny out."

Shay smiled and took off the dark shades she never went without these days. She couldn't take the chance. Without them she'd be distracted and sometimes scared by the colors, but Mr. Henderson was okay. She already knew what his colors were, yellow and blue and happy.

She took a deep breath and looked around her. Luckily no one else was in the store. "I need another tube of Spackle."

"More? What are you doing up there?" Astonishment raised his voice, and his grayish-green eyes bulged a little under salt-and-pepper brows.

"Grams's place must be on a fault line. Cracks keep forming in the walls, especially on the east side of the house."

He crinkled his already heavily lined forehead, creating fissures as deep as the ones in her walls. "You might want to get someone out there to look at the foundation."

"I will," she said to appease him. And she would as soon as she got the money, which wouldn't be anytime soon. "Thanks, Mr. Henderson." She took the Spackle and headed toward the door.

"Let me know if you need any help out there, okay?" Concern softened his voice.

She smiled, and wished not for the first time that Grams could have seen how much he'd cared for her, that they could have spent her last few years together. No one should live their life alone like Grams had.

Shay waved, slid the glasses back on and placed her iPod's earbuds in her ears as she left the shop and hurried down the street to Annie's Fresh Farm Grocery Store. Like so many stores in the village, the white clapboard two-story was adorned with flowers and antiques that made the building look charming instead of old and run-down. Annie's was a little overpriced, but it was better than driving to the large chain store down the highway. Besides, how much did one girl and her dog need?

Shay picked up a dozen fresh organic brown eggs and placed them in her basket, then perused the spinach and tomatoes before adding them to the eggs. As she picked up an avocado and gave it a gentle squeeze, the small hairs on her nape prickled—the telltale sensation that someone was watching her again.

Without making it obvious, she glanced around her, holding her breath and hoping she was wrong. For the past couple of weeks, she'd barely been able to leave the house without running into some kind of problem. Not just the uncomfortable sensation of someone's attention, which usually meant trouble, but suddenly people glowed. Everyone was surrounded by colors, some bright, some dull, some black. Black was the color she was afraid of the most. But the worst part was the noise. People's brains hummed and if a person was excited enough, their thoughts would burst right through the hum.

Shay *really* didn't want to know what people were thinking.

Mostly she heard a low buzz, all the time, everywhere she went. When it first started, she'd thought she'd go mad, but she'd learned to block it out. To never leave the house without her sunglasses and an iPod. It had been three weeks since the weird buzz and lights had started. Three weeks, and still they hadn't gone away. No one was paying much attention to her. No reason to warrant the nape prickling.

She took a few more steps when the soothing caress of warm energy brushed up against her arm. Gasping, she jumped back, almost dropping her basket. One of her earbuds popped out of her ear. She choked on the breath still caught in her throat and saw the man standing next to her. He was tall and slim with strong arms and snug-fitting jeans. Real snug. Real nice. Thick brown hair curled around his ears and astonishing pale blue eyes stared at her in concern.

"It's okay, I'm fine." She slapped an open palm to her chest to get the air flowing again and nodded, trying to look normal—when nothing about this situation, about this man, was normal. The most beautiful colors she'd ever seen surrounded him. Colors so bright she could even see them through the dark glasses. She couldn't recall ever seeing those particular shades of blue and purple before. Air burst out of her lungs and a feeling of calm settled over her. Better yet, the buzzing noise was gone. Her mind was completely at peace.

She turned off her iPod. Yep, not a sound was coming from him. How was that possible?

"I think that one is ripe. Probably even bruised by now," he said with a cocky grin.

She stared at him, stupefied, then embarrassment kicked in and she dropped the avocado into her basket.

"I—I don't think I've seen you around town before," she stammered, searching for something to say. He was awash in extraordinary colors. She could see right through the dark lenses of her glasses and it left her breathless and amazed.

"That would be because I just got here. I've been hired to oversee the remodeling of a new shop opening in the village—Tamara's Candles and Incense."

"Oh, nice," she murmured as her tongue thickened in her mouth. Obviously, it had been too long since she'd talked to people. Especially men. Drop-dead gorgeous men.

"You realize there's no sun outside," he said, staring at her glasses.

Geez, was it really that dark out? Preparing herself, she slipped off the glasses and dropped them into her basket. The man's aura was more startling than she'd first thought, and he had the most incredible bluish-gray eyes she'd ever seen.

"You have beautiful eyes. You shouldn't hide them," he said, staring into them with such intensity that a warm flush filled her face.

No one had ever said anything like that about her eyes before and she didn't quite know how to respond. So she didn't. She kept her mouth shut and her foot out of it.

"You don't happen to know where I can find a short-term apartment?" he asked, his voice rippling through her in an unusually intoxicating way.

She was staring, overwhelmed by the colors shimmering around his head and the fact that she couldn't hear his mind working. Not even the slightest buzz. Though for some reason he was affecting her body temperature. She let out a deep breath.

Amusement danced in his eyes.

"I'm…uh…sorry? Did you say something?" she asked, certain flaming-red must be filling her cheeks.

"An apartment?" he repeated.

"There is a real-estate office right down the street." She pointed in the direction he should go.

He had such a wonderful earthy smell, something she could almost place. What was it? Cedar? Cinnamon? Apple? All of the above mixed together in a cornucopia of goodness.

"Thanks, was hoping not to have to deal with leases and finder's fees and all that, since I won't be here for very long."

"Right." What was he talking about? An apartment? Maybe she should…? No. She couldn't. She wasn't used to being around men who made her feel so jittery and tongue-tied. Or like a complete idiot. No, she was better off keeping to herself. And she knew it. Just like she knew she was a complete and utter chicken.

Keep your head down, Shay. You never know when they'll find you. Her father's warnings rushed through her mind. Not that she ever knew who *they* were, why *they* were looking or even what *they* wanted.

But for this man, she could easily forget her daddy's warning. *Mercy!* With his dark hair streaked with a rebellious red, high cheekbones and wide, promising lips… She sighed. Not to mention strong shoulders that stretched from here to eternity. He was built and looked as if he could easily carry her and the world, and fight off whoever *they* might be.

And then she noticed his hands—large, strong hands. How she loved hands. Some girls liked chests and others liked butts. She loved hands. And his looked solid and capable. A warrior's hands. She sighed again.

"Well, hope to see you around," he said, after the long awkward pause she just realized had happened.

"Um, yeah. Right," she murmured, but too late. He was already gone. *Yep. Way to make a lasting impression, Shay. Not!*

She glanced around the small store once more before walking toward the cash register. Her handsome warrior must have slipped out. Feeling foolish and distracted, she paid for her groceries, loaded up her tote bag, then walked out the door and collided into someone walking in.

"I'm sorry," she muttered, looking up into a black fathomless gaze.

Shay's heart slammed against her rib cage. She'd been foolish enough to walk out the door without putting her glasses back on or her earbuds back in her ears.

An angry buzz filled her head, growing louder by the second. She shook her head, trying to dispel the distracting noise. Color—or the lack of color, more like a muddy darkness—surrounded him. Head down, she pushed past him. Gooseflesh raising her skin where she'd touched him.

Just go in the store, she thought. *Go in and leave me alone.*

She should have known that would be too much to hope for.

The man turned and followed her. Fear twisted and turned in her stomach as bile rose in her throat. They *are coming, Daddy.* They've *found me.* She quickened her step, trying to put distance between her and the man. It didn't work. He kept after her. What did he want?

She hesitated at the mouth of the alley between the two buildings that led into the parking lot and the quickest way back to her house. To Buddy. But she wasn't sure she wanted to go in there. And worse, beyond the alley, beyond the parking lot, she would be at the highway and once crossed, there was nothing but woods. She'd be alone. Where no one would be able to see her. Or hear her.

She screwed up her courage and spun around on the sidewalk to face her pursuer. Hoping he wouldn't be there.

But he was.

"Excuse me," she said in what she hoped was a strong, steady voice.

His clean-shaven face held no expression. With his

dress pants and polo shirt, he looked like any other tourist up from San Francisco. He certainly didn't look like something evil. But he was. She could tell by the dark shadows circling around his head and the slightly bitter, metallic way he smelled.

His nostrils flared as he sniffed the air around her, then he moved closer, his eyes a black void of nothingness.

"Can I help you with something?" she asked, a slight quaver shaking her voice as she took a step back from him.

He didn't answer. Just moved closer, uncomfortably close. She stepped back again and found herself at the mouth of the alley. She squared herself, planting her feet in a wide stance. All those years with her paranoid father teaching her everything from judo to how to shoot a revolver came rushing back. She dropped her tote bag, raised her hands, leaned her body weight slightly forward and loosened her knees.

"Turn around and get away from me," she demanded. "Now."

He stared at her with those obsidian black eyes that held no soul, and smiled. It was that smile, dripping with evil, that scared her more than anything he could have said.

What was he?

"What do you want from me?" her voice squeaked. She tried to stop looking at him. She didn't want to see the dark, shifting shadows encircling his head or what was moving within them. *What was that?* She could have sworn she'd seen teeth. And claws.

A violent shudder shook her.

He grabbed her arm. "This way," he snarled through a clenched jaw, and pushed her into the alley.

Fear, white-hot and molten, surged through her. She forgot her fighting stance, forgot every move she'd ever learned as her brain flooded with adrenaline. "Let me go!" She screamed, pulling and twisting, trying to break free from his grasp. But he was too strong.

He continued to push her forward, toward the large black van parked at the end of the alley. And she knew once they reached that van, once he got her inside, no one would ever see her again.

"Please," she cried and pried at his fingers, trying to loosen his grip on her arm.

"You heard the lady. Let her go."

The calm voice surprised and confused her. She looked up and saw the man from the store. Her knight in shining armor with the warrior hands stood not four feet away, watching them. Relief filled her, weakening her knees to the point she wasn't sure she could continue to stand. She tried to pull free once more, but the crazy loon still wouldn't loosen his grip.

What was wrong with him? There was a witness. Someone to help her.

Her rescuer set down his bag, took off his brown leather jacket and laid it neatly across the bag so it didn't touch the ground.

As if in a dream, she watched him, unable to comprehend what was happening. All she knew was that she no longer felt so afraid.

"You should do as she says," he said, walking toward

them, and planting one of his hands on her attacker's shoulder and squeezing.

She looked up at the man still holding her arm and could see the fear and anger surrounding him; it puffed up as a red cloud within the muddy darkness. Without looking at her, he dropped her arm, shrugged out of her savior's grasp, turned and walked away. As if he'd never stopped, as if he'd never touched her.

Shay stared after him, astonished.

"Does that happen to you often?"

She turned back to the man from the store, blinking. "No, but it's been happening more frequently lately." That man wasn't the first person with a black aura to take an unusual interest in her. But he was the first one who'd ever touched her. "Thanks for coming to my rescue."

"I was actually looking for that real-estate office you told me about. Luckily, I couldn't find it."

Luckily for her, but she might not be so lucky the next time. And somehow she knew there would be a next time. And like this time, she wouldn't be able to handle it alone. "How long did you say you'd be in town?"

"Hard to say. Anywhere from four to eight weeks, depending on how quickly I can get the job done. Why, have you thought of someplace?"

"It's not much and it's been sitting empty for a while, but I sure could use the money."

"No lease?"

She smiled. "No lease."

"Great. I can pay you by the week."

"Sounds fair. But don't you want to see it first? Then we can discuss price."

"Sure, should I drive? My truck's right down the street."

She looked toward his truck and shook her head. Her nerves were still too shaky to get into a stranger's vehicle. And yet, here she was taking him to her home. But for a reason she didn't understand, she trusted him. It had to be his aura, the warm vibrant colors surrounding him, so different from the muddy dark aura of her attacker.

"I really could use the fresh air, if you don't mind. It's not a far walk."

He gestured forward with an easy smile that immediately set her at ease. "Lead the way."

She took a step forward then stopped, turned back to him and held out her hand. "I'm Shay. Shay Mallory."

His large grasp enveloped her small hand, surprising her with its warmth. "Jason Stratton."

She turned and, for a moment, felt a prick of fear as she led him toward her home. An absolute certainty that everything was about to change.

Chapter 2

Jason was more than a little surprised when the woman offered her apartment so quickly. He wondered how long she'd been attracting the *Abatu,* men so lost and confused that it was easy for a demon to hitch a ride. Those types of lost souls were scary and bothersome, but were easily deterred. What would be worse was if the *Gauliacho,* higher-formed demons from the other side, found her. And from what he could tell, it wouldn't be long now until they did.

They crossed Highway 1 and started up the gravel road in silence. Shay couldn't have started her transformation too long ago. She wore dark glasses even though the day was overcast, so she could definitely see the colors. And he was fairly certain she was hearing the buzzing, too. Soon she'd be seeing and feeling a lot more.

Her scent and the vibrations she exuded were strong, making it relatively easy for him to find her. Unfortunately, it also made her an easy target for the *Abatu*.

But what concerned him more was how little she seemed to know about herself. Her dad, Dean, would have made sure she'd been properly trained. And yet, she'd been genuinely afraid of the *Abatu* when she could have taken him in an instant. She was strong enough. She just didn't seem to know it. Had Dean died before he had the chance to teach her what she needed to know? His stomach clenched at the thought. He hoped not.

They mounted the slight incline following a worn gravel road. Jason watched the gentle sway of her hips. Her snug shorts hugged her form nicely and showed off her long, strong legs. She was quite the beauty, and he had a feeling she didn't know that, either. She had her mother's bright blue, almost violet eyes. The effect of their deep color along with her long black hair was stunning. Her wide generous mouth drew his attention. On her mother, Lily, those lips had been easy to break into a smile, but on Shay, he wasn't so sure.

She didn't seem to have Lily's carefree easiness about her. It was that, coupled with Lily's bright smile, that had captured Dean's heart and refused to let go. A pang of regret thudded through Jason for his old friend. Dean had been foolish enough to break all the rules, fall in love with a human and then get her pregnant. For that, they had all paid the price. Maggie's smiling face and bright eyes slipped into Jason's thoughts. He quickly pushed them back out, but still felt the sharp ache of his wife's loss. He looked back at Shay and focused on her.

Dean's daughter. What had her life been like? He wished she could have grown up in The Colony, but half-breeds weren't allowed in the pack. They couldn't take the chance. Once the half-breeds were old enough, some would turn, some wouldn't. And if they didn't, the pack couldn't chance having humans living at The Colony, chance being exposed to the rest of the world.

It was one of the pack's oldest rules and one he still hadn't come to terms with. Family was family, human or not. Dean and Lily had been forced out on their own. A wolf living outside the protection of the pack didn't stand a chance. And now it was Shay's turn. She was changing, and soon her transformation would be complete.

As they walked silently through the woods, he considered asking her about her mother, but she didn't seem to be the type for mindless chitchat. Nor was she completely comfortable with him. He could tell by the subtle pinching of her lips that she was second-guessing her decision to invite him back to her home.

But whether she knew it or not, she needed him and fortunately she seemed to sense that. He wouldn't have long to convince her that she had to come with him to The Colony. He only hoped Dean or her mother had told her about them, about what she was, and prepared her for what was about to happen to her.

Shay stopped and picked up a large pinecone, twisting it this way and that. She was a beauty, every part of her from her slim graceful form, to her long black hair. Yes, Malcolm would be very pleased. For a second he felt a pinch of envy but quickly pushed it away. This she-wolf was for Malcolm. Her bloodline would ensure his continued leadership of the pack and silence those grumbling against him once and for all. Now that she was turning, all Jason had to do was get her to The Colony safely. Get her to Malcolm and let him deal with the fallout.

But to do that, he needed her cooperation. And he'd need it soon. As a small white clapboard house came into view, a large dog bolted through the trees toward them, breaking through the brush.

Shay stiffened beside him. "I hope you like dogs—"

Before she could finish, the dog, more wolf than Siberian husky, burst through the trees then skidded to a stop in front of them. It stared at Jason, its head cocked sideways, its large brown eyes studying him before it dropped whimpering to the ground. He lifted his massive front paw, up and down, up and down, as small little whimpers issued from his throat.

"Buddy?" Shay asked as she dropped to the ground next to her dog. "What's wrong, boy?"

Jason crouched next to them and rubbed the dog's brown-and-white head, letting him know he wasn't a threat to the animal.

"I have never seen him act like that before." Shay brushed the fur on the top of his dark ears. "Buddy, it's okay. This is Jason."

Jason gave the dog a pat on the shoulder then stood. As he did, Buddy stood, too, all his anxiety gone as his large tail beat the back of Jason's legs.

"Don't worry," Jason said. "Dogs like me."

"I guess so," she said, though she looked doubtful.

She was staring at him openly now, trying to figure him out. She could stare all she wanted, but in the long run, she wasn't going to like what he had to tell her. About him. About her parents. About herself. She pulled her arm back and chucked the pinecone, sending it soaring through the air. At full speed, Buddy took off after it. When they reached the house, they found Buddy sitting on the porch, the pinecone mangled between his paws.

Jason was mildly surprised not to sense anyone else inside. "Do you live here by yourself?"

"Yes. There's a small apartment above the garage. I haven't been in there in a while. It will probably need some dusting."

"I'm sure it will be fine," he answered automatically, and wondered where her mother was. If perhaps she was in another home nearby. He'd like to know how Lily had fared all these years without Dean. If she'd found happiness.

Or if, like him, she was more comfortable alone, preferring not to remember their past.

They walked toward the garage separated from the house by a small covered walkway and went up the stairs. He tried not to watch Shay's backside as she climbed the steps, tried very hard, but she offered such a nice view. He hung back as she opened the door and walked in.

Shay gasped as she stood in the doorway, her hand fluttering to her throat. Alarmed, Jason stepped past her

into the room and stilled. Buddy, who had followed behind him, whined, turned and ran back down the stairs.

Jason stared wide-eyed at the large cracks fissuring
the walls facing the house. They left long gaping frac-
tures in the Sheetrock.

"I am so sorry," Shay said, walking farther into the
room. "We live on a fault line that has been extremely
active lately. I've been having the same problem in the
house. I just bought more Spackle today." She lifted her
tote bag. "I'll take care of these right away."

Jason stiffened, trying not to show his reaction to the
voices whispering behind the walls and echoing through
his head. The *Gauliacho*. Couldn't she hear them, too?
No. Not yet. But they made her uncomfortable. As they
should. These weren't simple cracks. These were open-
ings, gateways to the other side. Soon they would be
wide enough that no amount of Spackle in the world
would be able to stop *them* from coming.

He couldn't stay there. And neither could she. Not
another day longer.

Shay stared in horror at the cracks shredding the
wall of the apartment. They were much bigger than the
ones in her house. These ones were almost big enough
to see through, but instead of wisps of pink insulation
or even a glimmer of studs behind the Sheetrock, all
she could see was darkness. She inched forward, clutching the Spackle in her hand, but as she took that first
step, fear, unreasonable and unexpected, swept through
her. Whispers filled her mind, unrecognizable and yet
somehow familiar.

She froze, her limbs stiff and unyielding as she listened harder, trying to grasp the sounds. Were they words? Yes. But how? Then the sounds became clearer, the syllables running together.

Abomination.

Fear strangled her throat, squeezing it within its fist to the point that she couldn't swallow, couldn't breathe.

Abomination. Abomination. Abomination.

Walls don't speak! Dizziness swam through her and she faltered. She tried to breathe, to force open her mouth and gasp a breath, but she couldn't. The room spun, nausea roiled through her stomach. Darkness filled the edges of her vision. And then Jason was touching her, holding her arm. Steadying her. She turned to him, her mouth opening but emitting no sounds, the question burning in her eyes.

Do you hear it, too?

With a whoosh, her lungs filled with air. She gasped, quick shallow breaths. His aura was strong, bright. Chasing away the darkness as she hung on to him. He didn't say anything and an awkward silence lingered between them.

"I...uh...I'll have to fill the cracks before you can stay here," she said, glancing back at the wall. "I'm afraid something in the walls is making me sick."

Even the air felt off and it didn't smell right. It seemed darker somehow, bleaker, and the scent of sour earth filled her nose. What was happening to her? She must be coming down with something. Tea and perhaps a nap and she'd be right as rain, as her grandma used to say. "The insulation must be toxic," she continued, muttering, babbling as she faltered again.

"It's going to be all right. I'll take care of you," he said, and before she could respond or even contemplate his words, she was up in his arms, cradled against his warm chest. She didn't know if the whispering had stopped or if she was so consumed by his body heat, by his heady, earthy scent that she no longer heard the disturbing whispers. She breathed his scent deep, holding it within her, as if it alone could protect her from the darkness.

She didn't know why, but she no longer felt sick or scared. She nestled close to him as he carried her out of the apartment, down the stairs and into the yard before he set her back onto her feet. She stood there, leaning into him, her hands on his chest, feeling his warmth beneath the palms of her hands. She didn't want to let him go. But she had to. She didn't even know him.

Once she stepped away and was standing on her own, embarrassment took root and spread quickly through her. She had never been one of those needy women who couldn't take care of herself, who needed a man around her. And yet that was what had just happened.

"I'm so sorry about this." She stammered, "I—I don't know what came over me."

He looked down at her, smiling. Which made it even worse.

"I really should get these groceries in the fridge." She patted the tote bag still slung over her shoulder then turned and quickly walked toward the house. After a second, she realized he wasn't following her. She turned back to him and found him standing in the same spot, staring after her, a look of concern on his face. Heat warmed her cheeks and quickened her already frayed nerves. "You want to come in for a cup of coffee?"

He nodded, an eager smile lifting his lips. "I think coffee would be a great idea."

He was concerned about her. Why? He didn't even know her. She climbed the steps up her porch and hurried into the kitchen with Buddy close on her heels. She went right to the sink and busied herself filling the carafe of the coffeemaker with water. Still trying to determine what had just happened. She'd become so lightheaded, she'd almost fainted and this man, this stranger, had caught her in his more-than-capable arms and she hadn't wanted him to let her go. She sighed. To make matters worse, this man who had shifted her libido into overdrive was sitting at her kitchen table.

She tried not to think about that. Or about the fact that she felt so comfortable around him. Sometimes he looked at her as if he knew her. As if she knew him. Crazy. And the way she felt when he touched her... She had definitely never felt like that before—all tingly and aware. She glanced at him, sitting in one of her kitchen chairs, his long legs stretched out in front of him. He looked good there. He looked...comfortable.

Once the coffee began brewing, she put a kettle of tea on for herself. Jason stood and perused her pictures on the wall. Photos of herself with her parents back before Dad had died and everything had become so hard for them.

"Your mom and dad?" he asked. His words were casual, but there was nothing casual about the tension in his shoulders. Why was he looking at them like that?

"Yep," she said and filled her grandmother's antique cream jar with milk and set it on the table with the matching sugar bowl. She used the set every day, trying to feel closer to her so she wouldn't miss her so much. Some days it worked; some days it didn't.

"Where do they live now?" Jason asked.

Was there more than idle curiosity in his voice?

"They aren't. Living, that is," she said more harshly than she'd meant to.

Confusion wrinkled his forehead. "Oh. I didn't know. Sorry to hear that." And he looked it, too. Much more than he should for someone who had no idea who she or her parents were.

Anxiety twisted through her as it hit her again that she'd invited a man she didn't know into her home. She was alone with a complete stranger. A too-good-to-be-true stranger.

And no one knew.

"I know what it's like to lose your family," he said as sadness filled his eyes. "To be alone."

She gave herself a strong mental kick for being so paranoid. Here was this nice guy, who had done nothing but help her and try to make small talk, and she was thinking the worst of him.

"I'm sorry about the apartment," she said, deciding the best thing to do would be to change the subject. "I'm afraid Mr. Henderson was right and I'll need to get the foundation checked. I don't think it's inhabitable."

For a moment he didn't say anything, just sat at the

table as she placed the steaming mug of coffee in front of him. She dropped into the chair across from him and added milk and honey to her tea.

"I am a contractor. I do remodels for a living and I don't believe the problem is with your foundation."

She perked up at that news. "Really? That would be great news because, honestly, I can't afford that kind of extensive repair."

She took a deep drink of the soothing chamomile. At first it hit the spot, but after a second her stomach flipped over on itself, sending a painful cramp slicing through her abdomen. She grabbed her middle and bent over.

Jason stood. "Are you all right?"

She tried to straighten but was in too much pain. She wanted to assure him that she was fine, but another racking wave shot through her. "I'm sorry. I must be coming down with something."

"You should lie down." He reached for her, his hand on her arm, pulling her out of the chair.

"Oh, I couldn't. We still need to discuss...." Sudden weakness and a spike in her temperature killed the words on her lips. But she had to say them. They had to talk. How could she sleep with a strange man in her house? And what was she going to do with him? He couldn't stay in the apartment, foundation issues or not.

"I insist." He slipped his hand around her waist, helping her walk. And once he did, once she stared up into those gorgeous pale bluish-gray eyes of his, she knew she couldn't fight him. But more than that, she knew she didn't need to fear him. Though, for the life of her, she couldn't imagine how she knew.

He led her into the living room and over to her large comfy couch. "Just for a little while," he said as she fell into the deep cushions. He pushed the hair back from her face and it took all the effort she had not to tip her head into his hand. To seek comfort from him.

"I'll check out the cracks in your apartment to see what needs to be done, then we'll talk." He looked around the room, noticing the cracks she'd tried to spackle on the wall above the TV.

Before she could respond, she started to drift off. She felt the warm familiar threads of her grandmother's afghan being pulled up over her shoulders, and heard him softly whisper in a deep, commanding voice, "Buddy, stay.

"You'll be safe for now," he whispered, and she couldn't help thinking what an odd thing for him to say, but before she could determine what he meant she succumbed to the dark.

Jason left the room with Buddy keeping watch over Shay and walked outside. The afternoon was growing late. With the shortened days of fall, soon it would be dark. He walked back down the road toward town and his truck, which he'd left parked outside the small grocery store.

His wolf scent was much stronger than hers. But with the crystals on his wrist, he had another day's protection from the *Abatu* before the stones stopped working. Then he'd attract the demons himself. If only it hadn't taken him so long to find her.

He had hoped he'd have more time to build her trust

before he had to drop the truth on her and explode her world. But time was a luxury they no longer had. From the size of those cracks on her walls and the way the change was affecting her, they would need to get on the road first thing in the morning or risk what would be coming through those walls after them.

He climbed into the truck and drove it back to her house, parking in front. He had all the necessary supplies he needed in the back—rope, knife, flashlight, water, extra food, extra clothes. He just hoped he wouldn't need to use any of them. But she was changing fast and from what he could gather, she had no clue who she was or what was happening to her.

How could Dean have been so careless? He knew the danger a fledgling wolf faced. How could he not have prepared her or at least told Lily what to tell her? He ran a hand over his face and wondered when Lily had died. Maybe they hadn't had time. That was the only explanation that made sense. Maybe they'd died too soon, when Shay was still too young to understand.

Grief tugged at his insides and he wished once more that Dean had chosen to stay at The Colony. Obviously if he had, he'd still be alive today and there wouldn't be as much dissention in the pack.

Malcolm was a good leader. A strong leader. But there had been grumblings about his methods, his integrity and honor. Not something anyone would ever have said about Dean Mallory. Dean had been as honorable as they came, which was why he'd left to marry Lily when she'd become pregnant. It was the right and honorable thing to do. The only thing to do.

As Jason sat there staring at the little house, thinking about Dean's daughter inside, he couldn't help wondering if Lily had known the truth about them. Had he ever told her? Or had he gone to his grave never letting the love of his life know his true nature? That he wasn't like everyone else. That he wasn't human.

Jason shook his head as the magnitude of what Dean could have done hit him. Had he really loved Lily that much? Had he made sure she never had to make the choice to give up her humanity, to give up her ties to her mother, to the outside world only to have to spend the rest of her life with wolves? That's when Jason knew the truth of his thoughts. Yes, he'd loved her that much and more. Only now his daughter would pay the price of his silence. Dean had gambled on the fact that, as a half-breed, Shay would never make the change, that she'd stay human. He'd been wrong.

Now it fell on Jason to have to tell her the truth about herself and her heritage. He would be the one to tell her it was time to give up everything and everyone she knew and move to The Colony with no forewarning of what was to come. Of what her future would bring, her responsibility to the pack and her need to marry Malcolm, the pack's leader.

He only hoped she'd come with him peacefully.

Chapter 3

Jason breathed in deep the salty ocean air. It had been a long time since he'd been able to enjoy the beach, the crashing of the waves, the sand between his toes. They were so close, he wished he and Shay could have even an hour together to walk along the shore and get to know one another better before he had to tell her about The Colony and about Malcolm.

It was imperative that she understood how important she was to the pack. Her marriage to Malcolm was the only way to bring peace to The Colony, to stop the grumblings and whispers of war. She was Dean's daughter; she was next in line as successor. As Malcolm's wife, they would rule together. Side by side, they could bring peace.

Jason walked back into the house. Shay was still sleeping as her body struggled to adjust to the changes going on within her. He sat in the chair next to her, watching her sleep while contemplating the best way to tell her she'd have to leave everything behind.

The crystals twined into the rope on his wrist began to prick his skin. He rubbed his wrist then noticed the faint scent of sulfur drifting into the room. He stood, his gaze immediately going to the cracks in the wall. Dammit, he'd thought he'd have more time. He hurried into the kitchen and, one by one, began pulling family pictures off the wall and placing them in the canvas tote bag Shay had used for her grocery shopping. She would want these and it would be a long time before she would be able to return to get them. If ever.

With the bag slung over his shoulder, he hurried back into the living room. It was time. It was almost dark and the whispers coming through the cracks were getting louder and almost…comprehensible. He sat on the sofa next to her and gently shook her shoulder. "Shay, you have to wake up. We need to go."

"Huh? Go?" she muttered, trying to rouse herself from a deep sleep.

"Yes, it isn't safe here."

"Not safe?" She sat up, rubbing her eyes and staring at him, her face crumpled with confusion. "What do you mean? Where do we need to go?"

"To The Colony."

"Where?"

Buddy whined at her feet.

He knew what was coming. The dog had enough wolf in him that he could smell the acrid scent filling the room, a cross between sulfur and vinegar, a sign of the demons getting closer, of barriers being breached.

"Where have I heard that name before?"

"The Colony? Hopefully from your dad. He used to live there. In fact, he sort of ran the place."

"What? When?" She started to stand but, unsteady on her feet, she quickly sat back down again. "I'm confused. Is that where you're from? This colony?"

"Yes, I've come to get you."

"But what about the candle shop remodel?"

"It can wait," he lied. "What's important is getting you to safety."

Her concern grew to fear as she came fully awake. He could smell it in the subtle shift of her scent. Could see it in the tensing of her shoulders and the way she kept moving her hands across her thighs.

"I didn't know I was in danger," she said, her voice soft enough to almost be a whisper.

"I'm sorry. I know this must seem strange, coming out of the blue like this from someone you've never met—"

"That's putting it mildly." She got to her feet and walked into the kitchen and toward the coffeepot. She took down a clean mug and poured herself a cup, then popped it in the microwave.

He'd spooked her. "I know how this sounds, and I wish I had more time for you to trust what I have to say, but I made a promise to your dad that... I promised I wouldn't let anything happen to you. I'm not about to break that word. We have to go, and we have to go now. Take only what you absolutely need. You have ten minutes, tops, to get your stuff together."

She stared at him with incredulity filling her face. "You didn't *know* my father. You're too young. How dare you tell me you promised him? I'm not going anywhere with you. Now I think you should leave."

He stepped toward her then stopped as fear widened her eyes and she backed up against the cabinets.

"I don't know why your parents didn't tell you about The Colony or about yourself, and I'm sorry for that, but I don't have time to explain it all to you now. Those cracks in your walls aren't caused by fault lines. They are doorways splitting open and leading into a demon dimension. Soon they will be wide enough for the *Gauliacho* to get through. Trust me, you don't want to be here when they do."

"Demons! Are you listening to yourself?"

"I know it sounds crazy."

"It doesn't just sound crazy. It is crazy."

"It's the truth. You heard the whispering. You breathed their air and it made you sick."

She stared at him wide-eyed and began shaking her head back and forth. "No. It's. Not. Now get out."

How could Shay have been so stupid? She knew better than to invite a stranger into her home. But she'd been distracted by his good looks and tempted by his cold hard cash. *Idiot.* Never before had a smooth-talking handsome man fooled her, and the one time one had....

And then she noticed the pictures that were missing off her kitchen wall and her fingers froze at her sides. "What have you done with my photos?"

He held up her tote bag. "I packed them. We're tak-

ing them with us. You shouldn't need them to prove
who you are, but it wouldn't hurt. Bring your papers,
too—birth certificate, driver's license and anything that
might have this symbol on it." He pulled up his sleeve
and showed her a tattoo on his forearm of a large swirling circle with five claws sticking out from the sides.

Shay gasped as her knees weakened. Coffee forgotten, she dropped into a chair at the table. The tattoo
was exactly like the one her father had worn. Her hand
fluttered to her neck, to the amulet hidden beneath her
shirt as she recalled her father's words the night he'd
given it to her.

*You're a big girl now, Shay. Big enough to wear a
big girl's necklace. Do you see this symbol?* Her dad
had swung the obsidian amulet in front of her. *This is
a symbol of a very special place. A place where your
daddy came from. If anyone ever comes to you and they
have a symbol like this, you must trust them. You must
go with them. Never take it off. Promise me, pumpkin?*

All these years and she'd kept her word. She'd never
taken it off. And now someone who had a symbol just
like hers was here.

You must trust them.

But how could she?

"I'm sorry I don't have time to explain everything
that is happening to you. Please trust me when I tell you
that you are in danger. We both are. What happened in
town today was just the beginning. We have to get out
of here. We have to get you back to The Colony where
you will be safe."

"Why?" She didn't understand. How could she? "Why this colony? Where is it?"

"The demons can't sense us there. It's protected."

Shay stood on shaky legs. "And you're saying that once I go there…" She couldn't finish the words.

"You might be able to leave. Like I can, but only for short periods of time. Most choose not to."

Unbidden tears filled her eyes. She didn't know why. She didn't believe him. She didn't have to listen to him, even if she could still hear her father's voice echoing in her mind. But it wasn't true. It couldn't be true. "This was my grandmother's home. It's my home. Buddy and I love it here. We can't just leave. We won't leave."

Jason sat back in his chair and took a deep breath. "What has been happening to you, the colors you've been seeing—"

A chill swept over and wrapped around her. How could he know about that?

"Have you started to hear the buzzing yet?"

She stared at him, unable to move. To breathe. Was it possible that he was telling her the truth? How else could he know these things?

"It's part of the change. Your body is transforming, and that transformation is what is attracting the demons. Soon it will draw the *Gauliacho,* too. They'll come through the walls, through the cracks. We can't be here when that happens. Please, Shay, pack what you absolutely must have and do it quickly. We have to go."

She shook her head. "Maybe you know some things about me that you shouldn't know, but that doesn't mean I am going to give up my home and run away with you.

I don't know anything about you. I don't believe what you're saying. I just... I won't go."

Silence thickened the air between them and she was finding it hard to pull in a breath. He was angry, she could see it in the bunching of his muscles, could hear it in the sharp intake of his ragged breath.

"I don't think you understand," he started again, his face tense, his eyes dark. Energy pulsed around him, making him look bigger than he was, stronger, more lethal.

How could she have invited him into her home? Why hadn't she seen this side of him? How big he was? How dangerous? And yet, he had the tattoo. And she had the echoes of her father's words playing around the edges of her mind. *You can trust them.*

"I...I just can't run off with a perfect stranger," she said again, though she wasn't sure if she was saying it for his benefit or for hers. No sooner had the words left her mouth than a rumbling shook the kitchen. A long crack split the wall where her family's pictures had once hung, forming a long gaping fracture.

Jason stood so fast his chair crashed to the floor behind him. "You have no choice, Shay. We have to go. They're coming! Hurry!"

Fueled by his fear, and her own, she ran to her room at the back of the house and pulled a duffel down from her closet. What was happening? She didn't know, and yet she started throwing things into the bag without much thought of what she was grabbing until it was overflowing. How could she choose in a matter of seconds which items of her life to take with her and which to leave behind?

She stopped, took a deep breath then picked up the duffel and dumped it upside down, shaking the contents onto the bed. She started again: her two favorite pairs of Levi's, her favorite sweater, socks, underwear, boots, a long-sleeved T-shirt, the book she was reading, her jewelry—not because she owned a lot of nice pieces but because most of what she did own had once belonged to her mother—a spool of yarn, her crochet needles.

"How are we doing?" Jason asked, appearing in the doorway; his eyes, wide with urgency, fell on the half-crocheted scarf in her hand as he shifted back and forth on his heels in his impatience to hurry her.

"Almost done." She grabbed some shorts and T-shirts and shoved them into the duffel, then ran into the bathroom and seized all her toiletries, sweeping them into a makeup bag, then hurried into the living room. She stood in the middle of the room staring at the brocade sofa, the soft leather wing chair that she loved. The antique sideboard filled with porcelain and crystal, her memories, her family's heirlooms, whether they were valuable or not, how could she leave them all behind?

Tears welled in her eyes and she collapsed onto the sofa. What was she doing? She dropped her head into her hands and tried to catch her breath and still her racing heart. This was crazy. He was crazy and somehow he'd sucked her into his delusion.

But as she sat there, listening to her heart thud in her chest and trying to get ahold of herself, she heard faint whispers filling the air. Like before, in the apartment, they seemed to be coming from the wall. From the crack. Slowly, she rose off the sofa and walked over to the deep fissure in the wall. The same wall that had been a supporting structure for this house for the past sixty years and suddenly it was broken.

And emitting a foul-smelling gas. She placed her hand over her nose and mouth and leaned in closer. *They are doorways leading to a demon dimension.* Jason's words filled her head and quickened her heart. But that was crazy! There was no such thing as a demon dimension. She leaned in closer, listening, and then she heard it again, the whispering that had filled the room with a strange rhythm that was almost a chant. The one word she could grasp clearly.

Abomination.

Chills scurried madly down her arms and across the back of her neck. But it wasn't just the chills; a strange vibration pulsed deep inside her ears, and the room began to spin. Darkness bloomed on the edge of her vision and her legs turned rubbery. Weakened, she turned and, on her way out of the room, grabbed her grandmother's afghan and her laptop case. She slung it over her shoulder with the duffel and hurried out the door and onto the porch. She quickly closed and locked the door then turned around and stifled a scream.

Jason stood on the porch's top step, the tote bag and a bag of Buddy's dog food under his arm. Buddy stood crouched a foot behind him, his hair bristling as he stared out into the yard. A lone wolf stood not ten feet in front of them, his head bowed, his teeth bared. Buddy whined, pushing himself next to Jason's powerful legs.

"What does it want?" Shay asked nervously.

"He's drawn to the smell of the demons."

"Why?"

"Because it's in his blood. He knows the smell, he fears it, but he doesn't understand why. He doesn't remember."

She didn't understand. How could she understand? It was nonsense. "Will it hurt us?"

"I don't know. He's confused and afraid." Jason stepped off the porch, walking slowly toward his truck. The wolf's eyes tracked him as he proceeded across the yard. Its upper lip lifted, showing a row of sharp teeth as it caught Jason's scent, then it snarled a warning that sent the hair on her neck standing on end.

Jason slowed, taking a tentative step forward. Then another, his eyes never leaving the wolf's. He was almost to his driver's door when another wolf stepped out from behind a large redwood tree.

Shay gasped a breath and held it to keep from calling out a warning. Very slowly and deliberately, Jason closed the distance to his truck and opened the driver's door. She didn't let loose the air burning inside her chest until he climbed inside the truck and slammed the door shut.

"Buddy." Instantly, he was by her side. A low growl rumbled in his throat as another two wolves stepped into the clearing and moved toward them. She leaned down and grabbed ahold of Buddy's collar. They had to get back in the house. But before she could take a step, Jason's truck roared to life. He flipped on the headlights and, in the dimming light of dusk, lit up the yard. The wolves turned and faced him, their eyes glowing greenish-gold in the headlight's reflection.

The truck inched forward, moving close to the porch, one tire riding up the bottom step. Jason pushed open the back door of the crew cab and yelled, "Come on, Buddy!"

In a flash, Buddy yanked out of her grasp and jumped into the backseat of the truck then slid between the bucket seats up front and positioned himself in the passenger's seat. Amazement surged through her at how easily and quickly Buddy obeyed him, which quickly turned to annoyance. She had no choice now. There was no going back.

"Come on, Shay," Jason yelled.

Before she could move, another wolf appeared on the porch from the side of the house not ten feet away from her. Without a second thought, she ran and jumped into the backseat of the crew cab, slamming the door shut behind her. Jason made a wide turn and carefully drove down the road as even more wolves stepped out from between the redwoods to watch them pass, their dark eyes following them.

Buddy whined and Shay repositioned herself, squeezing up into the front seat next to him. She put her arm around his trembling body. Though she suspected she was getting more comfort from his soft warm fur than he was getting from her. She laid her cheek against him and tried not to cry. More wolves stepped forward, flanking the road as they drove away from her home.

"Look at them all. In all the years I've lived here, I've never seen a single wolf. Now they're everywhere."

"They've come from far away, tracking the scent."

"What if they get into the house?" She turned around and watched them move toward her home.

"It doesn't matter. Not anymore."

Disbelief filled and angered her. "Yes, it does. How can you say that? They'll ruin everything. That is my home." As she thought of the damage they could do, to the antique sofa, the leather of the chairs, the wool rugs, she felt her control over her emotions slipping as tears spilled onto her cheeks.

"Did you shut the door?"

"Yes, but what if they break a window? We have to go back. We have to do something, call someone."

"We can't, Shay. I'm sorry. There's nothing we can do. No one we can call."

"Yes, we can! That is my home."

"No it's not. Not anymore."

She glared at him, feeling the hatred burning through her eyes.

"I'm sorry. That came out harsher than I'd intended. You have to trust me, Shay. As hard as it is to accept, life as you know it is over. You have no choice but to move on."

"That's not true. We always have choices."

"But not always good ones. I know it sounds insensitive, but—"

"You're damn right it does. I will never forgive you for this, for taking me away from my home. For not calling someone, for not helping me save…" And then it broke loose, all the fear and the anger she was trying to keep at bay. It filled her heart and overflowed, expanding into her throat. Gulping, painful sobs wrenched her chest, and tears flooded her eyes, scorching her cheeks.

Embarrassment engulfed her, merging with the fear

and anger and the deep sadness. Everyone in her family was dead and everything she had left to remind her of them was still in that house. And yet, she'd chosen to go with him, to turn from her home and get into his truck. *Fool.*

But what choice had she had? She thought again of the years, the memories with her grandmother. They were all she had left of her family. There was nothing else. No one else. But now the house was riddled with cracks, and foul-smelling odors and...wolves.

She closed her eyes and leaned her head against the window.

"I'm sorry," he said again.

"You already said that. It doesn't matter. It doesn't help."

"It does matter, Shay, because you're alive. If I hadn't come today, if I'd waited one more night..."

She turned to him. He was serious. He really believed she'd been in danger. She thought of the voices in her wall, of the feverish eyes of the wolves outside her door, and a shudder tore through her. Was he right? Was she that close to death?

If I'd waited one more night...

Chapter 4

Shay must have fallen asleep. She woke with her head pressed against the glass and Buddy's big body splayed across her lap. She dug her fingers into his fur, finding comfort in his softness. He was all she had left now. She looked out the windshield at the dark empty highway looming ahead of them.

"Where are we going?" she asked.

"To the most beautiful spot on earth. You and Buddy will love it."

Maybe. But they'd loved it where they were. Buddy had tons of empty forest to roam. They were a breath away from the beautiful blue Pacific with its soaring cliffs and giant black rocks. There were people she knew back there, people who knew her. She sighed. Who knew where she was going now? What it would be like. Why hadn't her parents told her about this place?

Would she ever be able to go back home? She had to. She'd take out a loan, make the repairs on the house, call wildlife control and take back her life. Running off with a stranger was beyond foolish and it wasn't like her. She was practical. Logical. She didn't let her emotions rule her actions. She didn't operate on instinct. She was a planner, so she was making a plan.

Except how could she plan for demons? She shook her head. Crazy. They were just cracks in the wall. *Cracks that whisper?* The question taunted her.

"Will we get there soon?" she asked, trying to stretch the kinks out of her neck and back. How long had she been sleeping? She looked at the radio's clock. Almost midnight!

"Not tonight. We will stop at a motel a few miles up the road."

She nodded, rethinking her plan. Perhaps she wouldn't have to go all the way to this colony. She was starving, and she had to use the restroom. First thing in the morning, she would call a car-rental place and take back control of her life. She didn't know who this man was, anything about him or where he was taking her. There was no reason she had to stay with him.

Except he had the tattoo.

But if it was so important that she trust him, go with him, then why hadn't anyone told her about this colony?

"Great. While I appreciate all you've done today to help us, this motel will be the end of the line for me and Buddy."

Jason turned and looked at her, his face unreadable in the dim light from the dash.

"Just because you have a tattoo that matches my necklace doesn't mean I'm going to give up my life and run off with you. I know nothing about you. Nothing about where you're taking me, or why I'm suddenly in so much danger."

"Fair enough," he said, his voice tense as he pulled into an old fifties-style motel. "But will you let me tell you more over dinner? Perhaps fill in some of the holes?"

"Those are some pretty big holes to fill," she muttered. She stared skeptically out of the window at the bright neon vacancy sign. "Blue Moon?"

"It doesn't look like much but it's clean and the cheeseburgers are to die for."

She sighed as her stomach rumbled and, with a pat on Buddy's head, climbed out of the truck. Jason ordered for them while she took Buddy to do his business then put him back in the truck. "We won't be long," she promised. "Then you can sleep with me. It's a pet-friendly motel."

Buddy barked once, then whined and dropped his head onto his paws. She filled up his bowl, which she'd found shoved into his bag of food, smiled at him and shut the door.

Jason was right. The cheeseburger was better than she'd expected, especially since she didn't usually eat meat, but suddenly she seemed to be craving it. She scarfed down the burger quicker than she would have imagined possible then picked at her salad.

"I can't believe how fast I ate that," she said, a little embarrassed. "I can't remember the last time I was this hungry."

He smiled. "I like girls with healthy appetites."

It was a nice smile, a charming smile. But it wouldn't work on her. Not anymore. She looked back down at her plate and speared a tomato. "So, what you said earlier…about my dad."

He looked up, his pale bluish-gray eyes catching hers, and she was almost afraid to continue, to know. "It almost sounded like you knew him."

"I did know him."

She stared at him, her salad forgotten. "When? How?"

"The Colony is a small town. Everyone knows everybody. Your dad was… He was the leader of our village. You would be, too—as his daughter it's your blood right."

Blood right? What was that supposed to mean? Suspicion wormed its way through her, leaving a trail of unsettling wariness. What kind of town had leaders based on blood rights?

"My dad died ten years ago. And we have never lived anywhere called The Colony."

"I know. He left shortly before marrying your mother."

"Okay, well, that had to have been twenty-three years ago. And you can't be a day over thirty. So how do you remember my dad?"

"He was a great man. He had a way of making an impression."

She leaned back into the red vinyl seat and stared around the fifties diner, the long row of booths lining the wall of windows, while trying to wrap her mind around this. Something just didn't sound right. Hell, none of it sounded right.

"Maybe you should tell me why you came for me. The real reason, because obviously you didn't just happen to bump into me in the grocery store."

"No, you're right about that." He swiped a handful of fries through a mound of ketchup and stuffed them into his mouth.

She waited, watching, her impatience growing by the second.

He swallowed, took a deep sip of his Coke and then smiled, a devastatingly charming smile meant to knock her off her feet. It wasn't working. Not even a little.

"I came to find you."

"Yes, I figured. Why?"

"To save you." He leaned back with a self-satisfied grin, obviously pleased with his accomplishment.

"Thank you," she gritted through a jaw growing tenser by the second.

"You're welcome."

"Why did I need saving?" She gripped the edge of the aluminum table to keep herself from jumping across the smooth surface and throttling him.

He looked around the room at the few other patrons scattered throughout the small diner then leaned in toward her. "It's the demons. They're after you."

She closed her eyes and took a deep breath. She was sitting in the middle of God knew where with an insane man. How had her life gotten so screwed up? "Fine, I'll bite. Why? Why do they live in my walls? Why do they want me? And why were there wolves surrounding my house?"

"I told you earlier, the wolves can smell the demons. But not only that—they can smell you."

Shock intensified her annoyance, and she wasn't sure how much longer she could hold on to her temper.

"It's not like that," he said quickly. "It's because of your transformation. They can smell the change coming. Once you've made the transition, once we get you to The Colony, you'll be safe. From them and from the demons, I promise."

Anxiety burned in her chest. "What change? What transition?"

He took another long swig of Coke and suddenly she could see it for the diversion technique it was. He didn't want to tell her. He was stalling! Because it was all lies.

"You have about thirty seconds to explain everything before I walk." The urge to give him a swift kick under the table was almost overwhelming, and she held on to her leg with both hands cupped around her knee. God, what was happening to her? She was so keyed up, so frustrated and angry, she felt like she could jump right out of her own skin.

He took a deep prolonged breath. "Your father, like all of us at The Colony, was…different."

"How?"

"Well, for instance, you've been seeing colors around people."

"Yes," she said, still surprised that he knew that.

"They are people's auras. By now you should also be hearing the energy coming from their brains."

The buzzing. "Yes…" But how did he know? "So, it's not a tumor?" she asked, giving voice to her biggest fear.

"Nope. We all went through it."

"And the people with the black auras, like that man at the store earlier?"

"He is a lost man, someone who doesn't know who he is or what he values. He's weak, and weak humans are easy vessels for demons to catch a ride in. We call them the *Abatu.*"

"Demons again."

"Yes. But, one-on-one, you can fight them. Easy. Please tell me your dad at least taught you how to fight."

"Of course he did," she snapped, not liking the reference that her dad was some kind of slacker. "So, my dad could see auras, too?"

"Yes. Once. Before he went through the change. And after, I think. Though he never really talked about it much."

"So, this change, whatever it is, why would that make us targets for demons?" She felt ridiculous even asking the question.

"Because the dimension where the demons come from, the place where the cracks in your wall lead to, is where our ancestors came from. Long ago. Our ancestors were sent here by the *Gauliacho* to spread fear through humans, to conquer and destroy them. They took the shapes of animals then transformed into humans, terrorizing the natives.

"Myths and legends were born. But our ancestors

liked it here. They liked running free. They even liked the humans. After a while, they didn't want to go back. In their human forms, they mated, started families, creating lives apart from the Demon dimension they came from. We are their offspring. We are the hated ones, the defiant ones. The abominations."

Her heart gave a little hiccup as he said the word. This couldn't be real, couldn't be true. "I, uh, I'm not sure I'm following. Are you saying we *are* demons?"

"Not demon, not human, either, but a little of both. Your dad wasn't human, Shay. Not completely. But your mom was. Once she became pregnant with you, your dad wanted to marry her. In order to do that, he had to leave the protection of The Colony."

She stared at him wide-eyed and stunned. "Why? I thought he was in charge. Your leader or something."

"He was. But your mother wasn't like us, and we couldn't know if you would go through the change or not. If you'd be more like her than him. Sometimes half-breed offspring do, sometimes they don't. But either way, humans must never know about us. As each year passes, as populations grow, our secret has become harder to keep. If human offspring were allowed to grow up in The Colony, it would be impossible.

"That's why it's imperative that we never mate outside The Colony. Your dad broke that rule. He saw your mom in a bordering town and fell instantly in love. He was lost from that moment forward. I promised him the day he left that if you changed, if you started your transformation, I would find you and I would bring you home safely."

She leaned back in the booth. "You realize how crazy all this sounds, right?"

"Yes."

"So according to you, I'm changing into some kind of demon hybrid and soon I will no longer be human?"

He nodded. "That's about it in a nutshell."

She slid out of the booth and stood. "Great meeting you, Jason."

"I understand how this all sounds."

"Do you?" She leaned in close to him. "And what about you, Jason? Are you some kind of demon? Are you not human, too?"

He placed a room key on the table and slid it toward her. "We're both tired. Get some rest. We'll talk more in the morning. You're in room fifteen. I'll be right next door if you need me."

"Don't worry," she said, snatching up the key. "I won't."

Shay put on her jammies and climbed into bed as Buddy settled himself onto the floor next to her. "Everything is going to be all right," she whispered to her dog. But was it? She had no clue what she was going to do. How could she believe a word Jason had said? It was crazy, and yet, somehow everything he'd said fit. He knew what she'd been going through with the colors and the sounds, and he'd said she wasn't the only one. The burden lifted off her by his words was substantial. She didn't have a tumor, benign or otherwise. She wasn't going crazy. She was just going through some kind of change.

But into a demon? How could he expect her to believe that? She switched off the light and touched the necklace around her neck. If any of this was true, why hadn't her father told her? Why hadn't her mother? Both had died when she was so young. First her father from a freak accident in which he'd fallen off the cliffs into the Pacific, and then her mother, killed by a drunk driver. Maybe they meant to tell her, but never got the chance. Maybe there was nothing to tell because it was all crazy.

She had no idea how much time had passed when she woke to darkness. She was dripping with sweat and wrapped in a wet sheet. Pain sliced across her middle. She groaned, bending over, cradling her stomach as images of the forest flashed through her mind. She could smell the damp earth, thick and musky in her nose, could feel the power in her legs stretching out beneath her, carrying her fast through the night as she chased after the acrid scent of fear from a scurrying rabbit.

She screamed as another sharp pain sliced through her insides. The images came quicker, the outlines of the ferns and the Douglas firs were easy to distinguish by the light of the moon. Even though it was dark, details were so much easier to see as her vision sharpened into focus.

Her breathing, rough and ragged, scraped across the inside of her throat. She moaned, curling up into a ball, bunching the damp sheets in her sweaty palms. The door connecting her room with the one next door burst open. On the outskirts of her peripheral vision she saw Jason hurry toward her. The bed sagged as he sat next to her.

"Here, eat this," he said, thrusting a large piece of jerky into her hand. "It's venison."

"I can't." She pushed it away as pain seared her insides. "I feel like I'm being ripped in two."

"I know, I went through it, too. We all did. I just thought we'd have more time before you would. You need the protein. Eat it," he demanded.

"No!" Her mouth was dry and filled with grit, there was no way she'd be able to swallow it. And even if she did, she wouldn't be able to keep it down.

"Sorry." He pushed the meat into her mouth. The woodsy flavor exploded across her tongue. She barely had it chewed before she was swallowing and greedily reaching for more.

He placed another piece between her lips. "No more salads for you. Not for a while."

"I love salads," she said weakly then cried out again as another surge swept through her. Her body temperature spiked, and she hung weakly on to Jason's arm, riding the wave of torment.

"Your body is changing. You need to give it extra fuel. Only protein from now on."

"Okay," she whispered, knowing she'd promise anything if he could only make the pain stop.

He gave her another piece of jerky. She chewed it more slowly this time, the gamey flavor satisfying her in a way she'd never imagined. She wanted more. And she wanted it now. She chewed and chewed, trying to concentrate on the fulfilling taste even as the pain swept over her, stealing her thoughts. Tears coursed down her cheeks, but she didn't care. This pain was sharper than when she'd broken her arm and deeper than anything she'd ever felt.

She cried out again as another wave swept through her, doubling her over until she just wanted to die, to close her eyes and drop off the deep end of oblivion. She felt herself being moved, being gathered up and pulled into Jason's embrace. He was lying behind her, holding her nestled against him as he murmured in her ear and continued to put small pieces of the meat into her mouth.

She tried to concentrate on the feel of him behind her. With the strength of his arms wrapped around her, his infinite heat seemed to melt her limbs into mush. His smell, woodsy and earthy, of pine and forest, reached inside her and she breathed deep, breathed it so far into her that she wasn't sure where she stopped and he began.

She touched the crystals on his wrist, fingering the smooth stones and rough twine. Dragging her fingers down to his strong warrior hands, trying to focus on the feel of them, their strength and their gentleness.

"I can help you if you'll let me," he whispered.

"Yes," she cried, as another wave of intense heat stole over her, bringing with it the racking nausea.

He stood and slipped out of his jeans and pulled off his T-shirt. She wanted to protest, to demand to know what he was doing, but instead she curled up and closed her eyes as she willed the pain to stop. And then he was pulling off her pajama pants, pulling her shirt up over her head.

"No," she protested, trying to cover her exposed breasts.

He slipped into the bed next to her and pulled her up against his hot skin. At first she tried to pull away from him. To put some distance between them, but then his hands began to move, soothing and caressing her skin. Moving up her body, and with each sure stroke, the pain and the tension began to ease. Warmth seeped into her clenched and strained muscles, appeasing the tension, until she began to relax and a new tension lit her nerve endings.

She felt each gentle touch so deeply it was almost as if she could feel the ridges of his fingerprints being imprinted on her skin. Nerve endings fired and tingled, leaving longing in their wake. His bare feet cupped hers, the backs of her legs pressed tight against the front of his, her backside nestled deeply in his center, his warmth melding with her as his hand moved up and around her hips.

His lips moved across the sensitive lobes and the outer shell of her ear as he murmured to her that everything would be all right. The pain wouldn't last. And he was right, it was finally ebbing. But a new kind of pain was starting, an exquisite burn of longing and need, and she pushed herself even closer to him as his fingers moved down her arms to her middle, caressing, loving. She moved her hand up behind her to his neck, drawing her fingers across his skin to cup his head and draw his lips down to hers.

And then she was pressing her mouth to his, her stomach tightening, her breasts drawing in, her nipples hardening. Her lips moved over his as his tongue filled her mouth. She took his hand and placed it over her breasts and he rubbed and tweaked and massaged until she thought she would burst with need. She shifted, turning until she was facing him, her hands cupping his face as his kiss sent her soaring.

He moved his hand behind her back, holding her close, and then finished the kiss. He pulled away from her and a small moan of protest left her lips. She tried to pull him back, but he moved farther and farther away, until he was off the bed and pulling the sheets up over her, covering her nakedness. "What is happening? Where are you going?" she asked.

"You are changing. But don't worry, the worst of it is over."

If it was over, then what was he doing over there and not back in the bed with her? "I am not a demon," she insisted.

"I know," he said, his words breaking over her, the deep timbre of his voice skittering across already frayed nerves.

"Nor will I ever be," she clarified, in case that was the reason he was pulling away from her. Because there had to be a reason. Didn't there?

"I know," he repeated.

"But you said—" she cried out as another twinge grasped hold and twisted, ripping and pulling her insides. *Not again!*

"The demon dimension was where we came from originally, but that's not why the *Gauliacho* are after us and that's not what we are now."

He gave her another piece of jerky. She ate that, too, and then another until at last she felt the wrenching pain subside. She pushed herself up against the headboard.

"But what does that mean? And why don't you come back to bed?" she asked when at last she caught her breath. Her body temperature dropped and her breathing returned to normal.

"It means you are changing, leaving your humanity behind and becoming like us."

"Like you? What are you?" She looked up at him with blurred vision. "What am I changing into?" She had to know, all this pain, this suffering—if she wasn't dying, then it had to be for something.

He brushed the hair back from her face, and for a second she wondered if he would climb back into bed with her. His pale eyes locked onto hers. Eyes that looked so familiar, that almost looked like...

"A wolf."

Chapter 5

A wolf? She took several deep breaths, trying to still the panic in her mind. "How can you possibly expect me to believe that?"

"Because you already know it's true. The buzzing you've been hearing, the colors you've been seeing. You dream of the forest, of running free. You know it deep inside. It's who you are. Who you've always been."

"It's not possible," she whispered, even as his words resonated deep within her.

"It is. You've already gone through the first modification. Things are going to be different for you now. Your sight, your hearing, your senses. After this last adaptation, you will be stronger. And when you're in wolf form, you'll heal quicker."

"Wolf form? Like a werewolf?" She thought of the

horror movies she used to watch as a teen where the actors' faces stretched into grotesque misshapen monsters, their jaws and noses elongating into a wickedly sharp tooth-filled snout. And they sprouted hair. *Everywhere*.

She shivered.

Buddy whined, placing his head on the side of the bed. Jason smiled and patted Buddy, comforting him. "No, not a werewolf. More like a shape-shifter. We can change form at will, anytime. We are not ruled by the light of a full moon and we do not crave human flesh."

"Great. That's the best news I've heard all day." *Not.* "This is really too much to believe." She tried to sit up and pull away from him, but a wave of dizziness broke over her.

She fell back into the pillow and willed sleep to return. She didn't want to hear any more, didn't want to think or feel.

He touched her head again, brushing his fingers across her hair in a soothing caress. "I would love to let you sleep the day away, but I can't. After this latest change, your wolf scent is even stronger. The sun is almost up. We have to keep moving."

"Why?" she asked, her voice treacherously close to a whine.

"The demons. Or have you forgotten them?"

No. She hadn't. She just didn't want to believe him. No matter what he said. No matter what kind of wicked food poisoning she'd had. The next thing she knew, his arms were under her and he was picking her up, lifting her up off the bed.

"Hey," she cried in protest as he carried her into the

bathroom and set her down on the toilet then turned on the water in the shower. She drew her knees to her, covering herself the best she could.

"Get in and take a hot shower. You'll feel better. Don't take too long, though. Here are my keys." He pulled his key ring out of his pocket and laid it on the counter. "When you're done, put Buddy and your stuff back in the truck. I'm going to take a quick shower myself, then head over to the diner to order us breakfast. We have a long day ahead of us."

"How do you know I won't take your truck and drive myself back home?"

He stopped on his way out the door and turned back to her. "Because I trust you. And deep down, you know you can trust me. You know I'm right."

"Fine," she grumbled as steam began to fill the room. "But don't be surprised if I don't eat. My stomach is still topsy-turvy."

"I'm not worried." His smile was annoyingly confident as he turned and walked out.

"Whatever," she grumbled as she heard the adjoining door close.

Apparently no more kisses for her. Or anything else. She sighed and stripped out of her underwear then stepped under the hot spray, and melted as the pulsating water massaged her muscles. A wolf. Ridiculous. All she needed was a hot shower and she'd be fine. Obviously, something she ate hadn't agreed with her, that's all.

As she stood under the hot water, her stomach growled as she thought of a thick slab of ham covered with over-medium eggs, and topped with a side of bacon and sausages. The little link kind. It had been years since she'd had sausages. How could she be thinking of food now, after all she'd been through? But she was. As impossible as it was for her to believe, she was starving.

In no time at all, she was out of the shower, dried off and combing her long dark hair when she noticed her arms did look different. She held them out and stared at them. They were suddenly well-defined. Muscular.

You will be stronger.

She looked away, brushed her teeth then put on a quick dab of lip-gloss and mascara. She wasn't changing. She just didn't feel good. She walked out of the bathroom, staying clear of the mirror as she dressed and repacked her duffel, then she and Buddy left the room for the parking lot.

"Here you go, Buddy," she said after he did his business. She poured some of his dog food into his bowl, put some water in a stray coffee cup rolling around in the back and placed it on the floor. "Everything is going to be just fine," she lied as she locked him in the truck and walked toward the restaurant.

The sky was beginning to show the first reddish-gold streaks of dawn across the horizon when she walked into the diner. She was surprised to find it already half-full with other patrons. She glanced through the long row of windows into the parking lot and saw several large diesel trucks. That made sense, especially if the diner's breakfasts were as good as their burgers.

The smell of coffee was strong and inviting as she dropped into the booth across from Jason.

"You're looking much better," he said with a wide boyish smile. She couldn't help remembering his arms wrapped tight around her, as he'd helped her through an agonizing night. The way his hands felt on her skin, heating her blood and everything else. Annoyance surged through her at the thought.

"I assumed you were hungry, so I ordered you the special."

She couldn't take her eyes off the soft red hue surrounding the man sitting directly behind him. The colors around all the patrons were much more muted than they had been yesterday, but even better than the muted colors was the fact that she didn't have to put in her earbuds. The buzzing sounds coming from them were so soft she barely noticed them. She could still feel the person's intentions, but the sound wasn't nearly as annoying or debilitating.

In fact, she almost felt normal.

She certainly felt better than she had in… Well, she didn't know how long.

"Good morning, hun." A rotund waitress with shockingly bright red hair placed a large steaming plate of food in front of her. "Coffee?"

"Yes, please." Shay's eyes widened as she took in the mound of food on the plate. "There is no way I'm ever going to be able to eat all this."

"Thanks, Marge," Jason said, offering her a smile as she filled Shay's coffee cup then refilled his.

She paused for a moment, basking in his attention, a pleased smile stretching her painted lips. "Anytime, hun," she said, then took her coffeepot to the next table.

Shay would have to remember that smile of his and make sure she didn't swoon over it. Irritated, she shoved a piece of ham into her mouth.

"Are you feeling better?" Jason asked.

"Yes, thank you," Shay said politely over the mouth-watering ham. When had ham ever tasted this good? Much better than the spinach-and-cream-cheese omelets she usually ate. And sausages. There were sausages, too, buried under the thick slab of ham, and strips of bacon. She smiled. Heaven. She was in heaven.

"I don't know why I'm so hungry," she said as she scooped scrambled eggs into her mouth. "I can't believe I can even eat after everything I went through last night."

"Your body needs the protein."

As she ate, she glanced out the window, surprised by how much clearer her vision was, especially in the dim light of dawn. She was seeing color slightly differently. Yet, somehow, she was able to see better, farther. And she could hear and smell really well, too. The rich scent of sizzling pork was making her ravenous.

She dug into her food, not stopping until the waitress was back refilling her mug with coffee.

"My goodness. Well, he did say you were hungry."

Shay glanced down at her plate and felt the heat of embarrassment rise in her cheeks. Her plate was half-empty. How had she eaten all that food, that quickly? "Please give my compliments to the chef," she said. The cook behind the counter turned and waved.

"Joe says thanks," Marge said, and laughed.

Shay took a sip of coffee and looked up at Jason, her eyes meeting his over the rim of her cup. Was it really possible? Could she really be changing? Transforming? *Into a wolf?*

"Okay, tell me more," she said, suddenly wanting to hear it all, even if she didn't believe. Even if she refused to believe.

"What do you want to know?" he asked, hesitation strong in his voice.

"Tell me about my dad. Did you really know him?"

"Yes. He was a good friend of mine."

"How is that possible? You were a kid."

"Because once you go through the change, you age differently."

"How do you mean?"

He leaned toward her, dropping his voice. "You age very slowly."

She stared at him, amazed by the implication of his words. "How slowly?" she whispered. "How old are you?"

"Eighty-five."

"Get out." She stared at him, at the plumpness of youth beneath his cheeks and eyes, the even tones and smooth skin. "Eighty-five? No way."

"It's true. Our life expectancy is somewhere around four hundred."

"Seriously?" She downed another sausage as she tried to absorb what he'd told her. *Four hundred.*

"I'm not sure I would want to live that long," she said honestly. She was only twenty-three and life had already been...hard.

"Shay, you're not alone," he said, seemingly reading her mind. "You have family waiting for you back at The Colony."

She looked up at him, her eyes widening, her heart afraid to beat. No, she was alone. She'd lost everyone, one after another until there was no one left. Just her and Buddy, in their little house in the woods.

"Your family is anxious to meet you. Grandparents. A cousin."

Shay shook her head, her breakfast forgotten, her mouth dry. "My dad said he didn't have anyone." The words came out a hoarse whisper.

"I suppose to him he didn't. He had to leave them behind and never look back. But they are still there, waiting for you. You even have a house—your dad's old house. It's a great place right on the lake. Your dad loved to sit in an old chair out on the end of his dock and fish. You and Buddy will love it there."

Tears watered Shay's eyes. She blinked. "I…I thought I—" A lump caught in her throat.

"I know I've given you a lot to absorb, but if you believe nothing else, please believe that you have family anxious to meet you, and they've been waiting to do so for a very long time. Will you come with me to The Colony?"

"Are you actually asking?" She couldn't help the smile lifting the corners of her mouth.

He nodded and leaned back in the booth, amusement dancing in his eyes and suddenly he looked as handsome to her as he had that first moment she'd laid eyes on him. "I'm asking."

She thought of her father's parents and knew she had to meet them. She had to see for herself. "Yes, I'd like to come. I'd like to see this place where my dad once lived, I'd like to meet my family. But I'm not promising I'll stay."

"Sounds like a deal to me."

She turned her attention back to her plate, but no longer felt the need to devour what was left. Instead she picked at her food while discreetly watching him. She didn't know if it was because of the way he'd held her through her pain, or the way he just seemed to know what she needed, but she was beginning to see him differently than she had before. More as a friend than someone who was dismantling her life.

Who was she kidding? Last night she'd wanted him to be much more than a friend. His sure touch, his warm hands had stroked away her pain and made her want so much more than just comfort. He looked up from his breakfast, his bluish-gray eyes locking on to hers and holding steady. Heat suffused her cheeks and she dropped her gaze back to her plate.

"Are you ready to go?" he asked with a strange hitch to his voice. She looked up at him and couldn't help wondering if he knew what she'd been thinking. "There's a whole community waiting for your arrival."

She nodded, not trusting her voice to speak. She finished the last of her coffee as he rose to pay the bill. A pickup truck had pulled into the parking lot and parked next to Jason's. Buddy was standing up in the front seat, barking at the two men who hopped out of the cab and were walking toward them. She didn't need to see the cloud of darkness swirling around them to know they weren't here for the food.

They were here for her.

She could sense it from the energy flowing from their minds, see it in the dark auras swirling around their heads. She looked at Jason standing in line at the cash register and then at Buddy going crazy, barking madly in the front seat of the truck.

She hurried toward Jason but just as she reached him, just as she turned to point out the window, another truck pulled into the lot with another two men, the same thought patterns issuing from inside them.

"Jason!" she hissed under her breath, and grabbed his arm.

He followed her gaze out the window, taking in the situation, then threw the check and a twenty on the counter. "Keep the change, Marge."

He turned her away from the front door, from the door closest to the truck, and with a hand on her back quickly led her toward the rear of the diner, toward the open-air walkway that led back to the motel. Away from the parking lot. Away from the truck.

"What are we going to do?"

"Make a run for it." He grabbed her hand, hurrying her forward toward the outside door. They reached it just as all four men walked into the diner.

"Now!" Jason said, and they bolted outside, running toward the truck. And they almost made it, would have made it, if one of the men in the diner hadn't chosen that moment to glance back out the window.

The next thing she knew, he was bursting out the diner's door, running toward them. They kicked into high gear, running faster than Shay ever thought she could and still the man reached the truck before they did.

"What is he, a track star?" she cried as Jason sprang into action, running at the man, bracing his hands on the hood of the truck and swinging both legs around and planting them square in the man's middle.

The man buckled over with a loud whoosh.

"Get in the truck," Jason yelled.

Shay ran past him and jerked on the door. It was locked.

"Dammit!" She fumbled in her jacket for the keys. Found them and pulled them out. She quickly hit the unlock button and pulled open the door then tried to climb up into the cab, but Buddy was moving back and forth across the front seats, barking ferociously.

"Move over, Buddy!" She pushed him back then slammed the door shut as he tried to plow across her lap. The other three men, seeing what was happening, were running toward them.

"Hurry Jason!"

Jason punched his assailant once more, sending the man soaring, then turned, rushing toward her, but before he could reach the driver's door, another man, a giant red-haired beast, grabbed him by the arm, swung him around and punched him straight in the face.

Jason hit the ground. Hard. The giant turned toward her, his hard green eyes narrowing as he spotted her in the truck. Quickly, she hit the lock button, locking all the doors.

He pulled on the handle anyway, jerking it up and down.

Another man appeared at the passenger's door, rattling it as he, too, tried to get in. Buddy was going nuts, barking and jumping at the window. And then the third and fourth men appeared.

She was surrounded.

"Jason!" she screamed, but she couldn't see him. Where was he?

Buddy sprayed spittle all over the driver's-side window, and jumping against it so hard, she was certain he was going to break the glass. What was she going to do? She couldn't just sit there. Surely Marge would see what was happening and call the police?

Wouldn't she?

"Jason!" Shay had to get out of there. She stood in her seat, trying to see beyond the front of the hood, but the men were surrounding the truck now, pushing against the doors and windows, rocking the vehicle back and forth. They were going to tip her over!

Shay blared on the horn, hoping someone would come running. Would help. "Jason!" she screamed again. Then she remembered the keys. She still had them. She pushed Buddy out of the way, stuck the keys in the ignition and turned them. The truck roared to life. She popped it into Reverse, quickly glanced behind her and then pushed down on the accelerator. The truck flew backward, tires squealing, smoke rising.

And still the men kept coming.

She saw Jason lying on the ground, his head torqued at an odd angle across the cement parking spot, blood dripping down his face. "Please let him be okay," she whispered. He had to be okay. Marge and a few truckers ran out the front of the diner. They would help him. They had to.

The men ran after her. Pushing her foot against the gas pedal, she floored it, pulling out of the motel parking lot and careening back onto the highway. She looked behind her to see if the men would follow her or if they'd turn back to Jason.

And if they did? Would the others help him? Could they? Before she could give it much thought, she saw them running toward their vehicles. They weren't after Jason; they were after her.

She drove down the highway faster than she ever had before then quickly pulled off at the next exit and skirted behind a gas station facing the highway where she waited for the two trucks to pass her. She didn't have to wait long. Within minutes the two trucks sped by, barreling down the highway.

Immediately, she gunned it, turning around and driving back to the diner, hoping the men wouldn't figure out what she'd done for at least another ten minutes. By then, she would have Jason and they would be gone.

If he was okay.

She pulled back into the parking lot, tires squealing, the truck pitching dangerously. But she didn't care. Quickly, she scanned the parking lot, but she didn't see Jason anywhere. Panic crawled up her throat.

"Shit, Buddy! Where is he?"

She lurched to a stop in front of the diner, throwing

the truck in Park; she jumped down and almost reached the diner's door when Jason came rushing out.

"Shay!"

Pumped up with adrenaline and so happy to see him standing, she ran into him, throwing her arms around him and holding him tight. "Oh, thank God you're okay."

After a second, she pulled back and looked at him, noticing the blood trickling from a nasty wound on his forehead. "Are you okay?"

He smiled, and her heart lifted. "I'll be fine. Where are they?"

"Hopefully still flying north up the highway."

He nodded, looking impressed. "Good thinking on your part."

"Thanks, though I don't know how long they'll continue on before they realize what I've done and double back."

"Then we'd better get moving."

"Can you drive?" she asked, eyeing that wound once more and the bloody towel in his hand.

"No problem. But we're going to have to take a different route. A longer, slower route."

"But I thought…"

"Yes, we need to get you to The Colony as soon as we can, and not just because Marge called the police. Each moment that you move closer to your transition, your wolf scent gets stronger. Add yours to mine and we have become a large neon target."

"And once we make it to this colony, they won't be able to sense us?"

"Exactly."

"Then we'd better get a move on," she said.

"My thoughts exactly."

Chapter 6

Jason hurried into the truck and they drove down the road, pulling off the highway at the next exit and heading east through the forest on two-lane isolated roads. They drove for miles, not seeing any sign of the men. They still had a long way to go. The good news was Shay finally seemed willing to take this ride, the bad news was he wasn't sure he'd be able to get her there.

He'd taken too long to find her, the crystals on his wrist were losing their power and would soon no longer mask his presence and she was changing too quickly. He glanced over at her. Her scent was almost as strong as his now. The two of them were bright beacons in a vast sea of darkness. All the demons had to do was run across one disturbed or lost human, hitch on and take a ride, becoming an *Abatu*. They would bide their time, tracking him and Shay until there were more of them, and then they'd attack. Just like they had at the diner. Only next time he and Shay might not be so lucky.

"I don't think I've ever been so scared," Shay admitted, turning to look at him, her blue-violet eyes filled with fear. "Those men weren't going to stop until they had me. I was afraid they were going to flip the truck over."

"You were great. You did exactly what you should have done."

"I hated leaving you."

"Luckily, I wasn't the one they wanted. Not then."

"Are you going to be okay?" she asked, concern betraying the fear in her voice as her gaze moved up to the wound on his head.

"I am a great healer. We are both going to be fine. Better than fine," he assured her with more confidence than he felt. It didn't help that his head hurt like hell and the bleeding wouldn't stop. If it didn't stop soon, he'd have to transform. He didn't want to do that, not in front of Shay. Seeing what he changed into, what the transformation really meant, would only spook her. It would be easier on her if he could get her settled with her family and in her new home before she had to face what her transformation would ultimately mean.

He'd have to call Malcolm. That was a phone call he didn't want to make. Malcolm wasn't a great leader, not like Dean had been—he was too heavy-handed and prone to a bad temper—but he wasn't a bad leader either. They'd had relative peace and prosperity for the past fifteen years. At least until now. Shay's cousin,

Scott, who had been too young at the time Dean had left to step up, now led a rival faction and was making a bid for pack leader.

Pack politics could be complicated, but Scott's bloodline was strong. He was well liked and he had some good and sound ideas. But Jason couldn't—wouldn't—abide Scott's tactics. An underground movement to unseat Malcolm and take over the pack's leadership wasn't the way they did things. There had been a few instances of violence that made Jason doubt if Scott was the right person to lead their pack.

Violence was never an answer. That's why there were rules. No wolf can ever cause the death of another wolf. If that happened, they were banished from The Colony to the outside world. They were on their own. As they should be. Some wolves had never left The Colony. They had no idea how dangerous it was out there. How chaotic.

Jason did.

Unfortunately, Malcolm was right. Getting Shay to come back, to marry him and to rule The Colony with him, was the only way to divert the bloodshed. No matter how much Jason was growing to hate the idea. Especially after what had happened between them earlier that morning. That kiss! It had taken all the strength and willpower he possessed to pull away from her. And he still wondered why he'd bothered. Why couldn't he be the one for Shay? Because he'd heard the whispers of rebellion; he knew what was coming. And Malcolm did, too. And right now, Shay was their only hope for peace or things were going to get really bad. He only hoped Shay would be on board with this.

He stole a glance at her long dark hair, the slim curve of her face, her high cheekbones and the slight russet shade to her skin. She looked exotic, stunning, especially with her brilliant blue eyes. But he hadn't expected her not to know anything about them, to have no understanding of pack loyalty and allegiance. These were tenets Dean had stood for. And values Jason never imagined he wouldn't pass on to his daughter.

Now it fell to Jason. But he couldn't tell Shay about Malcolm and her responsibilities to the pack yet. Especially not after what had happened between them. He'd just got the fear out of her eyes. If he told her what Malcolm had planned for her, she'd bolt the first chance she got. The woman was skittish. Beautiful. Independent. Feisty and strong. But very skittish.

Buddy sat up and whined. Jason went on immediate alert, checking the forest around them as they drove down the lonely road. They appeared to be alone, but he knew better than anyone that appearances could be deceiving.

"I think he has to go to the bathroom," Shay said. "It's been quite a while since we've had a break."

Jason checked his surroundings once more then reluctantly pulled the truck over to the side of the road. "Wait here."

He got out of the truck and walked off the shoulder into the trees, listening, smelling, sensing. Nothing. They were alone. He walked back to the truck.

"We need to be quick. We're vulnerable out here in the open."

"All right." Shay opened the door and Buddy jumped down. Within seconds he was off and running. "Buddy!"

Jason cringed at the way her voice echoed through the trees. "What is he after?" he asked as he pressed the bloody towel harder against his head. A wave of light-headedness rolled over him and he leaned against the side of the truck.

"I don't know," Shay muttered, heading off toward the dog. "Buddy!"

The dog came running back, appearing from the thickness of the trees. He ran up to Shay and jumped up on her.

"Buddy, get down. You know better than that." She turned to Jason. "I think he just wanted to stretch his legs."

"Well, if he's done now?" He gestured his head toward the truck.

"All right. Come on, Buddy. Back in the truck." Buddy didn't look happy and needed more coaxing, but soon they were back in the truck and on their way.

Nothing had happened. No one was there. Not an *Abatu* in sight. They just might make it after all, if they had no more unforeseen problems.

"Tell me more about The Colony," Shay asked, filling the silence in the truck.

That one was easy. "It's beautiful," he said. "It's nestled in a valley of soaring mountains and surrounds a lake of crystal-clear water fed by underground springs and snow runoff. Ice-cold most of the year, but so clear you can see several feet down."

"Sounds stunning."

"Most beautiful spot on earth. A hidden jewel and those of us who live there know it. We do everything we can to protect it from the outside would."

"That can't be easy."

"Nothing worth keeping ever is."

"So, why can't the demons sense us there?"

"There is a magnetic field in the mountains, a force field that makes us invisible to them. We also have crystals surrounding the perimeter of The Colony and a very special woman who has the power to energize and sustain them." He held up his wrist, displaying the stones intertwined within the black cord.

"This bracelet is made from those crystals—it prevents the *Gauliacho* from sensing my energy."

"But they can now?"

"Yes. The crystals' power has worn down. They need to be rejuvenated."

"How does she do it?"

"No one really knows. Some of us are born with the gift to see energy and manipulate it."

"Like the auras?"

"Exactly. Those are people's energy signatures. The different colors you see tell you about that person's soul. The kind of heart they have inside."

"Interesting." She smiled.

"What?"

"Your heart, it's very beautiful."

He stared at her for a minute, his eyes dropping to

her sweet lips. He wished he wasn't driving so his hands would be free to pull her close, to hold her in his arms as he had last night and to kiss her senseless. Obviously, he was losing it.

"Is this the only place where your people can be safe?" she asked, breaking his fantasy.

"*Our* people," he corrected, his gaze locking on hers. She quickly looked away. She still wasn't accepting.

"How long until we get there?" she asked.

Not soon enough, he thought. But he said, "Hopefully by midnight." They were approaching a small town. "Let's stop here, fill up with fuel and get something to eat. Plus I need ice for my head."

"It still hasn't stopped bleeding," she said nervously, leaning forward to look at his wound.

Close enough for him to pick up her delicate scent— lavender and chamomile with a touch of honey. "It will be fine," he rasped.

Concern filled her beautiful eyes. "Maybe you should lie down in the back and let me drive for a while."

"I would, but you haven't a clue where we're going. The way is a maze of logging roads."

"We could stay here for a while so you can rest. I am starving. I know that's hard to believe after that breakfast I devoured, but I suddenly seem hungry all the time."

He took a deep breath, fighting another wave of dizziness. "Don't worry, that won't last long," he pushed the words out as he pulled the truck alongside the gas pump. Speaking was beginning to take more energy than he had.

The gas station was attached to a small diner where they could get lunch. Maybe if he could send her inside, he could sit here and rest for a minute.

"Good, because at the rate I'm eating, I'll be as big as a house," Shay said, her eyes on the diner. Buddy whined from the backseat.

"Your body needs a lot of fuel for the cell restructuring."

"Cell restructuring? If you say so. You say I'm changing. But I still don't see it." She glanced down at her arms. "Much. And honestly, you look quite human to me."

Her eyes swept over his body and he saw appreciation there. And something more. *Desire.*

That would change. As soon as she saw him transform she wouldn't want to be anywhere near him. He pulled the blood-soaked rag away from his head. "Listen, I might need to show you my other side sooner than I'd planned. I don't want to, but I'm not healing. The bleeding hasn't stopped."

She took his hand and held it, surprising him. "Then maybe you should. Don't worry about me. I can handle it."

The earnestness in her voice, the concern in her eyes overwhelmed him and he felt the urge to lean across the cab and kiss her once more. The sweetness in her voice and the dewy wetness of her lips made him hate his orders, hate what he had been asked to do. Hate that he had to put Malcolm and the pack first. He sucked in a breath, but his resolve was weakening.

And what made it worse, she wanted him to kiss her.

He could see it in the way she was leaning into him, feel it in the expectation in the air. The memory of her touch on his neck, her lips on his assaulted him, battering his defenses. He wanted to touch her. To kiss her. To love her. He shook the images out of his head. He couldn't. She was meant for Malcolm. Malcolm had to be the one to help her with the final stage of her transition. Jason couldn't thwart that process. The pack needed him to be strong. Malcolm needed him. And he wouldn't let them down.

Not again.

No matter how enticing the she-wolf was.

"Will you run in and get us some burgers while I fill up?" he said, his voice catching in his throat. He had to put some distance between them.

"Are you sure you don't want to go in and rest for a little while?"

"We can't. The sooner we get to The Colony, the safer we'll be."

She sighed. "All right." She turned to Buddy and patted him on the head. "Stay here, boy."

Buddy whined and they both watched her get out of the truck and walk toward the small restaurant.

"She is a beautiful woman, Buddy," Jason said, appreciating the gentle sway of her hips and the nice way she filled out her blue jeans.

Buddy barked in agreement and Jason couldn't help smiling as he popped another two Tylenol. He got out of the truck and started pumping the gas when a wave of dizziness rocked over him, stealing his balance. He got back into the truck and sat there, waiting for the throbbing pain to ebb.

It didn't.

He took a swig from the large water bottle. Soon as he ate his burger, he'd feel better.

"Jason?" Shay asked as she opened the door to the truck.

He looked up at her. He must have fallen asleep. She eyed the bloody rag that had fallen to his lap.

"That really doesn't look good. Maybe we should find you a doctor."

"No. No doctors. I'll be okay." He got out of the truck and unhooked the fuel nozzle, took his receipt, then got back in. That small amount of effort took all the energy he had left. Blackness encroached, pushing in at the corners of his vision. His stomach flip-flopped.

"If you say so," she muttered. "Why don't you at least let me drive while you eat?"

He relented. He had no choice. He was in no condition to drive. He moved over to the passenger's seat while Shay ran around to the driver's side. He tore into his burger as she slid behind the wheel and pulled her bag of fries next to her. She adjusted the mirrors and put the truck in Drive.

"So where to?"

"Stay on this road for the next eighty-three miles. At that point you will see a small gravel road hidden within the trees to your left. Take that."

"Will it have a name?"

"Nope."

"Okay," she said. "Checking my odometer now."

"Thanks, Shay." He leaned back in his seat and closed his eyes.

"Don't thank me. Just get better. I'll wake you when we reach the road."

He took another big bite of his burger, hoped it would stay down then went back to sleep.

As Shay drove, she watched Jason out of the corner of her eye. He hadn't quite finished his burger and hadn't touched his fries, which wasn't like him. Every time she'd seen him eat, he ate *everything*. Especially his fries. His head was leaning against the window, and a steady trickle of blood rolled down his face and seeped into his shirt.

She was trying to keep up a brave front, but she was terrified. She didn't have to be a nurse or a doctor to know that that much blood loss was not good. It had been hours since Jason was hurt and the bleeding still hadn't stopped. He was pale and he looked as if he were comatose rather than merely napping.

And if he was? What chance would she have of finding The Colony, of getting them to safety before another whacked-out crazy demon person attacked them? When she woke him, she'd make him draw her a map. She pushed her fears behind her and pressed down on the accelerator. The quicker they got there, the better.

Several hours had passed since they'd left the gas station, and still Jason hadn't woken. She didn't like how pale he was or the way his head lolled to the side. But worse was his shallow, absurdly quiet breathing. She had to do something.

"Jason," she said softly, not sure if she should wake him. But the way he was sleeping scared her. "Jason," she said again, louder.

Still no response. She pulled over to the side of the road and parked then scooted up next to him. "Jason," she said, and then shook him.

Still he didn't wake.

Panic stole over her. She shook him hard. "Jason, wake up."

He groaned and tried to open his eyes.

"Thank God." She grabbed the water bottle out of the cup holder and held it up to his mouth. "Here, drink this. I think you passed out." She pressed it to his lips and poured a small amount into his mouth. Most of it dribbled back out.

"Jason, we need to get you help. You've lost too much blood and the bleeding still hasn't stopped."

He looked down at his shirt, now almost half-soaked with his blood. "I have to transition, Shay. Don't be afraid."

"Afraid. Why would I be afraid?" She tried to sound strong, but a quaver stole into her voice.

"You need to get off the main road. Have we reached the turnoff yet?"

She looked at the odometer. "Seventeen more miles."

"Go."

"All right. But don't pass out again. Keep talking to me."

He mumbled something she couldn't hear as she pulled back onto the road, driving faster than was safe, hoping to reach the turnoff before he went out again.

She didn't. They hadn't gone five miles and his head was back against the glass.

As soon as she saw the small road barely visible within the thicket of trees, she hit the brakes, skidding to an abrupt stop. Buddy whined as he hit the back of the seats. "Sorry, boy."

Luckily both she and Jason had their seatbelts on and they were alone on the mountain road. She made a hard left, turning onto the gravel road, then drove a half mile farther until they were out of sight from the main road and stopped.

"Okay, Jason. We're here. Wake up." She shook him again, and when he didn't respond, shook him harder. He didn't move an inch. Swallowing her panic, she climbed out of the truck and ran around the outside and opened his door. The cold air smacked him in the face and she saw his eyelids move.

"Jason!" she said again, grabbing him by the arm. "We're here. Do what you have to do. Change. Heal. Transform. Get better."

Jason's eyes opened and she gasped at how bloodshot they were. "Don't die on me," she pleaded. "Everyone dies on me."

"I won't," he said on a raspy breath. "I can't. I haven't been tortured enough yet." He reached for her and half fell as she tried to help him out of the truck.

"Jason!"

"Don't be scared," he whispered as he leaned against her, then he slumped to the ground. "Help me take off my shoes."

"Your shoes?"

He struggled to reach the laces. She swatted his hands away and undid them, then pulled them off.

"Socks, too."

Without saying a word she pulled off his socks and laid them by the shoes. Next followed his shirt when she saw him struggling with it. It was so bloody, she just threw it to the side.

"Get back in the cab," he rasped. "I don't want you to see."

"Don't be ridiculous. I can't leave you." She helped him out of his pants. What was going to happen? And why didn't he want her to see?

"Please, Shay," he whispered, his voice barely audible.

"Why not?" Now she was getting scared.

He didn't answer. He couldn't. She could see it was taking all his strength to argue with her.

"All right, Jason. You win." She left him there and went back around the side of the truck and climbed into the driver's seat. She was only there a few minutes when she heard Jason cry out in pain. She grasped the steering wheel, her knuckles whitening as more sounds reached her—cries, whimpers, growls…howls.

The hair stood on the back of her neck. Agitated, Buddy paced, whining, his ears twitching as he roamed back and forth across the backseat.

"It's okay, boy," she said, patting him on the head. But was it? What was happening to Jason? What really was this change he kept talking about? And why didn't he want her to watch?

Now she was more afraid than ever. Not knowing,

just imagining was far worse than seeing. "Oh, to hell with it." She got out of the truck and ran back around to where she'd left Jason. Only he wasn't there. Lying on the ground next to the pile of Jason's clothes was a very large gray wolf with blood seeping through a nasty wound on his head.

Shay grasped the side of the truck. Her heart lurched in her chest as Jason's words echoed in her disbelieving mind.

You'll change into a wolf.

Chapter 7

The wolf turned and looked up at her, its pale bluish-gray eyes gazing directly into hers. "Jason?" It wasn't possible. But the more she stared into eyes that looked so much like Jason's, and then there was the wound that was the same shape and in the same spot on its head... She slumped against the truck. It couldn't be.

He'd told her, but she hadn't believed him, not really. How could she? Even after everything else that had been happening to her. How could she believe *she* was turning into a wolf? That she wasn't human? What was she supposed to do now?

Run. The word screamed through her head. Get in the truck and drive away. Get as far away from him and all this craziness as she could.

She took a step away from the animal. The large wolf

that looked so much like the wolves that had surrounded her home. And then she knew she couldn't go back. The wolves were waiting for her back at her house and so were the voices. She couldn't run from this problem, because there was nowhere to run to. Nowhere to go.

Anxiety laced with a heavy dose of fear crawled through her, quickening her breath and accelerating her heart rate. She couldn't do this. She didn't want to become like *him*. But did she have a choice? An option? Perhaps there was a way to stop the transformation.

The wolf, still watching her, whined. A sad, weak sound that reached inside her and plucked at her heart-strings. It lifted its paw toward her then dropped it.

Was Jason still in there? Did he know who she was? Or was he just a wounded wolf? She took a tentative step forward. Would he bite her? Was that why Jason wanted her to stay in the truck?

"Damn, Jason, you could have given me a little more info," she muttered.

The wolf lifted its head and whined again. Buddy was standing in the passenger's seat looking down at them, howling in agitation and making a mess out of the windows again.

"Well, I don't know what to do," she said both to the wolf and to Buddy. She took another step toward. "What am I supposed to do?"

With great effort the wolf got to his feet. It turned and looked at her, expectantly, as if waiting for something. When she didn't move, he placed his paw on the truck's door.

"You want in the truck?" she asked, fairly certain she

didn't want it in there with her and Buddy. She glanced at the truck's bed and wondered how hard it would be to get him up there. She wasn't sure if the wolf knew what she was thinking or not, but it pawed the door again, then lifted its head and gave a long low moan.

"All right," she said, stepping forward. She leaned over him, her arm brushing the top of its large body, and held her breath as she pulled open the door, half expecting the wolf to bite her hand off.

But he didn't. Instead he tried to get into the truck. Jumping up only to slide back down again. He tried twice, then let out a sharp yelp before collapsing back onto the ground. Shay's heart broke as she watched the ragged rise and fall of the wolf's chest as he lay there. He didn't have the strength to get into the truck.

"Oh, no," she muttered, and knew it was foolish, beyond foolish. Crazy. But she couldn't just leave the poor thing there. She couldn't leave *Jason* there.

"Come on, boy, let's try one more time," she said, and bent over the animal. Tentatively, she placed a hand on the wolf's body, lightly stroking down its side. When the wolf didn't move, she slid her palm around its back and slipped it under his rib cage. She watched the wolf's face, expectantly waiting for any kind of reaction, any hint that he didn't want her touching him.

She caught her breath as the wolf came dangerously close to her face. And then he licked her. She exhaled deeply, and slipped her other hand under him. She had to help him. She couldn't just leave him there on the side of the road.

"We can do this," she said. "You and I together. Okay,

boy?" She applied pressure underneath the wolf and lifted slightly. The wolf let out a soft whimpering sound then tried again to get to his feet. He was barely able to stand this time, his legs wobbling as he stepped forward. Shay steadied him.

He was heavy, and almost slipped through her grasp, his legs pumping at the air, his nails scratching the metal kick plate in the opened door of the truck. Finally his foot found purchase. Using all her strength, she hefted the wolf up into the cab. Buddy whimpered, staring at the animal that was lying motionless on the front seat.

Shay took a huge relieved breath, grabbed the pile of clothes off the ground and put them in the backseat, shut the door and then ran around to the driver's door. Buddy was going nuts in the backseat, whining and sniffing, not knowing what to make of the animal. "It's okay, Buddy. It's Jason," she said, feeling more than a little foolish saying the words out loud.

The wolf looked up at him and whimpered. Eyes bright, Buddy stared at him, then sniffed him, sticking his nose right up next to the wound, and then he started to lick.

Shay stroked Buddy's head. "Good boy," she said, knowing his saliva would help in the healing. She put the truck in gear and started to drive back down the road. "I sure hope we are supposed to stay on this road for a while."

Somehow, the wolf moved his head, inching it forward until it was resting on her lap. She stroked his soft fur, burying her fingers in the deep fluff. He was so beautiful, his eyes so much like Jason's, white tufts of fur intermingled with black and gray strands lining his face.

"Just get better. Heal. Everything is going to be all right," she whispered. It had to be, for both of them.

The wolf licked her hand and she smiled. She would get them there. The only problem was she wasn't sure exactly where "there" was. She kept driving down the gravel road, trying to put as much distance between them and the main road as she could while heading for the crest of steep mountains in the distance.

"Don't worry, Jason. Buddy and I won't let anything happen to you."

Buddy barked in agreement.

Shay maneuvered slowly down the rough and winding road, afraid of hitting one of the deer that were constantly jumping out of the trees in front of her, or a raccoon or possum whose eyes shone yellow and red in the headlamp's reflection. Once it had gotten dark, all kinds of animals were coming out of the trees and her constant vigilance was making her exhausted and to make matters worse, she didn't have a clue where she was.

The wolf on her lap had been sleeping for the past three hours. His bleeding had finally stopped. She didn't know animals could sleep so deeply. As she approached another bumpy bend in the road, she dropped the car's speed to a crawl, trying to see beyond the curve. Once through, she stopped. There was nothing but trees in front of her. The road had come to an end.

Damn. Apparently she should have taken one of the

many side roads off this one. But how could she have known which one? There were no markers, nothing to show the way. She needed to turn around, but when she looked into the darkness behind her, she realized even with the reverse lights she wouldn't be able to see well enough to maneuver in such a narrow space.

She sighed. She was exhausted and scared. Surely no one would be able to find them or sense them way out here in the middle of nowhere. Right?

She considered waking the wolf, but what good would that do? Her eyes drifted closed as her options circled around her mind. She shook herself awake. She couldn't sleep. Not yet. Not with them stuck there. She had to at least get the truck turned around just in case. Her eyes slipped closed again. Ten minutes, she promised herself as fatigue washed over her. A quick power nap. She leaned forward and turned off the truck.

A cold wet nose pushing against her neck woke her. She opened her eyes to the dim light of dawn and a soft whine. Then she turned to face a very large, very awake wolf standing six inches from her face. She gasped and pushed herself back against the side window.

Buddy barked with excitement. She looked at them both, at their lolling tongues and wagging tails and realized she was not in danger. All they wanted was out.

"Okay, all right. I'm awake," she muttered, and made the mistake of opening the driver's door. Both the wolf and Buddy bounded across her lap, trampling her in their haste to get out the door. "Don't mind me!" she said as one paw after another dug into her stomach and thighs.

They both tore off into the woods. Shay leaned back against the seat and closed her eyes again. She had to go to the bathroom, but didn't exactly like the idea of going out in the woods where Jason could run up on her at any moment.

She squirmed in her seat while she waited for them to return and watched the golden-red streaks of dawn shimmering through the leaves, lighting up the dew and making the forest sparkle with early-morning light. She cracked her window, closed her eyes and breathed deep the scent of pine and cedar.

A soft knock on the glass startled her. She turned and saw Jason standing outside the window. *Naked.* Her eyes widened and her breath caught painfully in her throat. She coughed and quickly looked away. She didn't know what she'd expected, but she certainly didn't expect to see him standing there, looking gorgeous in all his natural glory.

She tried to block the image of his body from her mind, tried really hard, but the vision of him, *all of him,* would be scorched onto her brain. *Forever.* She grabbed the steering wheel and focused her gaze forward on the trees—the tall trees with the pinecones dangling from the branches, lots and lots of pinecones—in front of her.

She swallowed, her mouth going dry as her thoughts immediately went back to her hotel room when he'd been lying in bed with her, his hot skin against hers as he stroked her body, soothing her aches, taking away her pain and setting a new fire exploding within her. A fire that still hadn't burned out.

"My clothes?" he asked. "Unless you'd rather I didn't put them back on?"

Oh! She could hear the smile in his voice, but she wasn't about to look and see if she was right. Cheeks burning, she turned and reached into the backseat, grabbing his pile of clothes and the shoes, then opened the window. Not trusting herself, she squeezed shut her eyes and thrust his clothes and shoes at him.

"Thank you." He took the pile and as hard as she tried to keep her gaze forward, she still managed to catch a glance of his very tight, very perfect backside through the side-view mirror. Her mouth fell open and she made a slight blubbering noise. Kind of like an *aww* and an *ooh,* but coming out all confused. Damn! She quickly turned away as heat suffused her cheeks.

He sure did look good. Too good.

She scooted out the other door. "I'll be right back," she called. "Just…uh…just stay there." She grabbed her pack then bolted into the woods. She ran as far as she dared until she could no longer see the truck through the trees.

She quickly undressed, did her business, then searched through the pack for fresh clothes. Oh, what she wouldn't give for a hot shower right then. A hot shower with him! She pushed the thought out of her mind and stretched her arms up above her head, this way and that until her back popped. She slipped on a pair of cotton capris and a button-up blouse then ran a brush through her long hair, wrapped a hair band around it and twisted it up onto her head. Piling everything back into the pack, she headed to the truck. She had to get ahold of her libido before she made a complete fool of herself. She wasn't a woman who threw herself at unsuspecting gorgeous men and she wasn't about to start now.

When she stepped onto the road, Jason was standing there, shirtless but dressed and brushing his teeth with water from a water bottle. Of course, he didn't have to make it so difficult on her. Surely the man had an extra shirt. Though she had to admit, she sure liked the view. As she drew closer, she noticed the wound on his forehead had become nothing but a slight scab surrounded by dried blood. Amazing.

She focused on the scab and tried not to stare at his gorgeous, well-defined chest as she started brushing her teeth. But he was incredibly beautiful. Strong, hard muscles shimmered beneath his skin every time he moved. Her fingers itched to touch him, to see if his skin was really as smooth as it looked. How was it possible that just minutes before he was a wolf—fur, pointed ears, long nose, claws and all? She saw Buddy sitting beneath a tree next to him and wondered what he thought of all this.

Forcing herself to turn away, she put her bag with her toiletries back into her pack. After a minute of fumbling in the pack looking for nothing, she glanced up at Jason as he washed the dried blood off his face. He'd missed a spot. She stepped forward and reached up to help him. She'd been wrong. There wasn't a scab where the wound had been. There wasn't even a scratch.

"You're completely healed," she said with wonder in her voice.

He placed his hand over hers. "We heal quicker when we're in wolf form, though it took much longer than it should have. I'm sorry about that. I was worse off than I'd thought."

"I'll say. You scared me, Jason. I wasn't sure you were going to make it." She remembered how much he'd bled and how pale he'd been and out of nowhere a tremble shook through her. Yes, she'd been scared, but more than that, she'd been terrified.

"Is that the only reason you were afraid?"

His eyes searched hers as he waited for an answer. She knew what he wanted to hear. What she needed to say. "Yes. I was afraid you weren't going to make it. I would be lost and alone out here."

"And…" he prompted.

"I wasn't afraid *of* you," she muttered. "If that's what you want to know. I was just surprised. Very surprised."

He stepped closer and reached for her, slipping his hand around her waist. "I never would have hurt you."

"I know." *I think.*

He pulled her to him as if it was natural, expected. As if they belonged together. She leaned her face against his very warm, very smooth chest and smiled. It felt wonderful against her cheek, as good as she'd imagined it would.

"I'm here to protect you, to get you safely to The Colony. I'm very good at what I do. Nothing is going to stop me from getting you to your dad's house." The deep timbre of his voice reached inside her, caressing. *Soothing.* "A few demons aren't going to stop us."

"Promise," she whispered.

He pulled her tighter against him. "Promise."

She looked up at him. "There was so much blood, Jason. I was so afraid you were going to die…."

"Shh." He leaned down and suddenly his lips were against hers, gentle and sweet. And everything else disappeared. The ground beneath her feet, the cool morning breeze on her cheeks—all she felt was the warm smoothness of his lips against hers, of his skin beneath her fingers.

"It's okay," he whispered, breaking away. "We're both here. We're both safe. That's all that matters."

She nodded and smiled a shaky smile, twined her arms around his neck and kissed him again. Longer this time, feeling his mouth tentatively open, his tongue reach inside and meld with hers. Warmth dropped over her as her insides ignited. She held him tighter, pressing herself against him. She didn't want to let go. Holding him like this, being with him, feeling his heat surrounding her felt like the most natural thing in the world. Like she was exactly where she was meant to be. There was no awkwardness. No second guesses. Happiness bubbled up inside her, and she knew she could spend the whole day standing in his arms, feeling the sweet touch of his lips against hers.

She dropped her hands and slipped them up his back. Just as quickly as he'd started, he pulled away, breaking the kiss and leaving her wanting more. "We should really get going," he said, his words sounding husky and strained.

Not exactly what she wanted to hear. She looked up into his face and wondered what he was thinking. Was he feeling the same as she? Was he feeling anything at all? "Jason…I'm not sure if it was because you got hurt, or because I saw you in your…um…your other form, but I feel close to you. I know I can trust you. I believe you when you say you'll take care of me."

He brushed her hair back from her face. "I'm glad."

"Then what is it?" she asked, because there was something, a sudden detachment, a sense of regret.

He eased back, taking a step away from her, putting distance between them. "I, uh, that's good. I'm glad. Like I said, I won't let anything happen to you."

She smiled, but it was forced. That wasn't what she wanted to hear. What she wanted to know. He was hiding something from her. Worse, he was retreating. She shouldn't have spilled her guts like that. Since when did she ever do anything on instinct? She was not an instinctual person. She was a rational, logical person, and rational, logical people didn't spill their guts just because they kissed a guy. "And?" she prompted.

He looked at her blankly, that wide-eyed, unable-to-move, deer-caught-in-the-headlights look.

"I've seen you face down demons and a pack of wolves and you look more afraid right now than you did then. What is it? What's going on here?"

"It just that this… Us… We can't." He spread his arms wide. "It's complicated."

He reached past her into the truck for another water bottle. She felt struck. Dismissed. Worse. Inconsequential. What was wrong with her? She didn't even know this man. Obviously the stress of everything was making her think things, feel things that weren't real. Especially where Jason was concerned.

"Where are we?" he asked, obviously ready to move the conversation to safer ground. *For him.*

"I'm not sure," she admitted, unapologetically. "I followed the road you had me turn off on and it just ended. You didn't give me very much information."

"I know." He looked around him. "And you left the shirt I was wearing where?"

"Really? It was covered in blood. Unwearable. Why would you care where I left it?" Now she was getting pissed.

He stilled, seemingly reading her annoyance in her tone, or maybe it was the way she was staring sharp daggers at him. "It's important."

"I must have left it back at the beginning of the road. Right when we turned off. Right where you…" She couldn't say it. Couldn't say what he'd done. Because she still didn't know or entirely understand. All she remembered was that she had helped him out of the shirt and, not wanting to get the rest of his clothes bloody, she'd laid it on the ground behind her.

He sighed. "That will make it easier for them to track us."

"How?" Fear crept in, overshadowing her annoyance.

"They'll be able to smell it."

"Oh." Dread stole through her as she tried to absorb the idea of humans hosting demons that could smell blood hundreds of miles away. What were they? Supernatural bloodhounds?

No. *Supernatural wolves.* And she'd led them right to them.

Jason turned the truck around and, in the faint light of early morning with sunrise painting deep strokes of pink and red across the sky, drove back down the road. He tried to focus on the sky, on the road ahead, on anything but Shay. But he couldn't. His mind was whirling with her scent. Her taste, soft and sweet, was still on his tongue just as the warm feel of her body was imprinted on his arms and against his chest.

Her skin felt like silk against his, but more than that, her touch sparked a connection in him, a need to touch her, to be near her, to forge that contact. Even now, he yearned to reach across the seat and take her hand. But he couldn't. She was the pack's hope; he couldn't thwart that, couldn't interfere with what needed to be done. But as he looked at her, at the perfect curve of her neck and jaw, at the sweet plumpness of her lips, he wanted to kiss her again. He *needed* to kiss her again.

He shook off the thought. It would get him nowhere but in trouble. Like he'd said, this whole situation was too complicated. Even if he wanted to defy Malcolm, he couldn't. Her being with Malcolm wouldn't just affect him, it affected the whole pack. They needed to silence Scott and his people once and for all.

But she wants you. The words whispered through his mind, and he knew they were true. Could see it in the sparkle of her eyes, in the stolen glances, in the expectation thickening the air of the cab. And she was right; there was something between them. Something he'd felt when he'd first seen her in that grocery store wearing those insanely dark sunglasses, and when they'd been together that morning at the hotel.

But it didn't matter. It couldn't matter. Even if she was the one. His one. After all this time. He couldn't have her. She was meant for Malcolm. She was the pack's only hope for peace.

"Jason?" Shay's voice was hesitant.

He stiffened, hoping she wouldn't ask him about the kiss. About them. About all the things he couldn't tell her. Not yet. Not until she was safe with her family, in her new home and he wouldn't have to worry about her leaving.

"I'm turning into a wolf. A real wolf. Is that what this change is all about?"

He looked at her, at the fear and wonderment shining through her beautiful eyes that looked more purple than blue in the early-morning light. It's what he'd been trying to tell her. What she wouldn't, couldn't, believe but had to accept. "Yes."

"When?"

"You're changing a little every day, getting stronger, leaner."

She looked at her arms, holding them out in front of her, turning them this way and that. "Other than feeling starved all the time, I can't tell too much difference. Any way to stop it?"

"Do you want to?"

"I don't know."

He gave her a weak smile. "Here, have some jerky." He opened the glove box, his arm reaching across her legs, touching her.

Big mistake.

He had to force himself to sit upright, to break contact. When all he really wanted to do was pull the truck over, sweep her into his arms and kiss her the way she deserved to be kissed, the way he should have kissed her the moment she'd confided to him how she felt about him. But no, he'd been a coward. And he was a coward now. He couldn't tell her the truth of why he was holding back.

She was upset. But he couldn't tell her how he really felt. Even if Malcolm wasn't in the picture, he couldn't let himself take a chance on love again, not after what had happened with Maggie. Even if he wanted to, even after all this time. Especially with the way everything was stacked against them. She was Malcolm's only hope. Jason's best bet was to focus on that, and not on how much he wanted to touch her.

He handed her the bag of seasoned beef. "Thanks," she said and snatched it up.

She was so different from the reserved, guarded woman he'd met only a couple of days earlier. Yes, she was changing, she was changing a lot.

"So, if I don't have a choice in the matter, when will I make my final transformation? And will it be as painful as what I went through the other night?" She took a bite off a piece of pungent beef.

"Maybe. It's hard to say. Each person is different."

She was looking at him expectantly. Waiting for more. He didn't want to give her more. To have to be the one to explain how it all worked. He shouldn't be the one. But if he did, maybe it would stop what was happening between them. She needed to know, he just wished she didn't have to know right then.

"Jason, what aren't you telling me? When will I transform?"

He took a deep breath, planted both hands on the steering wheel and stared straight ahead. "You'll make your final transformation when you mate with another shifter."

He heard her strangled gasp. "Excuse me?"

"It's nature's way. I had nothing to do with it. Swear."

She laughed. Surprised, he turned to her, enjoying the twinkling sound reverberating through his truck.

"If you had grown up in the pack, just being around all the others would have started your transformation a lot sooner," he explained. "You would have had years to train your mind and your body. You would be much more in control of what was happening to you."

"You mean instead of being broadsided with excruciating pain."

He smiled. "Exactly."

"Will I be different than the others?"

He looked at her, his eyebrows raised. Though he suspected he knew what she meant.

"Because I'm half-normal."

"Normal?" he jested.

"Human."

"Yes. You will never be as strong. But it's not a difference that will slow you down or impede you in any way."

"Well, that's good to hear. I guess. Although I'm still having a hard time believing it, if I hadn't seen you…"

"Yeah, sorry about that."

"Don't be sorry. You were…beautiful."

Her words touched him in a way he hadn't expected. He saw sincerity shining in her beautiful eyes, and giving in, he reached over and grabbed her hand. Heat shot through him and a sense of rightness filled him with a feeling that everything was well with the world, with *his* world, in a way that it hadn't been in a very long time. That feeling was strong enough to spark a sense of fear in him. What if she was right? What if there was a connection between them? And the more she transitioned into her true self, the more she came into her nature, the harder it would be for either of them to resist the lure of what they shared.

"Don't worry," he said, pulling back his hand and putting some distance between them. "Everything is going to be all right." He said the words but he wasn't sure he believed them. Things would only be all right as long as he could get her back to The Colony, unscathed and untouched.

Especially by him.

Chapter 8

Shay sat in the truck next to Jason trying not to think about what he'd said. *When you mate with another shifter.* But no matter how hard she tried, the words were front and center and replaying over and over in her mind. She couldn't stop thinking about them. Couldn't stop wondering. It didn't help that he was sitting next to her with his strong muscular chest bared for her to see. Like a delectable dessert of frothy cream and chocolate, she just wanted to touch and taste and explore.

She sighed deeply and imagined how it would feel to lie under him, to feel his weight pressing down on her, his heat surrounding her, his hands caressing her. She sucked in a deep breath and shifted uncomfortably in her seat then turned to look out the window. She had to stop thinking about him like that. If she didn't, in another few minutes she'd be crawling out of her skin or throwing herself at him. How embarrassing would that be?

But how could she stop? He'd just said when she made love to another shifter she would make her final transformation. So the real question was, how soon did she want to transform? *Did* she want to transform? Did she have a choice? He said she didn't, but how long would she have to draw this out to keep her humanity? How long could she hold out and not give in to her feelings toward him? To her desire that was growing as strong as her need to eat? Of course, he said when she mated with another shifter. He didn't say when she mated with *him*.

"Jason," she said, her voice coming out in a squeak. She cleared her throat and tried again. "Is there any reason I should hold off, that I should wait?"

"Wait?" he asked, the word breaking as he said it.

She leaned closer to him and touched him, running her fingers over his arm, surprised by how hard his muscles were beneath the smooth skin. She wanted to feel that rock-hard arm around her. Holding her tight, pulling her closer.

"If I have to mate with someone to give up my humanity, I'd like that someone to be you." There, she'd said it; once more she'd laid it all out for him. She waited expectantly for his reaction, for what he would say, and hoped he'd pull the truck over and ravage her.

But he didn't do any of those things. He just continued staring straight ahead, focusing on the road ahead. Seconds passed, a full minute and still he didn't say a word. Tears of rejection, embarrassment and humiliation stung her eyes. She turned back toward the window and leaned her forehead against the cool glass, willing her emotions to calm.

Then she felt his hand on her hair, lightly stroking the back of her head. "It's not that I don't want to." His voice sounded strained and husky, as if his jaw was clenched and he was trying to push his words through rock.

"Damn!" Jason cursed.

She turned and looked out the windshield. A truck was barreling toward them down the dirt road, kicking up a plume of dust behind it. Four men inside the cab.

No, not men.

Demons.

Her insides clenched and she grasped the dash. "Can we fight them?" she asked, a quaver in her voice.

"Not four."

"What are we going to do?"

"Grab the pack in the back. Put the food in it. We're going to have to go in on foot."

She looked into the woods surrounding them and cringed.

"How far is it to The Colony?" she asked, though she was afraid of the answer.

"Far," he said evasively, which told her more than she wanted to know. Buddy was growing more and more agitated by the second. Shay reached behind her and patted him on the head then grabbed the big backpack off the floor, hefting it up onto her lap. She pushed the packet of jerky inside. There were already two large bottles of water, another packet of meat and one of nuts.

The truck coming toward them turned a hard right, swinging across the road and stopping, effectively blocking their way.

"You ready?" Jason asked.

"As ready as I'm going to be."

"Hold on!" he yelled, dropped the truck into four-wheel drive and turned off the road, driving over bushes and through trees. Shay bounced so hard in the seat she hit her head on the cab's ceiling. She looked behind them and saw the others following them, though their truck wasn't as big or as powerful as Jason's was. Yet they were still keeping up.

For now.

After another ten hard minutes, the other truck had fallen far enough behind that she could barely see them. "I think we've outrun them."

"They won't give up. And we won't be able to continue like this much longer."

"No?" And then she saw why. They'd reached the base of the mountains where the trees grew too thick to drive the truck through.

"We can continue on through this meadow for a little while, just to put some distance between us, but it's taking us farther away from where we need to be. It will only make our walk longer."

"Any chance of finding the road I missed last night?" she asked, the hope ringing loud in her voice.

"Not without going back. The trees are too thick."

She sighed as she looked at the steep incline in front of them. "Let's do it."

"You sure?"

"Do we have any other choice?"

He smiled and then stopped. "Nope." He grabbed the pack off her lap then got out of the truck. Buddy jumped out behind him.

"Shouldn't we try to hide the truck or something?"

"It wouldn't matter."

"Why not?"

"Because they're tracking us by smell. They'll find us no matter what we do."

"That doesn't sound very promising."

"It wasn't meant to be. We just have to be ready for them when they do."

"Great." She looked behind them and a chill rocked through her body. She started up the steep hill in front of them, wondering how she was going to make it. How was she going to climb all the way to the top with four men chasing after her? Buddy and Jason ran ahead, easily navigating the precipitous terrain. As she watched them, perfectly in sync, she knew she was going to be the weak link, the one to slow them down. When the demons finally caught up with them, it would be because of her.

The mountain was easier to climb than she'd expected it would be. She walked a lot, so she wasn't totally out of shape, but she certainly didn't walk up steep inclines, and yet she seemed to have more power in her legs than usual, more stamina. They stopped for a water break and she devoured another piece of jerky.

"Do you think they've given up?" she asked, knowing it was too much to hope for, but needing to voice it anyway.

Jason stared at her as if she'd just said she could fly. "Not a chance."

"How much farther do we have to go?"

"A good twenty miles."

Shay swallowed. "Twenty miles of this?" She pointed to the small deer path they'd been following. "That will take all day."

"Even more at our pace."

"You mean we could still be out here tonight?"

"Most likely."

Panic expanded in her chest. "This is never going to work. We're not going to make it." A snap sounded behind her. She spun around, looking between the trees, her nerves bunching and stretching as she expected to see the men coming toward them.

No one was there.

"It was just a falling pinecone. But we should keep moving," he said.

She looked at the briars and branches, at the multitude of scratches on her arms. "I can't do this. There must be a different way."

Jason grabbed her hand. "You are doing great. And yes, you can do this. You are stronger than you think. Here." He handed her the water bottle.

She took it and drank one last swig of water before falling back into step behind him once more. She watched the sweat glistening on the bare skin of his back and tried to think of anything other than who or what could be coming up behind them at any moment.

After a while of watching him move, thinking of nothing but his long legs and how effortlessly they seemed to carry him up the mountain, she wondered if they would have a chance to be together, to continue what they had started with their kiss earlier that morning. Or if he'd continue to pull away from her. His words echoed in her mind. *We can't. It's complicated.*

"Jason?" She ran ahead to catch up with him, but once she did, she had to take a minute to catch her breath. The air was getting thinner as they rose in elevation. Breathing, moving, was getting more difficult.

Impatience flashed across his face. Clearly, he wanted to keep moving. He started to walk.

The words she'd been about to ask froze in her throat as she struggled to keep up with him. "How much farther? What's the plan?" she asked instead.

"To keep moving. We don't have time to stop and talk."

"Why not? We're obviously alone here."

"No, we're not."

Fear scuttled across her back. "What do you mean?" She glanced behind her, peering into the gaps between the trees, but didn't see a thing. And she couldn't hear anything beyond her labored breathing and the blood rushing through her ears.

"We're being tracked right now. He's about five hundred yards behind us."

"Just one?" Her voice came out in a hoarse whisper.

"Yes. They must have split up, each one taking a different route."

"What are we going to do?"

"I've been thinking about that."

"And?"

A stitch of pain arced through her middle. They'd been keeping the same quick pace for too long. She needed to rest. But she knew she couldn't take a break. Not yet. Maybe not at all. She was slowing them down, and by the time the demon man caught up with them, she'd be so exhausted she'd be useless.

"Do you see those large rocks up there at the top of the hill?" He pointed straight ahead.

"You mean way up there almost near the top? Barely," she muttered.

"If you and Buddy continue straight up this hill heading for those rocks, I can double back around and ambush him."

"But won't he know you're coming? Can't he smell you, or something?"

"Only if I'm in human form."

She stared at him, at the sheen on his beautiful chest, at the startling pale blue eyes, and knew what he meant.

"You're going to change back into a wolf?"

"I'll be faster and quieter. He'll continue to track you and I'll be able to sneak up on him."

She shivered at the thought but knew it was the only chance they had. "Then do it," she said. "Because honestly, I don't know how much longer I'm going to be able to keep up this manic pace."

Steely determination entered his eyes and suddenly she saw him differently. She saw him as what he could be, a deadly protector.

"Just head for those rocks, steadily and as quickly as possible."

"And if I run into another one of those things?"

"Then scream and fight, using every technique your father taught you, and try to hold him off until I can reach you."

"All right." She nodded, trying to look brave and confident, but she didn't think she was fooling him.

"Here." He pulled a knife out of a side pocket on his pack and handed it to her. "Use it if you have to. Don't be squeamish."

She took the wicked-looking blade from him, turning it over in her hand, hoping if she had to she would have the courage to do what needed to be done. But would she actually be able to push the sharp steel into someone? Honestly, she wasn't sure. She grimaced at the thought then straightened her shoulders and nodded. "Absolutely. Don't worry about me."

Jason took off his pack, placed it on her back. She grabbed his arm as the weight of the pack knocked her off balance.

"Jesus, what do you have in this thing?"

"Just some supplies we might need. It's mostly the water weighing it down."

"Then maybe I should drink some."

He smiled and touched her cheek. She stared up at him, suddenly not wanting him to leave her.

"What if something happens to you? What if you don't come back?" A tremor shook her voice as she spoke.

"There is a satellite phone in the pack. Make it up to

the rocks. Continue behind them and to the left. There is a cave hidden behind two tall redwoods joined together as one. Call the number for Malcolm, tell him what happened, tell him you're in the cave and wait for him."

"What's so special about this cave?"

"The *Abatu* won't be able to smell you inside. But you must go in as deep as you can. There's a flashlight in the pack."

"All right. I can do that. But Jason—" she placed her hand on his chest, feeling his heat and the strong beat of his heart beneath her palm "—promise me you'll come back. We still have a lot to talk about."

His eyes held hers for a long moment and then he leaned down and touched his lips to hers—warm, gentle and holding the promise of everything she'd ever wanted. "I will," he said softly. "Now go on, and don't look back."

Shay didn't want to leave him. And she certainly didn't want him to leave her, but what else could they do? "Come on, Buddy," she said, when she thought the dog might follow him instead of her, and then she did as he asked and continued straight up the hill without looking back.

She didn't make it very far, though, certainly not far enough, when she heard a loud howl breaking through the woods. A chill cut down her spine followed by a surge of adrenaline pulsing through her blood. Her heartbeat sped up and a strange prickling peppered her palms.

She hurried even faster, reaching out to touch the

nearest tree for balance as the pack weighed her down, making the climb even harder, if not impossible. She considered dropping the pack and leaving it for Jason to get on his way up, and after another five minutes of struggling, that's exactly what she did. She dropped it to the ground next to a large tree, resting for a moment as she unzipped it.

She dug inside and pulled out a bottle of water and a packet of jerky. Before she could dig further to see what else was in there, the snap of a twig sounded from behind the tree she was squatting next to.

She froze. Buddy whimpered softly and she placed her hand on his neck, pulling him to her. "Shh," she whispered against his head, and then set the jerky and the water bottle on top of the pack and pulled out the knife Jason had given her. She peered around the large tree.

No one was there.

She stilled, listening intently. All around her the woods were alive with the sounds of animals rustling through bushes, birds with their constant chatter and the occasional cry when a hawk got too close to their nest. Every animal in the forest was either looking for food or trying not to get eaten by something stronger and bigger. She was beginning to understand how that felt and knew that even with her father's training she wouldn't be able to protect herself. She had been too young when he'd taught her to fight. But even if she had been old enough to remember the moves, she wasn't strong enough to fight a demon.

Buddy whined, his ears twitching, his eyes alert and

scanning. Was it Jason? No. She could still hear him in the distance, sounds of growls, barking and the occasional yelp. But the truly frightening part was that he didn't sound that far. In fact, he sounded a lot closer than he should. Had she really not made that much progress?

Taking a deep breath, she shoved the knife back in its sheath and clipped it on her jeans' belt loop, snatched up the water bottle and jerky and ran.

Behind her, a howl ripped through the air, turning into vicious growls. She looked up the hill at the outcropping of rocks in the distance. They were still too far. She had to put some distance between them, because if Jason didn't win, if he couldn't stop the demon, then she'd never make it to the top before the demon found her.

She put her head down, barreling forward, watching her feet, following the narrow path through the thick trees. Despair bordering on hopelessness filled her as another painful stitch cut through her side, and her lungs burned with each breath. She had to stop thinking bad thoughts. Jason would make it. He would come back to her. He would help her navigate this new life. He had to, because she couldn't imagine doing it without him.

The growls and barks behind her intensified. Fear clenched her insides tighter. Buddy stopped and barked, looking behind him, obviously anxious to go back and help Jason. "Shh," she said, patting her side for him to follow, and tried to break into a jog, anything to put some distance between them, afraid of the demon and terrified Buddy would leave her and go back for Jason.

And if he did, and something bad happened to them both, then she really would be alone.

And that was something she just couldn't handle.

"Come on, Buddy," she called when he lagged behind her. He sprinted up ahead of her, easily maneuvering through the terrain. She watched him with his sure footing and boundless energy. He wasn't tired at all. She needed to be like Buddy. She needed to be like Jason. She needed to be a wolf.

Now.

If she were able to transform, she could easily make it the next twenty miles, and the best part would be that the demons wouldn't be able to follow her scent.

Then they'd all be safe.

But in order to make that final transformation, she'd have to make love. And she wanted to make love. To Jason. Buddy ran in circles around her, his growing agitation obvious. "You stay with me, Buddy," she demanded and forged ahead, her hand clutching the handle of the knife as she hoped and prayed she wouldn't run into another one of the demons. But she knew if she could hear the loud battle going on behind her, then the others could certainly hear it, too.

And come running.

Her gaze flitted through the dense woods around the tall pine and spruce trees. She peered beyond the thicket of bushes. They could be anywhere. Suddenly all sound ceased. Shay stopped, looking behind her, listening intently.

But she could no longer hear the growls and yelps of battle. "Jason?" she whispered as fear stole into her heart and squeezed. Buddy whined and rubbed against her legs. She listened for a moment longer and still no sound reached her. Not even the rustling of an animal cowering in the bushes or the song of a bird in flight.

The squeezing fear blossomed into panic. She rushed forward, climbing up the steep hill, moving toward the rocks above. Her safe place. Her haven.

This had been a dumb idea, she thought, struggling to hear anything over her labored breathing. She and Jason should never have separated. She could have helped him. They worked well together. She shouldn't be out here on her own. She skirted around a massive tree and skidded abruptly to a stop, her arms pinwheeling as she struggled to keep her balance on the uneven ground. Her heart lodged painfully in her throat as she stared at the large man standing directly in the path before her.

Chapter 9

The man didn't say anything. He just stared at her through dark, menacing eyes, a black cloud swirling around his head. She knew what that was now, knew the glimpse of teeth she saw within the maelstrom of darkness was the demon. A demon sent to kill her.

She dropped the water bottle and jerky then gripped the knife with white-knuckled fingers, pulling it from its sheath and shifting it back and forth in front of her.

Buddy started barking ferociously, lunging forward, his paws digging into the earth as he held his ground. "Get away from us," Shay warned with as much bravado as she could muster.

Her dad had trained her for this. She could take him, she told herself, though she didn't believe it. Not for a second. He stepped toward her and she saw how big he was, at least six feet three inches of sheer muscle. His biceps were as big as bowling balls. And when he flexed them, like he was doing now, they rolled, moving like something alive was buried beneath his skin.

She shivered and looked around, contemplating her options. He was blocking the path directly in front of her. What if she headed back down the mountain? Could she outrun him? Would the momentum help her or send her flying? If she could find the truck, could she drive back out to the road? Back to the store? Back to help?

Not without a key. Before she could finish weighing her options and decide what to do, the man lunged. He grabbed hold of her, his teeth sinking into her shoulder.

What the hell! She screamed and pushed against him, slicing his arm with the knife. Buddy went nuts, barking like Cujo. The man pulled back, laughing, her blood painting his lips. She tried to sidestep him to put some distance between them but instead tripped over a root, lost her footing and fell to the ground with a teeth-jarring thud. Terrified, she stared up at him. His smile deepened. Before he could pounce, Buddy jumped, his teeth tearing viciously into the man's arm. He roared and turned, then kicked Buddy hard, sending him flying with a loud yelp.

"Buddy!" Shay screamed, then tightened her grasp on the knife, jumped up and ran at the bastard. He could hurt her all he wanted but no one messed with her dog. She thrust the knife toward him but before she could connect, he swung round, hitting her with the force of a Mack truck and knocking her back to the ground. Her head hit the trunk of the huge tree. Pain shot through her skull. Blackness swirled around the edge of her vision.

The ground shuddered as he came at her. She shook her head, trying to clear her sight and instead sent a bolt of pain pinging through her brain. She touched her head and her fingers came back wet and sticky. *Blood.* Lots of it. Through a haze she saw the man bend over her. She tried to move, to jump to her feet, to get away from him and fight. But her legs weren't following her brain's commands.

She struggled to rise, pushing against the tree for purchase, swimming through the dizziness, but it was too late. It didn't matter now. The struggle. The fight. It was over. She wasn't going to make it.

She braced herself for another blow. But it didn't come. From behind her a gray blur flew through the air, crashing into the man's chest, pushing him backward to the forest floor. *Jason.* The wolf's teeth tore through the flesh of the man's neck. He screamed, an agonizing howl of pain.

Then the giant wrapped his arms around the wolf and pulled it down away from his neck, his face turning red with the effort, his teeth clenched together. The wolf continued viciously snapping and tearing. The man's arms, encircling Jason, squeezed until his face turned purple with the effort. Hell, he was a freaking machine.

"Jason!" she screamed. But she could do nothing as the two fought, rolling over and over across the ground. The giant *Abatu* was trying to crush Jason even as Jason tried to rip out his throat. The battle was taking too long, too painfully long, to watch. Shay couldn't tell who had the upper hand, but she knew she had to do something.

Acting on a spike of adrenaline, she rushed forward, her knife clutched in her hand as they rolled back and forth along the ground, rolling away from her then turning back toward her again. Somehow, she had to distract the monster, to weaken him before he squeezed Jason to death.

As they rolled away from her once more, she jumped forward and thrust the knife into the man's shoulder and then jumped back out of his way, falling into the nearest tree as a wave of dizziness broke over her. The man roared in pain, flailing his arm out to his side, trying to grab for her, for the knife still stuck in his back. His hold on Jason loosened. It was all the leverage Jason needed.

Jason scurried forward, crawling up the belly of the beast, his back paws scraping against the man's legs as he pushed himself up his body, toward the massive neck where the wolf's powerful jaws clamped down in a vicious tearing bite.

The *Abatu* thrashed his head back and forth, trying to pull free from the wolf's brutal grasp. Blood flew everywhere, in every direction, and still the monster wouldn't stop. He continued to fight, but he wasn't nearly as strong as he had been, and not nearly as fast.

The wolf pulled back and barked at her, staring deeply at her with those pale blue eyes. Surprisingly, she was almost certain she knew what he was thinking, what he wanted. Leaving the knife where it was, she ran past them both as quickly as her swimming vision and the pain in her head would allow and hurried over to Buddy. He was sitting up, licking his wound in his side.

"You okay, boy?" Gingerly she ran her fingers over his wound. He would be sore, but it didn't look too bad. He licked her fingers then stood up. The two of them continued up the hill, toward safety, toward the cave. But neither one of them was moving as quickly or as steady as they had before.

Piercing pain arced through her head with each pounding step. Blood trickled down her forehead, running into her eyes and stinging them. And on the back of her head, where she'd hit the tree, the skin had split. There was more than a trickle of blood running down the back of her neck. Her wounds would make her scent stronger, make it a lot easier for the other two *Abatu* to find them. She had to make it to the top of the mountain, to the cave before they did, or before her legs finally gave out from under her.

Jason hurt everywhere. He tried to stay in his wolf form as long as he could, but there was no way Shay could keep up with him and he kept having to circle back to her. Worse, the other two *Abatu* were close. Every now and then, when the wind shifted, he could smell them. Somehow he had to get Shay up to the cave before the demons reached them.

Fighting off two or more of them, especially if they were together would be problematic, if not impossible. Especially the way he was feeling. Shay stopped and leaned against a large tree to try to catch her breath. She was hurt, he could see it in the way she moved, could smell it on her skin. She needed to rest and heal, but they still had too far to go. He needed her to transform.

But to do that he'd have to make love to her.

He wanted to make love to her. He hadn't been able to think about anything else since their kiss earlier that morning. The kiss that still burned on his lips and coiled tightly in his gut. But to think of her that way... He stopped himself.

He couldn't not think of her that way. He had never wanted a woman as much as he wanted Shay right then. Not even Maggie had heated his blood with such an unquenchable desire. Guilt seared through him at the thought.

He'd loved Maggie. She'd consumed his life from the time they were both eight years old in Ms. McKenzie's class. But his love for her had been as steady and strong as the river that fed their lake in The Colony. It was never turbulent or filled with unpredictability. With Shay, he wasn't sure what he would do, how he felt or if he could stick to his convictions. All he did know was that he wanted to hold her, to keep her safe and to make love to her all night long.

How could he let Shay be with Malcolm? Especially given the way he felt about her now. Even knowing what it would mean for the pack. How a relationship with Malcolm would help smooth the building tensions and ensure Malcolm's leadership. Perhaps, Malcolm could find a new way. A different way.

They forged ahead. He continued his wide arc around her, making sure no one got close to them, but she kept dropping farther behind as her pace slowed to a crawl.

Finally he walked up alongside her, pushing into her legs, letting her lean on him as he pulled her up the steep incline toward the peak.

When at last they crested the top, she stopped and leaned against a tree then slumped to the ground. She wasn't going to make it any farther without him. Not wanting to scare her, he walked behind the tree and reluctantly changed back, shifting easily from wolf into man.

"Come on, Shay," he whispered softly, holding out his hand to her. "It's not far to the cave now."

She opened her beautiful blue-violet eyes and stared at him, her gaze sweeping him from head to toe, a crimson blush filling her pretty cheeks. And yet, she liked what she saw. He could read it in the quick intake of her breath and the slight puckering of her lips. Her pupils dilated as she looked shyly up at him.

"Sorry," he said. "But I lost my clothes somewhere on the mountain. I have an extra set in the pack, but we need to get you into the cave as quickly as possible."

"All right," she murmured, standing, then gasped a quick breath.

"What is it?"

Panic-stricken, her eyes met his. Her sweet mouth opened then closed. That's when he noticed she wasn't wearing the pack.

"The pack. I, uh, it was too heavy. I left it on the mountain." She turned and looked back down the steep slope into the thicket of trees below. "I'm so sorry. I meant to tell you…."

"It's all right," he assured her while quietly thinking of the phone and the extra food inside the pack.

"But you can't…" She stared at him, her eyes widened with dismay.

"What? Walk around naked?"

"Well. Yeah." She was trying to look everywhere except at him.

He couldn't help the grin pulling at the sides of his mouth. "Why not?" he teased. "Afraid you won't be able to keep your eyes off me?"

He didn't think she could turn any pinker, but she did.

"I'm really sorry," she gushed, but even as she said the words, her gaze slipped down his body.

He quickly turned before she could see the physical effect she was having on him. "You're still bleeding pretty heavily. We best get into the cave as soon as possible," he said, and hurried forward. *And not just to escape the demons.*

Shay tried not to stare at Jason's well-defined muscular behind, but she couldn't help herself. She was so intent on not watching his very appealing backside that she barely noticed as he vanished into the side of the mountain. One moment he was in front of her and the next he wasn't. If she hadn't watched Buddy disappear into the rocks right after him, melting into the darkness, she never would have known the entrance was there.

She followed behind them, stepping cautiously through the small, barely noticeable opening. She stood still for a moment, waiting for her eyes to adjust. She couldn't see a thing and hoped there wasn't anything big inside waiting for her. But then, after fighting demons, a bear really didn't seem all that scary.

She hovered around the opening, reluctant to step too far inside. There was something heavy and confining about the utter darkness. She stretched her hands out in front of her and moved slowly forward, blindly scraping her fingers along the rough stone wall. She shuffled along, straining her ears to hear Jason or Buddy, but she heard nothing. She saw nothing as the utter darkness stretched forward without an end. An eternity of nothing but cold, damp air.

After a few minutes, her senses adjusted and she heard drops of water hitting stone. Light wavered in the distance layering the deep blackness with various shades of gray. "Jason?" she called. She didn't have to wait long and he was standing before her, a flashlight in his hand and wearing a pair of jeans, shoes and a fresh shirt.

"You have clothes?"

"Disappointed?"

"Not in the least," she said, thankful that the light wasn't on her face.

"Are you sure? I can take them off again if you like."

Now she wished she could see his face. Was he flirting with her? She felt as if she'd been pulverized by a semi then picked over by vultures. Not to mention that she needed a hot bath. Bad.

"Come on, the chamber is this way." He and his light turned and walked away from her, descending deeper into the cave.

Chamber? She wasn't sure she liked the sound of that. "Are you sure it's safe in here?" she asked, her voice trembling a little. No one knew where she was, and worse, in here no one would ever find her.

"There are no *Abatu* in the caves—of that I am sure."

"What about anything else?"

He turned back to her and laughed. It bubbled forth and rebounded off the rocks in the cavern.

Buddy looked up at him, his tail wagging and springing against the wall. Apparently he was feeling better. How he could have the energy to wag his tail, Shay didn't know. She felt as if she could collapse at any second. And she hurt…everywhere.

"It's just a bit farther up ahead," Jason said, as if sensing her need to drop where she stood.

"What is this chamber?" she asked as they meandered deeper into the cave, turning this way and that. She realized she had no idea where she was or if she'd be able to find her way back out. She only hoped she wouldn't need to. Wherever he was taking her it had a flashlight and it had extra clothes. Maybe it would have water and something to eat other than jerky, too. But honestly, right then, she was too tired to care if there was nothing.

Up ahead, the light dimmed as Jason squeezed through a small opening in the rock wall and disappeared out of sight. Not wanting to be left alone in the dark, she hurried after him into a small room. A chamber.

A battery-powered lantern lit up the small space. There was a trunk against the wall and inside was a jug of water, another bag of jerky, clothes and a large blanket.

"Wow, what is all this here for?"

"We've used this cave for shelter and protection for a long time. We've always kept fresh clothing and water in here, just in case anyone ever needed it." He laid out the blanket next to a small fire pit then lit a fire from the stack of wood standing in the corner.

"Won't those men or whatever they are out there smell it?" she asked.

"Maybe, but they won't know where it's coming from. The smoke will go out the very top." He gestured toward the ceiling and she saw a thin sliver of light bleeding through the rocks.

"Feel free to use the water to wash up. There are some towels in the trunk."

Thankful, she reached inside the trunk and picked up a small cotton cloth, doused it with the cool water and ran it over her face and arms. After suffering the dust and dirt sticking to her skin while climbing up that hill, the cool damp cloth felt heavenly.

After a moment, Jason took the towel from her. He washed her forehead, her arms and the various cuts and scrapes where the demon had torn her skin. Then he inspected the wound on the back of her head.

"You need stitches. There's quite a gash."

"Will it get infected?" she asked as he tried to clean out her wounds.

"It looks pretty bad." He kissed her forehead gently. "If you transform, you will heal."

"I'm not sure…" she said hesitantly as apprehension

stole into her, tightening her insides. She wavered as another wave of dizziness stole over her.

"You've lost a lot of blood, Shay. I'm just not sure we'll be able to make it out of here if you don't."

She stilled, barely breathing as his nimble fingers unbuttoned the top button of her blouse then the next before he slipped her shirt away from the bloody wound on her shoulder where the demon had bitten her. His face darkened as he ran the cloth over the bite wound on her shoulder slowly and gently until it was clean. Then he kissed her skin around the wound and warmth, slow and languid, crept through her. She should step away. Stop him. This cave, this time—it wasn't right. Not for what she was thinking of and hoping for. Not for what she hadn't been able to stop thinking about ever since she'd seen him standing in front of her at the store.

She'd wanted so much to touch him, to run her hands down his smooth skin, to feel and touch and kiss every part of him. Her heart thudded and her breath caught in a net of expectation that expanded in her chest.

They couldn't. Not here. Not now.

I'm just not sure we'll be able to make it out of here if you don't.

His lips found a soft spot on her neck and lingered, his tongue gently caressing. Her knees weakened and she grabbed on to his shoulders, holding tight. His mouth fell over hers and then she was lost. A blast of heat blazed through her skin, moving downward. Every nerve ending sensitized to the point that she quickened at the slightest touch; even his hot breath on her neck felt like a gentle caress.

She inhaled deeply, breathing hard and fast, and ran her hands down his beautiful chest, slipping her fingers beneath his T-shirt and across his hot skin. She knew what his body looked like. His exquisite, perfectly sculptured form would be forever emblazoned in her mind. Now she wanted to feel him, to touch him with her fingers, her lips.

Deepening their kiss, she swept her tongue inside his mouth, sparring with his, moving, dancing, tasting. She pushed her fingers farther beneath his shirt, scraping across the ripples in his abdomen, exploring the surge of his strong pecs, slowly, thoroughly, eliciting a gasp from between his lips. He kissed her even deeper, stronger and with more force, shooting fire down to her core.

She threw her head back and gasped a deep ragged desire-laden breath. He yanked off his clean shirt and unbuttoned his trousers. And then her arms were around him again, holding tight, holding her balance. She needed to be close to him, skin against skin, heartbeat against heartbeat, with an intensity she couldn't explain or even understand.

It was almost as if all her years alone were preparing her for this moment, for this place, for this man. "Jason," she whispered as he pulled her down to the blanket next to the fire. How could she explain how she felt, this odd connection between them that had clutched ahold of her with unrelenting tenacity and refused to let go? And if she did, if she tried to explain, would she scare him away?

On their knees, he slipped his hands under her blouse, his warm touch gliding up her skin, his lips following close behind. "I'm here for you, Shay. Just me. Only me." His mouth found hers again, and he kissed her until all rational thought slipped from her mind.

Chapter 10

Her taste consumed Jason, pushing the heat coiling in his center outward in a fiery explosion of urgent need. Dean had always said that the moment he kissed Lily, he knew she was the one for him and that he'd never be able to let her go. Jason had never understood his friend's absolute certainty. Until now.

Until Shay.

Not even when he was with Maggie. Though his love for her had been strong, the heat of her touch had never consumed him. Not the way he was burning now. How could he let Malcolm have Shay after all they'd been through together? He pushed all thoughts out of his mind and slowly…carefully…finished unbuttoning Shay's tattered, bloodstained blouse until it fell free of her shoulders and dropped to the ground.

He gently pressed the wet wash cloth against her bite wound and felt anger surge within him for what that demon had done to her. "You will heal," he whispered and ran his lips down her neck and gingerly across her collarbone, absorbing the taste of her and the softness of her skin. He felt her quick intake of breath and heard the staccato rhythm of her heart. She was nervous. So was he. He eased her onto the blanket then lay beside her.

"I want to make love to you," he whispered in her ear then gently took her sweet lobe into his mouth.

She looked up at him, her blue-violet eyes wide and vulnerable.

He trailed his lips down the elegant column of her throat. His fingers played with the lace on her bra, slipping inside to find her pert nipple hardened and waiting for his touch. His blood raced as he caressed it, his body stiffening. Her quick gasp of breath told him she felt the same; she wanted him as much as he wanted her. He smiled, then leaned down, pushed the lacy fabric aside and took her sweet nub in his mouth, rolling it across his tongue, grazing it gently with his teeth until her back was lifting up off the blanket.

"Jason," she breathed. "You said we couldn't be together. That it was complicated." A soft moan escaped her lips.

He sighed, wishing she would forget, wishing he could make her forget. "Are you sure you want to hear about it now?" he asked, running his tongue along the top of her breast that pillowed above her bra.

"No," she said on a sigh. "But something tells me I should."

"All right. The quickie version." He reached around to unclasp her bra. The very quick version. "Our Colony is run by an alpha leader. Your father was once that man." He paused to clasp his lips over her nipple, not wanting to wait a second longer. He thoroughly kissed them, first one and then the other, leaving her breathless and squirming as heat pulsed through him.

"After your dad left, as sheriff it was a natural transition for me to step forward, but things…didn't work out. I had to leave for a while, and Malcolm stepped in for me. He picked up the reins and has led the pack ever since. He was my right-hand man. He knew how to do the job. He knew what needed to be done."

Jason touched her again, running his hands down the curve of her hips and around her firm bottom, where he lingered. He was finding it hard to focus, to keep track of what he was saying. He couldn't help himself, she was just so…enticing, and then his lips were surrounding the soft peaks of her breasts once more, licking, sucking, loving. As fire burned through him.

And then she was touching him, fingers moving down his arms, across his chest, and lower. He had to get out of his pants. He had to get her out of hers.

She moaned softly as he fumbled with her buttons. "What else," she asked on a deep breath, her hand falling over his, stopping him.

Torture. She was torturing him. "Some people aren't happy with Malcolm. They say power has gone to his head and he's too domineering. Your cousin, Scott, has claimed his right to usurp him and take his rightful place as leader."

"And this Malcolm person obviously doesn't want that to happen."

"Right. And neither do I. Scott, your cousin, is young. Inexperienced. A troublemaker. Malcolm believes, as do many of his followers, that if he can marry you, that will give him the lineage he needs to stay in control."

"Is he right?"

"Yes."

She pulled back. "You're telling me I'm supposed to marry this Malcolm person? Tell me I have a choice in this."

"Yes, of course. Malcolm was counting on you wanting to fulfill your duty to the pack. He... None of us could have imagined that you wouldn't have been brought up understanding your lineage, your duty as a Mallory and the ways of the pack. If you did mate with Malcolm and marry him, you wouldn't just be his wife, you'd lead the pack with him. The two of you, together." His voice broke over the words. "If we do this...if we continue..." He took a deep breath. "It's a lot for you to give up. It's selfish for me to want you to give it up for me."

Shay stared at him, her eyes wide in the firelight, her lips swollen from his kisses. "Wait. So let me get this right. You were bringing me to The Colony to marry this...this domineering pack leader?"

Jason smiled, amused. "After spending the past few days with you, Shay, I'm sure you could handle Malcolm."

"Handle? I want more out of a partner than a bully

that I will have to handle. If that's my future, I think I'd rather take my luck with the demons."

"Malcolm wasn't the only reason I came to get you. I promised your dad that if you started your transition and he wasn't there to do it, I'd go after you and bring you home."

He sat up and pulled her onto his lap, his arms wrapping around her body as her back nestled against his chest. He slipped his hands over her breasts, feeling their weight, caressing them until he elicited a moan from her. His hands slipped down her stomach and lower, while his lips found the soft, tender spot on her neck.

"Jason," she said on a deep breath. "Won't this complicate things?"

"Oh, yes. Malcolm will be furious. Many in the pack will feel betrayed and let down. I can take it. But, if I transform you, it will also create a strong connection between us. Whether you are married to Malcolm or not, we will always be aware of one another—our thoughts, our emotions. We will be able to feel each other, and be joined emotionally whether we are together or not. Are you sure you can handle that?"

She sighed, her head falling back on his shoulder. "When you're touching me that way, how can I be sure of anything?"

Shay gasped another breath as fire spread through her, heating the urgency in her blood. His skin against hers, his heat…his power. It was overwhelming and all-consuming. And yet, there wasn't anyplace else she wanted to be, no one else she wanted to be with.

His hand moved down her belly, stroking, caressing, fueling the fire within her. He unclasped her capris. She brought her hand up, moving it over the smooth skin of his chest, down his rock-hard biceps.

No, she wasn't sure about what he said, or what their future would bring. But she knew she wanted him right then more than she'd ever wanted anything. But if she gave in to her desire for him, would she regret it later? How much did she really know about him? About this world of his?

"Don't be scared," he murmured, deftly moving his hand inside her pants, finding her sweet spot and sweeping away all her doubts with his quick sure strokes that stole her breath and had her body temperature spiking.

"I'll take care of you." He slipped her pants down her hips, and in one quick movement had them off her. He removed his own, then pulled her on top of him, pressing her against his rippling muscles. She felt them moving as he shifted, pulling her closer, nestling his large hardness between her legs, making her tingle with expectation.

She pushed her hips against his while his lips fell over hers. She swept her tongue inside his mouth, searching for more, for the release only he could give her. An urgent need heated her blood, sending her reeling and gasping for more. The sensation was stronger than anything she'd ever felt or imagined. She wanted this man, wanted him now.

He flipped her onto her back and slid his finger inside her, making sure she was ready for him. He needn't have bothered. She'd never been more ready for anything ever. She ached to have him inside her. To feel the thick length of him nestled within her moist heat.

He entered her slowly, with teasing strokes, pushing in then pulling out. She cried out in protest, wrapping her legs tightly around him until he entered her fully in one swift movement. She threw her head back on a deep moan as he gave her what she wanted, pushing himself deep inside her. He stilled for a moment, letting her body expand around him, the fiery burn exquisite, turning molten within her.

Then he began to move again, his breadth filling her until she thought she would split. But she didn't. Instead, she molded herself to him, her body fitting perfectly with his. So snug that with each slight movement, each breath, her nerve endings fired with delicious sensations that made her want to scream and cry and never let go.

They rocked, moving in sync, the two of them fitting together as if they were meant to be together, interlocking, inseparable. *Connected.* She held on tight as his hips moved in a rhythmic dance, her hands sliding down around the smooth skin of his buttocks. His muscles tightened as he moved faster, pushing harder as he reached closer to his climax.

Hot desire surged through her. Her legs cradled him as she clung to his waist. He took her on his ride, pulling her out of her mind and to a place where there were no thoughts, only sensations—a building crescendo of feelings she didn't want to end. The heat. The longing. The need.

The tension between them built so long, so high and strong that with a last shuddering gasp it snapped and she fell, reeling into an abyss that was rich with the scent of pine and earth and a taste that was both sweet and salty. Liquid warmth filled her from the inside out, sluggish and thick. How could she ever want to be anywhere else, with anyone else?

She couldn't.

She didn't.

And then her pleasure peaked again, falling over her and she screamed her passion as it raced through her, sending her over the brink and into oblivion where she wasn't even sure if her heart was still beating, if her lungs were still expanding or if she could even move.

As she lay there, he shifted, pushing forward one last time, finding his release and piercing through her, spilling his love and breaking through some invisible veil. The room exploded, and all she could see was the fire and the pale blue light of his eyes. She smelled Jason's rich, earthy pine scent.

But there was more; she was surrounded in the smell of rain in the forest, the richness of the earth when burrowing deep within, the cleansing scent of a young sapling just sprouting its leaves. It was the smell of a field of wildflowers just beginning to bloom.

Her muscles pulled and flexed, popping, bones cracking. She stretched her toes, her feet, her ankles and calves, up her legs—every joint, every tendon felt tight and bunched. She arched her back, reaching high above her, flexing as her blood raced in her ears, flooding out all sounds but the roar of the change igniting within her.

"You are going to be fine," Jason whispered, his voice a soothing caress across frayed and tattered nerves. "I'm here. I won't let anything happen to you."

She reached for that voice, knowing it was her lifeline, knowing it would pull her back from the darkness and help her find her way.

"I'm here, Shay. Right here, holding you."

Her nerves burned as fire raced through her body. She tilted her head back and screamed, but the scream changed, becoming a howl. Anxiety shot through her, and it took everything she had not to get up and run in a full-blown panic. But warm arms tightened around her and she held on to them with everything she had. Her heartbeat raced, thundering in her ears and then suddenly she could hear the pumping of Jason's heart and her own pulse blending together, becoming one.

Her blood was racing in her veins; her skin was suddenly too hot. A wave of pain exploded through her. Something was wrong. Fear detonated a mushroom cloud that grew and grew until it encompassed every cell in her body, stealing all thought, all reason. Instinctually, she curled up in a ball, barely feeling Jason as he cradled her against him, murmuring in her ear.

She had to get away from him. Get out of this room, this cave. Everything was too confining, the air too thick, the light too dim. She needed to run, to feel the earth beneath her feet, the night air filling her lungs. She took a deep breath and felt her lungs expand, and then she was up and running. Out of the chamber, away from Jason, away from the fire and into the darkness.

Buddy was next to her as she broke out of the cave and into the fresh night air, racing through the dark, aware of the intensity of the smells around her. The deep rich earth, the sour, heady scent of an animal buried deep in the brush. She raced forward, eager to stretch her legs, to hear the sounds of the night forest around her. And then Jason was next to her, running by her side, a beautiful gray wolf.

She could feel him, hear him, not a buzz, but a warm current of energy that grew stronger the closer he got to her. And then she caught the scent of a rabbit and she was gone, chasing after the elusive smell, thrilling in the game, the speed with which she ran, the dig of her paws in the earth and the ease with which she could see in the dim light.

Water ahead. Beautiful. Dark. Fresh, clean. She skidded to a stop next to the pond, staring at the reflection lit by a full moon shimmering off the glassy surface. She saw Buddy standing next to Jason and another wolf. A wolf with long flowing whitish light gray hair, and then she realized with a sense of startled excitement that she was the other wolf.

She was no longer human.

She was beautiful.

Shay didn't know how long they ran through the night, through the forest, before they ended up back at the cave. She followed the pull of energy leading her into the chamber, back to Jason. He lay on the blanket.

Human. Naked. The dim glow of the fire's embers lighting his beautiful skin.

Jason smiled at her. "Walk around the fire and as you do, imagine walking upright, imagine walking on feet and not paws, imagine yourself in your human form." She did as he said and it was that simple, that painless to make the change back from wolf to human, complete with her limited senses. The room's chill hit her and immediately she wanted to change back.

"When can we do it again?" she asked. "Why did we come back here?"

"Because that was your first time. You need to take it easy, give your body time to adjust."

"Adjust? Why?" She knelt on the blanket next to him, though she was still too keyed up to sit for long. "Why couldn't we have run all the way to The Colony?"

"Transforming requires a lot of energy and resources. It's a long way to The Colony. You're still too new. If there's any other way, I'd rather not take the chance if we don't have to. Not yet."

"But I want to run, to feel the night air in my lungs, the earth beneath my feet. It was magical. It was exhilarating."

He laughed and reached for her, pulling her into his arms.

"Why would you ever want to change back?" she asked, lying next to him on the blanket, nestling into his warmth.

"Because you have to. If you don't, if you stay in wolf form too long, you'll forget your human side. You'll forget what it's like to *feel* human, or that you ever were human. Then there will be no coming back. You will stay a wolf. Always."

She thought of the wolves surrounding her house, attracted by the scent coming from the cracks in her walls, and shivered. He held her tighter, and she sighed as his lips found hers. His warm energy, which she'd felt while in the forest, cocooned her and she was thrilled it was still there. This connection between them.

And now, in her human form, she could recognize it for what it was. His happiness. His joy. Her heart lifted and she kissed him deeper, pulled him closer, until he was making love to her again. Filling her with his need. His want. His heart. It could have been hours that they lay there next to the fire that had burnt down to the embers, lost in each other's touch, exploring, touching, feeling, loving. She'd never been happier. She knew she'd made the right decision, didn't have a doubt in her head. Not even when she heard Buddy's low growl.

She looked up and saw two men standing just inside the chamber's opening, their faces filled with shock and anger. *Demons?* Shay gasped and grabbed the blanket around her naked body. She stared at the men, but didn't see a dark aura surrounding them. Was it because she'd changed? Did she no longer see auras? Or was it because of the dim light in the cave?

Jason stiffened next to her. He stood, stepping into his jeans. "Mitch."

"Jason," the taller of the two men answered.

Surprised, Shay looked up at him. How did he know their names?

"You mind waiting for me outside?" Jason asked, his body tense, his tone harsh.

Shay waited for the men to turn and walk out of the chamber before turning back to Jason. "Do you know them? Who are they?" she said, her tone hushed.

"They're Malcolm's men," he grumbled, obviously not happy.

"Isn't that good? Doesn't that mean we're almost there, that they'll help us? That we're finally safe?"

"Perhaps," he said evasively, pulling on his jeans. "Get dressed and ready to go. I'll be right back."

"All right." She stood.

The warm current connecting them was now sharp, edgy and prickling. She didn't like it. She stepped into her capris, grabbed a fresh T-shirt out of the trunk and pulled it on, surprised to see that, as Jason had said, the bite mark and scratches from her fight with the *Abatu* were gone.

She picked up the blanket and quickly folded it then put it back into the trunk. She grabbed what was left of the food and three water bottles for herself, Jason and Buddy. Buddy whined low in his throat. She patted his head and gave him a piece of jerky, then plopped another in her mouth. She was starving. Beyond starving.

"It's going to be all right, boy," she said, more to make herself feel better than him. He had to be as hungry as she was. Maybe even hungrier. She couldn't help wondering what he thought about her "other self" or if he'd even realized it had been her. She poured some water into her cupped palm and he drank greedily. "We are going to get through this." They had to. But the prickling sensation coming from Jason seemed to be growing stronger.

She tried to block it, to put it out of her mind as she stood and kicked dirt over what was left of their fire, when she heard raised voices.

"She was meant for Malcolm," one of the men said.

"There are *Abatu* after her. At least two that we know of are left on the mountain looking for us right now," Jason said. "We needed to hide out here, to rest…to heal. She was hurt pretty bad. We had no choice."

"No choice but to bed a beautiful woman?" the man sneered. "There are always choices, Jason. And you know that's how Malcolm's going to see it. You're a traitor now and traitors aren't tolerated. Not in The Colony."

"I am not a traitor. You know it and so does everyone else at The Colony. No one will see it that way."

"From where I sit, all that matters is how Malcolm will see it. He counted on you. We all counted on you and you let us down. Again."

"I've always been there for you and for the pack. You know that."

"All I know is that if I were you, Jason, I wouldn't come back."

Shay felt slightly sick, and it wasn't from the overwhelming hunger gnawing at her stomach. When Jason stepped back into the chamber, she hurried toward him. "Is everything okay?" she whispered.

He looked troubled.

"I wasn't eavesdropping. I just heard."

"I know. Your hearing has intensified now."

"Yeah?" She wanted to smile, but couldn't. He was

too upset. She could smell his anxiety, but more than that, she could feel fear rolling off him.

"What is it?" she asked. "What's bothering you?"

"We might not be able to drive straight into The Colony as I'd planned. We might need to be more evasive, keep our presence a secret, take refuge with your family."

"Why?"

"I don't trust Malcolm, not after what I've just seen. His men reacted much more strongly to us being together than they should have. They weren't listening to what I had to say. They didn't care how much danger we were in. In fact, I think they would have preferred it if we didn't come back at all rather than come back with you already transformed." He sighed. "With you as my mate."

She walked into his arms and he held her close, his heat encompassing her. "What are we going to do?"

"First off, we're going to go back down to the truck. But instead of driving straight into the Colony, we will find a different way in. I'll take you to your grandparents' house and together we will figure out what to do."

Excitement filled her as he said the word *grandparents*. She really did have a family. "Are you sure? What about the *Abatu*? Aren't they still on the mountain?"

"There are only two left. They are no match for us now. If we have to, we will change so they won't be able to follow our scent."

"If we do change, it would make the trek down the hill a whole lot more pleasant," she added, smiling.

He kissed her then, long and hard, stealing her breath

and making her almost giddy with lightheadedness. "We're going to be okay."

"I know." How could they not? Because even with the trouble they faced, she was happier now than she had ever been. But even as she said the words and kissed him one more time, she heard a loud ripping sound behind her. Stunned, she turned and saw a large crack splitting the wall of the rock chamber. A crack that looked a lot like the one in her living room and kitchen back home.

"Oh, my God! How is that possible?"

"It's the *Gauliacho*. They've found us."

Chapter 11

They ran out of the chamber and had just cleared the rocks outside the cave's entrance when Shay heard the crack of a gunshot. A piece of the rock flew into the air, barely missing her. A wave of fear slammed into her. She scurried to the edge of the clearing toward Jason. Another shot came dangerously close. She hurried down the hill following after him as fast as she could with Buddy right on her heels.

"Change!" Jason demanded, disappearing into the thicket.

"Change?" Just like that? She couldn't. She ran after him. He must have heard the hesitation in her voice, for, as she passed a fairly large tree, he was standing on the other side waiting for her.

"You can do it," he said, taking her hand.

"I know I can. I just don't know...*how.*"

"Focus. Concentrate."

A twig snapped off to the right. "Jason, those men were shooting at us."

"I know. You need to hurry."

She turned and saw a man in the distance coming toward them. *Abatu* or wolf? She didn't see a gun, so she had to assume *Abatu.* "Jason," she warned as panic crawled through her.

"It's okay, Shay. Take off your clothes and close your eyes. I've got you."

Take off her clothes? Feeling extremely vulnerable but knowing she had no choice, she did as he said, quickly looking around her as she stripped out of her clothes. The *Abatu's* footsteps were getting closer. She pushed aside her fear and the overwhelming instinct to run and instead put her trust in Jason's words, in the strength in his tone, in the security in his touch.

"Focus on your heartbeat right here." He placed his hand over hers and then rested it on her chest. "Focus on the breath filling your lungs and then leaving your mouth. Think about last night. About how it felt to run through the trees, the cool night air against your face, the scent of the forest deep in your nose."

She did as he asked, letting his soothing voice wash over her.

"Think about all those things. Picture them in your mind and then run." She opened her eyes and then, hand in hand, they started running down the hill. She focused on the blood racing through her body, on the breath rushing through her mouth, on the forest around her. And soon, she wasn't thinking about her nudity or about the *Abatu* behind them, or even about the man with his gun. She was running on all four legs, loping through the forest, a feeling of exaltation bursting through her chest.

With Buddy next to her, she followed Jason, giving a joyous bark as they brushed their faces against each other. Soon the sounds and the scents of the forest overwhelmed her and she no longer thought about why they were running or where they were going. All she could see was the beauty surrounding her and the multitude of hiding places for all the different kinds of burrowing animals, animals she wanted to chase and catch and eat.

In the distance she heard the rush of water. Compelled, she wanted to run toward it, to jump in and see what she could find. The scent was intoxicating. She started to turn, to run that way when suddenly Jason was by her side, nipping at her neck, pushing her forward, keeping her on the path. Right. Yes. For a wonderfully blissful moment, she'd forgotten about everything but the forest around her. And for that brief time, everything had been *perfect*.

For a long time, she ran next to Jason down the mountain. After a while, they stopped near a river and took a long drink from the crystal-clear, icy water. It tasted wonderful and soothed her raspy throat. But before she could finish drinking, something quick and dark skirted past her, brushing against her skin.

A shadow. Her nerves tensed, her heart quickened. It was only a shadow, but was it? No. It moved, a cloud of darkness, darting through the trees. The sound of the wind, pulling at the bushes and rustling the leaves, changed, turning into the echo of a whisper. A chanting that raised the hair on her skin. Low voices in discord, all saying the same thing.

Abomination. Abomination.

Fear, dark and menacing, grabbed her by the scruff of her neck. Shay turned to Jason. Anxiety had his lips quivering, his snarl low in his throat. She whimpered, but before they could move, two men stepped into the clearing. Immediately, Buddy started barking, but the men still continued forward.

Buddy lunged toward them. One of the men rushed forward and kicked him viciously out of the way. Buddy flew against a tree and landed in a heap below it. Instinct taking over, she sprang forward, hurling herself at the man. He kicked at her, too, but missed. She lunged, leaping for his neck.

He grabbed hold of her, trying to wrap his arms around her, to squeeze her like the other had done Jason, but she snapped at him, feeling her canines rip into his skin, tasting his blood as it seeped into her mouth. She wouldn't let him get his arms around her. She saw what had almost happened to Jason before. She fought with even more ferocity, twisting this way and that, when burning pain sliced through her side.

She yelped and fell to the ground, licking her wound. The man came at her again, a bloody knife in his hand, a demonic smile on his face. She turned to Jason, but he was savagely fighting off the other man. She wanted to scream but all she could manage was a bark and whimper. He couldn't help her any more than she could help him.

She struggled to her feet, watching the man come toward her with the knife, trying to think of a plan. But she couldn't think. Couldn't focus. He wanted to kill her. He would kill her, if she let him. They circled round, him stepping forward, her stepping backward, only to lunge forward and snap at his feet. If she could get her jaw around his Achilles tendon, if she could bring him down, he wouldn't stand a chance.

He pivoted, a move she didn't see coming. Pain shot through her shoulder. It was a shallow wound, but he came at her again. This time, she jumped up, throwing all her body weight into him, knocking him off balance. He faltered and she lunged again. No holding back. No thinking as she went for his neck.

He threw up his hands to guard his face, the bloody knife still clutched within his grasp. He thrashed it back and forth, trying to stab her. She couldn't get the upper hand. From out of nowhere Buddy came rushing forward and bit down on his leg. The man screamed, flailing out with the knife. She bit his arm, wrenching with her razor sharp teeth, and tore into his skin. The knife flew out of his hand.

Before she could move, Jason was there; his steel-trap jaws locked around the *Abatu's* thick neck. Not taking any chances, she ran toward the knife, picked it up between her teeth and turned back to Jason. He stood watching her, her attacker lying on the ground, not moving.

Jason turned and ran. She and Buddy were close behind him. They were a good ways away from the men when she finally dropped the knife from her mouth. The cuts and bruises she'd sustained hurt, but not enough to stop her or even slow her down. She wouldn't think about those men, about what they'd done to them or the salty taste of blood in her mouth.

Or the black shadow that had raced by her, preceding the attack. She knew on some instinctual level what it had been, what had finally come through the walls. What had led the *Abatu* to them.

The Gauliacho.

After a while, Jason slowed. He stopped by a large redwood with an opening within and slipped inside. A second later, he came back out and stood in front of it, gesturing for her to go in. She and Buddy went inside the hollow. Jason whimpered and she had the impression he wanted her to stay put. She dropped to the ground and placed her head on top of her tired paws. Buddy followed suit.

She watched until Jason disappeared into the trees then closed her eyes and tried to listen to the sounds around her. His soft footfalls could barely be heard above the racket of the birds in the trees and the cacophony of insects. But she could smell his fear, his sense of frustration and sadness. A low keening wail escaped her lips. Buddy pushed himself against her, and she dropped her head once again. By loving her, by saving her, Jason had risked so much.

After a while he returned. He stood before her, naked and beautiful with the last of the sun's rays shining on his beautiful body. She looked up at him and knew in that instant that she wanted to spend a lot more time with him, getting to know him. All of him. He had done so much for her, had risked everything just to save her. She walked out from the hollow and approached him. His large, warm hand brushed the top of her head.

"It's all right. We're alone. You can change back now."

She focused on his touch, on the warmth of his hand on her head, and remembered what it had felt like on her skin. Touching her. Caressing her. And then she was standing in front of him, wishing he'd touch her again.

He pulled her into his arms and ran a gentle touch along the shallow knife wounds on her shoulder and her side. "You're hurt."

"They're not bad."

"I'm sorry."

"You keep saying that but it's not your fault."

"I just wish all this was over and that you were home in The Colony and safe."

She smiled, trying to imagine it. Trying to imagine being home with him. As they reached the truck, he walked forward and she couldn't help watching the strong line of his back, down to his incredibly well-defined butt. No man should look that good. He crouched behind the back bumper and pulled a hide-a-key box out from beneath the truck bed. Soon the door was open and he was rummaging in the backseat for a T-shirt, shorts and a pair of boxers. He handed her her duffel.

"The last of my clothes," he said. "I've lost a lot more clothes than I'd expected to on this trip." He quickly dressed, covering that gorgeous body. She sighed, sorry to see it go, but as he said, they would be at The Colony soon enough. A hot shower and his bed was definitely something she was looking forward to. She pulled on a T-shirt then slipped into a pair of jeans. She was getting low on clothes herself.

"Would it be too much if I mentioned I was starving? It seems to be a constant state these days."

He smiled as Buddy barked in agreement. "Sorry, no place to grab something to eat between here and The Colony."

She reached into the back and scooped a handful of dog food out of the bag and into Buddy's bowl. Buddy devoured it instantly. "How long till we get there?" she asked, giving Buddy another scoop of dry food.

"Shouldn't be too long. Depends how many more complications we run into." He put the truck into gear and headed back out across the meadow toward the dirt road.

"I'm not sure I can take any more complications," she said truthfully.

He looked at her, his gorgeous pale eyes locking on to her and causing a quickening in her chest. "You've been...great."

They sat in silence as the truck barreled over the uneven ground. Shay held tight to the handle above the door to keep her teeth from rattling. Then very slowly became aware of a heavy sensation pushing down against her chest. Pushing so hard she was having trouble catching her breath.

Wide-eyed, she turned to Jason. "What's happening?"

"What do you mean?" he asked, turning to her, looking all relaxed, like he didn't have a care in the world. But she knew better. The oppressive sensation of anxiety was rolling off him and onto her with such force that she felt as if she might be pushed through the truck's floorboard.

"Why are you so afraid?" she asked. "After everything we've already been through, what else could happen to us?"

He stared at her for a moment, his gaze examining her face before his eyes widened with surprise. "You can feel my emotions that strongly?"

"I've never felt you so afraid. And I've never felt your emotions…physically. In here." She touched her chest. "Just tell me what's going on," she insisted.

"Yes, it's true I'm worried, but there isn't anything we can do about it until after we talk to your grandparents."

"Will they help us?"

"I'm not sure. I just hope they'll understand."

"About?"

"About us."

"Of course they'll understand. How could they not?"

He smiled. "Exactly."

She still didn't understand, and he still hadn't told her much, but after a moment the uncomfortable tension dissipated and she relaxed. "How much of *my* emotions can you feel?"

"Not a lot," he admitted. "Only when you're highly stressed or emotional do the feelings break through."

"Are you highly stressed, then?"

He looked at her, his eyes thoughtful. "No. Not really. Not enough for you to have noticed them. You might be extra sensitive."

"How?"

"I don't know. Some people are. There's no reasoning. You are part human. That will make you different. As we grow closer and spend more time together, this connection between us will strengthen."

"I'm not sure I like the sound of that," she admitted.

"For me, it was the hardest transition to make. Knowing I wouldn't be able to hide my feelings from the person I was connected to. It is a loss of privacy. But I learned how to block it, and you can, too. I'll show you."

"Is that what you're doing with me now? Are you blocking your feelings?"

He hesitated then admitted softly, "Yes."

"Then perhaps you should tell me what you are so worried about. Who was shooting at us and why? I don't remember the *Abatu* having guns but those men you were talking to did."

"They work for Malcolm. I knew Malcolm sometimes crossed the line in his pursuit for power, but I never dreamed he'd go this far. Shooting at us goes against every tenet of the pack. We have rules against this. Extreme rules. If what they did was discovered, all those involved would be banned from The Colony and not allowed back in."

"Where would they go?"

"Out here. To the outside world."

"But the demons…"

"Exactly. That's why we take our laws very seriously. We don't last long out of The Colony on our own."

"And that's what happened to my dad? He was sent away?"

Jason turned to her, his eyes heavy with sadness. "He chose to leave. But knew that once he married your mom, he could not stay."

Anxiety pinched her insides. "Then why would my dad do it? Why would he fall in love with a human and take that chance?"

"Sometimes you can't help who you fall in love with. He loved your mom more than he feared the *Abatu*. He thought he could outrun them. He believed he could find another sanctuary where our kind could be safe."

"That must be why we kept moving."

"Yes. It was always unimaginable to him that there would only be one spot on this planet that had the right combination of elements to protect us. He wanted to form another colony, one where humans and wolves could live together side by side."

"Sounds ambitious."

"Yes. Unfortunately, most thought he was crazy."

"We never found such a place," she whispered.

"I know. But I'd always hoped he had."

"You didn't know he'd died?"

"Not for sure. Though I assumed. Letters and pictures stopped coming a long time ago."

They sat in silence for a moment as memories of her childhood flitted through her mind, bringing with them the fear and loneliness she had always lived with. And then his hand found hers and tightened around it as they pulled out of the meadow and back onto the dirt road.

"We're going to be okay," he said. "We're going to make it."

"If you say so," she grumbled. Blocking or not, she knew he was lying. Between the *Abatu,* the *Gauliacho* and the wolves gunning for them, there was a strong chance that they wouldn't make it to The Colony.

Buddy whimpered again and jumped into the front seat and sat next to her, pressing against her side, taking most of the space. His body trembled and she realized he, too, could sense her emotions. She hugged him tight and willed the fear growing inside her to ease.

Easier said than done.

"Okay, tell me the game plan," she said.

"The game plan?"

"Yeah, what we plan to do when the big bad wolves out there or demons attack again? If we're a team now, you need to start sharing your plans with me. You need to start being honest with me. Otherwise, I'm just sitting here suffering through your anxiety attacks and not able to do a damn thing about it."

The corner of his lip tilted up. "Have you always gotten this grumpy when you're hungry?"

"My hunger pangs aren't the issue here. Just answer the question. What's the plan?"

She didn't wait for him to talk, but forged ahead with the thoughts swirling around in her mind. "What do we tell the others about what happened on the mountain? If we can get these men kicked out of The Colony, then they are going to need to make damned sure we don't get there to tell anyone about what they've done. And if that's the case, won't this Malcolm person have people waiting for us?"

"Johnny works the front gate. He always has. He is not one of Malcolm's men."

"Maybe not, but do you really want to take that chance? If you were Malcolm, wouldn't that be the best place to wait for you? He knows you're coming back. You have to. You have no choice."

Jason stared at her, contemplating her words. "I hate to think Malcolm would go that far."

"I would think he'd be desperate by now. They shot. They missed. And you certainly never thought he'd go *that* far."

"True."

"Is there another way in?"

"Yes, there's a town on the other side of the mountain where your dad met your mom, but it would take us too long to get there."

"All right, then what are we going to do?"

"We'll have to hike in through the woods."

She groaned. "Not again. How far?"

"It's seven miles from the front gate to The Colony. A nice buffer to keep out hikers."

"Is there a fence?"

"Yes."

She sighed as he turned off onto another road, the one she'd missed last night. If only she hadn't. Everything would have been so different. They wouldn't have had to climb the mountain or sleep in a cave. They wouldn't have been chased by monsters, hurt and almost killed. They wouldn't have made love by firelight.

She wouldn't be a wolf.

The thought made her smile. She hadn't had time to think about what it all really meant. Time to doubt or be afraid. It had just happened; in an instant her whole life had changed and she was no longer human. She was a shape-shifter. She was in love. And from where she sat, next to this incredibly honorable and brave man, even with the threat of demons, her life had changed for the better.

Chapter 12

"You were right." Jason hopped back into the truck and quietly shut the door. "Malcolm's men are at the front gate. Johnny is nowhere in sight."

"I'm sorry," Shay whispered, wishing for his sake she hadn't been.

"Don't be. I shouldn't be surprised."

"What are we going to do now?" She looked at the chain-link fence disappearing through the trees.

"We're going to have to climb the fence."

She looked down at her bare feet and cringed. "What about Buddy?"

Ears pricked, Buddy looked up at them and whined.

"We'll manage. Somehow," he muttered. "At least once we get beyond the perimeter the *Abatu* will no longer be able to track us."

"And that black shadow?"

"That was the *Gauliacho*. Demons from the other side. It came through the crack in the wall of the cave and apparently wasn't alone."

A shiver tore through her.

"Don't worry. Once we're beyond the gates they won't follow us."

He started the engine and drove for another five minutes before hiding the truck in the woods outside The Colony's perimeter. They walked along the fence for a long time as they searched for a way in. Shay was growing more nervous by the second, peering through the trees, on constant alert for danger. Finally, they found a downed tree. "This could work."

"You're sure?"

"Yes, and once we're on the other side, we're safe."

She stared at the large tree lying on the ground, then saw what he meant. Together, they hefted the tree up against the fence, then transformed it into a bridge, climbing up it. Showing Buddy how it was done.

At last, they were in The Colony and running free. It was hard to accept, but finally there was no more fear or worry that the *Abatu* or *Gauliacho* could find them. There was only her joy as she explored the sounds and smells of the forest. Everything was as it should be as they ran through the woods while the sky dimmed to dusk. They tracked for miles alongside a rushing river that flowed into a large and clear lake, the most beautiful lake she had ever seen. The reflection of the snow-peaked mountains shone in brush strokes of reds and purples across the glassy surface.

They turned inward, running through the woods until finally they stopped in front of a small house nestled within the trees. Smoke billowed invitingly from a stone fireplace.

Jason stilled amongst the large cedars and pines, lifting his nose into the air, catching the different scents. She and Buddy sat next to a tall tree and waited while Jason circled round the house. After a moment, he came back changed into his human form.

He crouched down in front of them. "Stay as you are until I'm certain it's safe and I can get you some clothes."

She nuzzled his hand, and together they walked up to the front door. She as a wolf. He without a stitch on. She supposed people here must be used to that. She didn't think she'd ever get used to it. Jason knocked and after a long moment of anxious expectation, an older man with a face that looked a lot like her dad's pulled open the door. Her heart swelled inside her with a strange mixture of expectation and apprehension. What if he didn't like her?

What if he didn't want her there?

He greeted Jason, looked down at her and Buddy then stepped back, inviting them in. He handed Jason a quilt off the sofa then disappeared into a back room. Anxiously, Shay looked around the small room, instantly aware of the pictures on the wall, pictures of her dad, of him and her mom, and even some of her as a very young girl. Shay whined. She no longer wanted to be in wolf form, she wanted to change back, to look at her grandfather with human eyes.

Seeming to understand what she wanted, Jason said something to her grandfather when he came back into the room, carrying a pair of pants and a fresh shirt. He handed them to Jason then looked at her with widened eyes. He gestured toward the back of the house, and Jason led her into a back bedroom where she changed immediately. She didn't need any coaxing or guidance. She wanted to change, wanted to be able to speak. To hug her grandfather. To meet her family.

Jason opened the closet, then handed her a flannel shirt and a pair of sweat pants. Quickly, she slipped into them, running her fingers through her tangled hair. "I need a shower," she muttered.

"You and me both," he said while stepping into the clothes her grandfather had given him. "You're going to be fine." He pulled her into his arms and kissed her.

She melted into his warmth. "I'm so nervous. Do they know it's me?"

He nodded. "Robert does. Kate, your grandmother, is still in the kitchen. She is going to love you." He kissed her again. "Everything is going to be okay. You're home now."

"Home," she whispered, and felt a flutter of expectation light her chest.

"Yes. So come see your family. They've waited a long time to meet you."

Shay took a deep breath, then walked back into the living room. Her grandfather, Robert, was standing next to an older woman who had tears running freely down her face. She hesitated for a brief second, but that was all it took, and her grandmother was rushing forward, pulling her into her arms and holding her tight.

It was like a dam had burst inside her, and Shay was flooded with emotion. There was no holding back. No judgment, no tiptoeing around, trying to figure her out. They knew nothing about her and yet they instantly welcomed her into their family and home.

Her grandmother, Kate, wouldn't stop talking and smiling and touching her. As if Shay might disappear again at any moment. Shay knew how she was feeling because she was feeling it, too. For a long time she couldn't speak for fear that if she did, she'd just start crying and never stop. And then she couldn't stop speaking, blathering about nothing, about everything all at the same time as she walked around the room looking at the pictures.

"Come," her grandmother said, sitting on the couch and patting the cushion next to her. "Have your tea."

Shay took the cup and sat next to her. Her grandmother was nothing like her grams. For one thing, she was younger and beautiful with her long black hair so much like Shay's. She'd always wondered about her hair since her mom's had been fair and wavy. As had been Grams's. Shay had always been dark.

"So, you made the change, then? We weren't expecting that," her grandfather, Robert, said from his dark leather chair in the corner. His jaw was hard and concern filled every line in his face.

Uneasily Shay looked to Jason, knowing this was what Jason had been fearing. "We had to, Robert," Jason said. "There was no choice."

"We were being attacked, it was horrible," Shay added. Suddenly nervous as tension bunched Jason's shoulders. She felt an uncomfortable current coming off him and wanted to go grab his hand, to assure him that she was there for him. But as she looked at her grandfather's disapproving face, she held back. Biting her lip.

"Otherwise, I would have waited," Jason said, sitting forward on the edge of the sofa.

"We both would have waited," Shay added, making it clear that it was their decision. Together. Jason almost sounded as if he was apologizing, then he started explaining about the cracks in her walls, about the *Gauliacho* and the *Abatu*.

"Oh, my," Kate said, her hand fluttering to her mouth. "My poor girl."

"She'd been hurt," Jason said, looking down at his hands.

Shay ran her fingers along the back of her head, expecting to feel a scab or a bump, anything. But nothing was there. "Yes, it was pretty bad. A lot of blood, but honestly, I think those men with the guns were worse."

Shay took a sip of her tea but the cup froze on her lips as she noticed the subtle change in the room, the air of shock and expectancy. They were all staring at her. Her grandfather shifted, his brows drawing down in a thick black line.

"Guns?" Kate said, her dark eyes sharp.

"It was Mitch and Louis," Jason explained. "Outside the caves."

"No, it couldn't have been." Kate stood and started to pace. "They know better. They know the rules."

Robert shook his graying head. "I must admit I'm not surprised. The real question is whether or not Malcolm put them up to it."

"I did wonder the same thing," Jason admitted. "I didn't want to believe it but when we got to the gate, Johnny wasn't there. Malcolm's men were in his place. Three of them. I know Mitch couldn't have arranged that without Malcolm's help. I just have a hard time believing Malcolm could be involved."

Robert shook his head in silent disgust. "I'll call Scott."

"Are you sure that's a wise move?" Skepticism lowered Jason's voice.

"There have been other incidents while you've been gone, Jason," her grandfather said. "Malcolm is out of control. The time is now for Scott to make his move. Especially if Malcolm has his hired guns shooting at the only people who have a chance to unseat him."

"I can't believe it's come to that."

"Trust me, it has."

"All right," Jason relented, reluctance strong in his voice. "But make sure Malcolm's men don't see him coming."

Nervously, Shay stood. "If we're having more company, would anyone mind if I took a shower and got cleaned up?"

"Of course not," Kate said.

"I'll show her." With a soft touch to her back, Jason stood then led her to the bathroom. "Are you okay?" he asked softly.

Before she could answer, Kate appeared in the doorway. "Here's a fresh towel and toothbrush. Let me know if there is anything else you need."

"Thanks," Shay said, and took them from her.

She turned to Jason, slipped her hands around his waist and leaned her head onto his chest. "I'm exhausted."

"Just a little longer. I need to fill your cousin in on what happened and see what he wants to do about it." He leaned down and kissed her deeply.

Shay's limbs melted, and she wished not for the first time that they could crawl into bed together and put this day to rest. Then, before she knew it, he was gone. Shay hurried as quickly as she could. She wasn't sure she was ready to meet this cousin who wanted to take on the leadership of the pack. She couldn't remember what Jason had said about him, but thought he wasn't quite sure about him. She had just finished brushing her teeth and pulling her hair back into a ponytail when she heard a knock at the front door. She took a deep breath and walked into the living room as the man she assumed was her cousin entered through the front door.

He was big with dark hair and copper skin. He had huge arms and a massive chest and looked quite frightening. But that wasn't what concerned her about him; it was the way he kept staring at her, with wariness shifting in his black eyes. What was it Jason had said about the pack leadership being her birthright? Was she a threat to this man? As she took in his hulking form, she sure hoped not.

"Shay, I'd like you to meet your cousin, Scott," her grandfather was saying, but Shay barely heard him. As

Scott walked into the room, his gaze intent on hers, she was too distracted by colors swirling around his head. She'd thought once she'd transformed she wouldn't see the colors any longer. She hadn't seen anything around Jason or her grandparents, but this man was surrounded by a dark red cloud.

Her heartbeat burst into a racing canter and she had to force herself to stand still instead of taking a large step back. She reached for Jason, but he was too far. She glanced toward him, but he was oblivious to her distress and didn't seem the least bit concerned himself. At least not that she could tell. But there was a weird energy coming off him. Trepidation hummed through her system, though she wasn't sure if it was coming from him or if it was coming from herself. She dropped her hand to her side.

"Welcome home," Scott said, sounding courteous and perfectly normal.

But he wasn't. Shay didn't know how she knew that, but she did. She forced a smile and nodded her head. "Nice to meet you."

He nodded back, but luckily didn't move toward her. She didn't think she could stand it if she had to shake his hand.

"Scott, how is Natalie?" Kate asked, walking toward them.

Scott's face looked troubled for the briefest moment before it hardened once more. "Healing," he said. "Thank you for the basket."

She patted his arm. "I'll be going by to see her again tomorrow."

"She would like that."

"Come on, Shay," Kate said, taking her arm. "Let's go into the kitchen. You can help me finish dinner."

Relief mushroomed inside Shay as she left the room with her grandmother. She was happy to get away from the men, especially her cousin, and thrilled at the prospect of dinner. Buddy barked in agreement and they walked into the warm kitchen where Shay helped Kate cut up vegetables for the stew.

"The meat has been cooking all day. I just need to add the vegetables and it will be done in no time," Kate said, stirring the pot.

"It smells wonderful," Shay admitted. She felt as if one side of her stomach was eating the other.

"It's the fresh thyme, it's my favorite."

"Mine, too." Shay sat at the table watching her grandmother, feeling a strong kinship with her. She just wished her mom could be there and her dad, that they could have met long ago and have had a normal life free from running and hiding and living in fear. She'd never even known what they'd been running from. She sighed. That was probably a good thing.

Once the vegetables were cooking in the pot, Kate refilled her cup from the kettle on the stove. "Now sit down and tell me everything. Leave nothing out."

Shay laughed, feeling lighthearted and happy for the first time in ages. She talked and talked, telling her grandmother everything about her life. Crying with her when she told her about her dad, and about how young she had been when he'd died. "At first I didn't believe Jason when he told me that I had family I'd never heard of. In fact, I didn't believe anything he said. I didn't want to go with him, until he told me about you." She reached across the table and took her grandmother's hands within her own. "I thought I was alone in the world. If there was even the slightest chance that he was telling the truth... I'm so glad that I found you."

Her grandmother's eyes misted. "Not nearly as glad as we are that Jason brought you home to us. We were so afraid we'd never get to meet you. It's been so long." She rose from the table, turning her back on Shay to stir the stew.

Shay gave her a moment. "If you don't mind my asking..."

"You can ask me anything," her grandmother said, turning back to her, her eyes damp. "I know this all must be very strange to you."

"Yes, well, how come you look—" Shay couldn't finish the words.

"Old?" Kate asked, a twinkle lighting her dark eyes.

"Well, older," Shay admitted. "Jason told me that once we make the change we age differently. Slower."

"Yes, that's true. But Robert and I stopped making the transformation a while ago. We no longer felt the urge to run. We knew if we didn't force ourselves to change, then the aging process would begin for us again. After losing your dad and then our daughter, Maggie, well, we no longer cared. We'd lost our joy. Our bliss. We didn't see any reason to prolong our time here. Not without them."

Her words resonated within Shay, drawing deep into the empty well of sadness she had lived with for so long. She knew how it felt to be alone in the world. To lose everyone you loved. The loneliness. It could be debilitating. "I'm so sorry," she said. "I know after a loss like that, nothing seems to matter much anymore."

"Don't be." Kate patted her hand as she sat back down at the table across from her. "We've been given a second chance at a family. You can't imagine how happy that makes me."

Shay's heart ached and unbidden tears burned her eyes. "Me, too." She fiddled with the napkins on the sideboard, pulling them down and placing them on the table.

Without saying another word, Kate walked over to the cabinet above the kitchen counter, pulled down several large bowls and handed them to Shay. "I'm sorry if I got too mushy. We are both just so happy you're here."

"Thanks," Shay said over the lump in her throat. She placed the bowls on the table, noticing there was an extra one for Scott. "But I'm not sure my cousin shares your feelings on that one."

"Oh, pooh. Don't worry about Scott. He is obsessed with unseating Malcolm and is afraid that if Malcolm forces you to marry him, it will solidify his position so that Scott won't have a chance at taking over leadership of the pack."

"How could Malcolm possibly force me? Don't women have rights here?"

"Yes, of course we do. But Malcolm has his ways of getting what he wants. He always has."

"Well, you don't have to worry about me on that account. I'm with Jason now and we're very happy."

"I saw that," her grandmother said. A shadow passed in front of her eyes and Shay couldn't help remembering

Jason's fears that her grandparents might not understand their being together. Though she couldn't imagine why.

"He is a great guy. I feel very lucky to have found him," she prompted, hoping her grandmother would say something to help her understand.

"That he is," Kate agreed.

Shay stared at her. There was more here. More she wasn't saying. Her grandparents obviously liked and respected him, so why wouldn't they want them together?

"He saved me from an incredible nightmare. There was this horrible buzzing all the time and I kept seeing colors around people. I thought I was losing my mind, and then the *Abatu* attacked. But Jason stopped them. Not just once, but over and over again. He'd been hurt pretty badly, too, and yet he still got me here. You should have seen him." She was rambling. And smiling too wide. She knew that, she just couldn't seem to help herself. "He was incredible."

Kate didn't seem as impressed as she should have been. Was Shay reading something into her grandmother's reaction that wasn't there? Or was there something more going on? Whatever it was, Shay had to know. She took a deep breath to ask when she noticed her grandmother's eyes drifting to a picture on the sideboard, a picture of a beautiful woman with dark brown curls and smiling eyes. For a second, heartbreak filled her face so completely, it was almost as if her grandmother had left and had been replaced by someone else. And then just as quickly the look was gone. She turned and walked toward the door to the other room. "Let's call the boys in to dinner. You must be starving."

* * *

"Malcolm will not let this go," Scott said to Jason. "That girl in there is the only chance he has of maintaining his leadership."

"Malcolm will understand we had no choice," Jason assured him, though he wasn't 100 percent sure he believed it. He looked toward the kitchen. He hoped dinner would be ready soon. Now that he knew Scott's plans to take over the pack, he wasn't sure he wanted any part of it. The man was a loose cannon. He would set them back to the dark ages if he could. No internet, no TV, no communication at all with the outside world.

"You are a fool, Jason. Malcolm won't understand, nor will he care. All that matters to him is staying in charge. Hell, Celia took off and left him over this. She's gone and that only leaves us with one Keeper of the Crystals. If it had been up to me, she'd never have been allowed to leave."

"Celia left the Colony?" Jason asked, unable to believe what he was hearing.

"She is the only one who can. With her gift of regenerating the crystals, she'll be able to secure a perimeter for herself."

"Yeah, but for how long?"

Scott's black eyes hardened. "Long enough for her to get over that bastard Malcolm. This pack has never been more vulnerable and I place that solely on his doorstep."

Jason couldn't believe what he was hearing. How could Malcolm have gotten so out of control? The man was losing everything. "I will talk to Malcolm in the morning."

Scott laughed, a short annoying bark. "Are you sure that will do you any good? Time for talking is over."

"I get how you feel about this, Scott, but are you sure you're not letting your animosity toward Malcolm skew your judgment? You want to be pack leader as badly as Malcolm wants to keep it. But both of you seem to have lost touch with what's best for the pack."

"Are you sure about that? I'm not the one who went to the council to ask for a marriage permit to marry a girl I haven't even met. Who may or may not even agree or want to."

Jason stilled. "Did they give it to him?"

"Yes. They want peace as much as everyone else, and it appears will do anything to keep it. Just because you helped her through her transformation doesn't mean Malcolm still won't claim her as his."

"He can't," Jason whispered.

Scott looked at him and shook his head. "He already has."

Chapter 13

Dinner had been wonderful and hit the spot. Before Shay could finish, exhaustion had set in and she hadn't been able to take another bite. Luckily, Kate had seen it and sent her straight to bed. Even Buddy was content lying in the corner of the guest room, snoring away. But the best part was climbing into this big soft bed next to Jason and snuggling up into his arms. She'd been through hell, but it appeared the worst was behind her.

She was surprised how happy she was that Jason was there with her, even if her grandparents seemed more than a little shocked and surprised when Jason had said he wanted to stay with her. Of course, he'd wanted to take her back to his house, but they wouldn't hear of it and had finally relented and let him stay. She had to admit, she wouldn't have minded seeing his house and lying with him in *his* bed, but she really was too tired to move. She rested her head on his chest and listened to the thudding of his heart. "Is everything going to be okay now?" she asked after he'd been silent for too long.

"Scott is going to come by with his people in the morning. They are going to fill me in on their case against Malcolm, what they believe he's done and what their evidence is against him, before I go see him. They want to strategize a plan for his removal from power."

"You don't sound like you are sure that's what you want."

"I'm not. But before today I never would have believed Malcolm was capable of the things he's done. I guess I'm not sure of anything, except that I want you to be safe." He pulled her closer, tightening his arms around her.

She sighed in contentment as her eyelids grew heavy.

"I want to marry you, Shay. If you agree, we could approach the council tomorrow and apply for a marriage permit, and let them know in no uncertain terms that we want to be together."

"A marriage permit?" Suddenly awake, Shay pulled back and looked at him, stunned. "Why? What's up? Isn't this a little fast?"

Jason laughed and nuzzled her neck. "Yes."

Happiness bubbled through her, but she didn't believe it. Didn't trust that what she was feeling was real. "Why so soon?" But even as she said the words the answer came to her, stealing her happiness and leaving doubt and insecurity in its path. "This has something to do with Malcolm."

He was silent for a moment and his arms tightened around her as he pulled her back to him once again. "Yes, I know he wants you for himself and I want to ensure that he can't touch you. That he can't take you away from me."

She smiled indulgently. "That would never happen. I won't let it. We have been through too much."

"I just want to be certain," he said, his voice soft.

His tone was starting to scare her. He was worried about something. "Shouldn't we go on a date or two? A normal date like with dinner and movie where monsters and men with guns are on a screen instead of trying to kill us?"

Jason stilled, and she could feel his trepidation in the gentle current filling the air around him. And yet, he still wasn't telling her everything. "I'm afraid it's the only way to protect you from Malcolm."

She sat up, drawing her knees to her chest. "This isn't exactly how I'd dreamed about getting engaged. How do I know you aren't just marrying me to keep someone I've never met from claiming me? What if Malcolm wasn't in the picture, would you still be asking? We just met."

"I'm sorry. I shouldn't have sprung this on you so soon."

"Does that mean you would have eventually?" She smiled, though she was fairly certain he couldn't see it in the darkness of the room. Excitement was growing inside her, but she didn't trust it. Didn't want to believe in it in case it wasn't true. In case the bubble burst and it didn't happen.

"I'm not certain you should want to marry me," she warned, trying to give him an out. "You don't know anything about me. You could marry me, then two months later be kicking yourself in the butt for your impulsiveness."

"Good point," he said, and her breath caught. "But I think I know enough."

"Really? Do you know I don't cook?"

"Sure you cook. You eat, don't you? I saw you buying food at the store."

"Yes, I cook eggs. It's my specialty. And I make soup."

"Soup is good," he said, sitting up next to her, close enough that their shoulders were touching.

She smiled and buried her face in his neck at the doubt in his voice.

"What else should I know about you?" he asked.

"I hate to clean house. I'm not going to be one of those women who spends all day cooking hearty meals for her husband and scrubbing floors."

"Okay," he agreed. "I like housework. We should fit together fine."

"No one likes housework. And I spend a lot of time on the computer."

"Oh?"

"In fact, as soon as all this is settled, we need to go back to the truck and pick mine up. I have accounts I need to maintain."

"What do you do?" he asked tentatively.

"Graphic design. You know, websites, blogs, brochures."

"Sounds…interesting."

"Will that be a problem?"

"No. We have computers. Internet. For now. I'll be able to get your stuff in the morning."

"For now?"

"It's one of the changes Scott will make if he takes over. He feels constant access to the outside world is… damaging. Especially to the kids."

Shay stilled. "I can't imagine not having the internet."

"You're not alone," he admitted.

"What about the demons? They know where they lost us. Will they be hovering around outside the gates, waiting?"

"I'm not worried about a few demons." She shivered, and he pulled her closer, kissing her forehead. "You don't have to worry, Shay. Sooner or later, you'll come around to my way of thinking. You'll realize that you won't want to live without me."

She grinned. "I will?"

"Yep. From what I hear, I'm quite the catch."

"Really?" she said. "From what you hear?"

"Yep. I'm a great provider. Not only that, I cook *and* clean. I'm very self-sufficient. I've had to be. I've had to live on my own for a long time now."

Had to? That was an odd way of phrasing it. "Well, I must admit, you do sound like you'd make the perfect husband." She leaned over and kissed him gently on the lips.

He deepened the kiss, making her muscles weaken and her stomach flutter. His strong, warm hands moved down her body, inch by slow inch, touching, caressing, stopping at all her sensitive places and giving them extra loving care until she felt liquid heat surging through her veins.

She ran her hands over and across his shoulders, feeling strong muscles beneath smooth skin. He was gorgeous. Irresistible. And he knew exactly how she liked to be touched. He rolled her on top of him, running his warm hands down the groove of her back, his strong fingers kneading, massaging. She let out a long sigh. Heaven. She was in heaven.

"You certainly are a good lover," she muttered, and melted all over him when his fingers explored places that hadn't been touched in a long time.

He spun her back over, kissing her again, deeply, his lips moving with certainty down the column of her throat, igniting a trail of fire in their wake. He touched her breasts, taking them deep in his mouth and sucking on them until her back arched up off the bed and a deep guttural moan rose from her throat. She reached for him, taking his hardness in her hand, stroking him until a low moan left his throat. She shifted him between her legs, anxious to feel him inside her, to quell the insistent need pulsing within her. She lifted her legs up around his back, straddling him. Pulling him closer.

"I think I need more convincing," she whispered.

He nipped her nipples, kissing and sucking until she thought she'd come apart if he didn't give her the release she needed.

"I want you now," she insisted as the urgency inside her reached the breaking point. Her skin popped and sizzled, and she was certain that if he didn't enter her right then, if he didn't ease the throbbing ache pulsing deep within, setting her nerve endings on fire, she would come apart at the seams.

And then he was lifting her, pushing his thickness inside her, surrounding her with his warm, hard body. And all she could feel was his heat, and all she could smell was his warm earthy scent, and all she could hear was his breath firing in her ear, and his heart thudding against her rib cage.

But more than that, she could feel his love for her, washing over her in a strong stream so overwhelming it brought tears to her eyes. And she knew that no matter what she'd said, she wanted this man to love her and to make love to her every night for the rest of her life. She trusted him, not only with her heart, but with all of her.

In one hard thrust he entered her welcoming body, moving fast and deep, his rhythmic bucking fanning the flame that grew hotter with each long stroke. Her legs clung to him, trying to pull him deeper, the rhythm of her hips increasing in tempo. They were dancing, swaying with one another, bucking, moving with such intensity she burned inside and out until the passion within her exploded in a fiery storm of aching need.

She heard herself scream before she buried her face in his chest, muffling her moans as her body shuddered along with his in a mind-jolting, seismic release.

"Oh…my," she whispered, feeling horrified and satisfied all at the same time.

He grinned, capturing her mouth with his and kissing her senseless. When he finally let up, she sucked in a deep breath. "Please tell me I wasn't too loud. That my grandparents didn't hear me scream."

Jason laughed, a low chuckle that reverberated through her. She clung tighter to him, not wanting him to leave her. Not wanting to separate. But they did. He rolled off her, lying next to her on the bed.

She repositioned herself, nestling against his chest, laying her head on his shoulder as her muscles relaxed into a pool of liquid warmth. "I suppose you are right," she said, relenting as her fingers caressed his warm skin. "You are a very good provider."

"Marry me, Shay, and I will provide for you whenever you want. And once you move into my house, you can scream as loud as you want and no one will hear you. There will be no holding back."

"Promise?" she whispered, smiling as she imagined the many nights of happiness and fulfillment ahead.

"Marry me and you can go to sleep wrapped in my arms every night. You won't regret it. I promise."

Happiness at his words bubbled inside her. "All right, Jason," she whispered as endorphins rushed through her brain, saturating her judgment in orgasmic pleasure. "I'll marry you."

He smiled and pulled her closer, kissing her again and again, and then they made love once more before they both dropped into an exhausted sleep.

The next morning the sun was shining through the lace curtains when Shay woke to loud voices coming from the front of the house.

"You can't come in here like this," her grandfather bellowed.

Jason jumped out of bed and pulled on his borrowed pants seconds before the door burst open.

Shay sat up, yanking the covers up to her chin as two men strode into the room.

"I'm sorry, Jason," a man wearing what looked like a sheriff's uniform said. "But you're going to have to come with us."

"Why?" Shay blurted.

The sheriff turned to her. "Ma'am," he said. "Please excuse the interruption." He turned back to Jason. "We'll wait in the other room while you get dressed."

They left, shutting the door behind them. Shay jumped out of bed, picking up the sweats and the flannel shirt she'd worn the night before. "Jason, what's happening?"

"I don't know, but don't worry. Everything will be all right."

"You're lying. I can feel the anxiety rolling off you."

He gave her a sheepish smile. "I can see I won't be able to keep anything from you. Stay here with your grandfather. I'll be back as soon as I can and then we'll go see the council." He leaned down and gave her a quick kiss then walked out of the room.

She finished dressing then rushed out into the living room in time to see, through the front window, Jason getting into the back of a Jeep. Whatever comfort she had managed to get from his words disappeared in an instant. "What are they doing?" she asked her grandfather, who was standing at the window beside her. "It looks like they are arresting him. Why?"

"Conspiracy, I suppose."

"Conspiracy? To do what?"

"To dislodge the pack leader."

"That's crazy! That's Scott, not Jason."

"The way they see it, his job was to bring you back here for Malcolm. Once Malcolm helped you make the transition, you would be connected to him. You would be his mate. His wife. Solidifying Malcolm's position. Now you are with Jason instead."

"That's absurd. Don't I get a choice in all this?"

His face troubled, he turned away. "Yeah, you could still choose to be with Malcolm."

Shay gasped, outraged. "No!"

"It might be the only way to help Jason."

Panic twisted her insides, squeezing. "That's crazy! No wonder my dad wanted to leave this place."

Kate made a strangled sound from the doorway, her hand fluttering to her lips.

Shame and embarrassment washed over Shay, flaming her cheeks. "I'm so sorry," she said, hurrying toward her. "I didn't mean that."

"No." Her grandmother stepped into the room, her voice and face resigned. "Don't be sorry. I understand your anger and confusion. There are a lot of reasons for the rules we have here. They may, at times, seem restrictive, especially to someone born and raised on the outside, but give us a chance. We have a lot of wonderful things here, too."

"There must be something we can do for Jason?"

Shay said, turning back to her grandfather. "Should we call a lawyer?"

"I'm going to see the council," Robert said. "I still have a lot of influence around here."

"Your grandfather was the pack leader before passing it on to your dad," Kate said. "We've always been a family of leaders, it's why Malcolm wants you."

Shay nodded, understanding more and more. "I'd like to go with you. Jason and I were going to talk to them this morning about applying for a marriage permit. Maybe it would help him if this council knew that."

Her grandparents didn't say anything. They just stared at her with a strange frozen deer-in-the-headlights look upon their faces.

"Married? I hadn't realized things had gotten that serious between you," Kate said.

"I, uh, think that would be a good thing," her grandfather said, before Shay could respond.

"Are you sure, Robert?" Kate asked, her brown eyes filled with worry, reminding Shay of her suspicion that they were keeping something from her. Something about Jason.

"Yes," Robert said to his wife. "Shay's right. We need to help Jason. Maggie would want us to. Not only for Jason, but also for our granddaughter. I won't have her married to that brute Malcolm. I'm going over to see Scott. Get dressed. I'll be back in an hour to pick you up, then we'll go visit the council."

Shay nodded, but as she watched him walk out the door, she couldn't help wondering what he meant. She turned back to her grandmother. "Who is Maggie? And why would she want you to help Jason?"

Kate hesitated a moment, watching her husband leave.

"Kate?" Shay pressed.

"Maggie was our daughter. And Jason's wife."

Chapter 14

Jason stood in Malcolm's large living room before the great stone fireplace, watching the logs burn, wondering how this was going to go. With Malcolm, one never really knew.

He didn't have to wait long. Malcolm strode into the great room. "Coffee?" he asked, gesturing toward the coffee service on the sideboard.

Without a word, Jason helped himself to a cup.

"I appreciate your coming to see me." Malcolm filled a cup for himself and lifted it to his lips.

"You didn't leave me much choice." Jason let his annoyance seep into his tone. "I don't appreciate you sending your goons to pick me up. You could have called. It would have been nice to have had a shower and get some clothes that fit me first."

"Yeah, sorry about that." Malcolm grinned, showing the charm that had gotten him where he was. But his charm didn't work on Jason. Not since that day in the seventh grade when he'd seen Malcolm charm Mrs. Huffington into an A on a paper that should have been a C.

"My men get a little carried away sometimes," Malcolm said with lazy arrogance.

Jason's grasp tightened on his cup as he tried to keep from exploding on him. Coming unglued and beating the crap out of Malcolm might make Jason feel better, but it wouldn't help the situation. And besides, they weren't fourteen years old anymore. "Mitch and Louis got a lot more than carried away up at the caves. They shot at us."

Malcolm's eyes widened. "I had nothing to do with that. I can't imagine why they would do that."

"I can imagine it easily. Mitch called you and told you he'd seen Shay and I together. You exploded, said a few choice words and hotheaded Mitch ran with it. Admit it, Malcolm. I've warned you about him before. He's a loaded gun with a hair trigger and one of these days, someone is going to get hurt."

Malcolm perched himself on the edge of a bar stool. "You're right. He's gone too far this time and I'll deal with him. This Scott thing has him on edge. Hell, it has us all on edge, but I had nothing to do with it. You are like a brother to me—you must know that. I would never order anyone to shoot at you."

Jason wasn't sure if he believed him or not. But one thing he'd said was true—he and Malcolm went way back. "What about the gates? When we got there,

Johnny was gone and three of your thugs were waiting for us."

"Yeah, well, I wanted to make sure you got here safely. I was hoping you'd stay here with me. We have a lot to talk about and I wanted to meet Dean's daughter."

"If that's true then you won't mind when I report the shooting to the council and make a formal complaint against Mitch and Louis."

"No. I won't stop you. In fact, I'll go with you."

Jason watched his old friend over the rim of his cup, trying to decipher what Malcolm's game was, if he had an agenda or if he was shooting straight this time.

Malcolm held his gaze steady. "I'd just appreciate it if you'd hold off a day or two. Give me a chance to talk to them. To try and find out what happened."

"Why?" Suspicion swirled with the coffee in Jason's gut.

"Because I want to know what really happened out there. What about Dean's daughter? Is she all right?"

"What happened is we were being hunted down from the moment I found her. Her scent was much stronger than a newborn's usually is. We were attacked relentlessly from all sides, even from the *Gauliacho*."

Malcolm whistled high and low. "Are you serious? Why?"

"I have no idea, but trust me when I tell you she had to transform. She was badly injured by the *Abatu* and we weren't making it off that mountain otherwise. We had no choice. I tried to explain that to Mitch, but obviously he didn't listen. We almost didn't make it as it was, and having your men shooting at us didn't help matters."

Malcolm stood perfectly still, his light green eyes boring into Jason's. After a long moment, he said, "I believe you, Jason."

"Well, that's good to hear," Jason responded, trying to keep the sarcasm out of his voice but not succeeding.

"Listen, Jason, I know better than anyone how much you've sacrificed for the safety of this pack, and now this little pup, Scott, is about to start our troubles all over again."

"I'll try talking to him," Jason said. "But he's hell-bent on his path."

"This has moved far beyond talking and you know it."

Jason sighed and emptied his cup. "Yes, I suppose I do."

"To make matters more complicated, two nights ago our warehouse was broken into. Everything was stolen."

"Who?"

"Scott is the only one that makes sense. It had to be an inside job. There were only forty-five minutes between the time the shipment was dropped off and when we arrived to pick it up. A forty-five-minute window and everything was gone. Do you know what this will do to our economy? The setback we're going to face? A lot of money was tied up with that shipment and now it's gone."

"But Scott? That's a little extreme, even for him."

"I've heard from an inside source that he's going before the council today to claim I'm mismanaging pack funds."

"I'm sure you can counter those claims. All our money couldn't have been tied up in TVs?"

"TVs, computers, washers and dryers, game systems, all the amenities people have been working hard to get. Now they're all gone. People paid in advance, Jason."

"But it could have been anyone."

"Could anyone have burned down his house?"

"What are you talking about?"

"The day before the shipment disappeared Scott's house burned to the ground with his daughter still inside. He's trying to blame it on me."

Jason took a deep breath while he tried to process the news. "Is Natalie okay? I saw Scott last night and he didn't mention it."

"Trust me. He's saying a lot. To a lot of people."

"What makes you think he did it? Burning his own house down, hurting his own child... I can't believe he'd do that. Scott loves that girl."

"I think he was more surprised than anyone that she was there. He thought she was staying the night at a friend's house, but she hadn't felt well and came home. Now the bastard is more determined than ever to pin it on me, so Natalie doesn't find out her own dad almost burned her to death."

"That's extreme."

"Tell me about it. I think he found out you were going after Dean's girl and became desperate. Stealing the shipment just added to his ammunition against me. I shouldn't have risked so much of the pack's money. I know that. But sales have been going really well. I just thought if I could get more products in advance, we could make even more money. When you buy in bigger quantities, the cost goes down significantly."

Jason rubbed a hand across his face. "So let me guess, this is why you want me to hold off telling the council about Mitch and Louis."

"It will just add fuel to Scott's claims. He'll say I put them up to it. If we can wait until we find that shipment, it will diffuse the situation. Mitch and Louis are out there tracking it now."

"On top of a mountain?"

"What better place than those caves to hide the town's goods?"

Jason had to agree with him there, though it wouldn't be easy getting them up there. Those old logging roads hadn't been used in a long time and were very overgrown.

"I just need to stall Scott and the council's inquiries a little longer to give Mitch a chance to find the shipment."

"What about the sheriff?"

"He's been down to the warehouse. He looked around but there was nothing to find. Right now he's busy doing everything he can to find out how that fire at Scott's house got started."

Jason closed his eyes. "How the hell did everything get so messed up? I was only gone for a few days."

"That's what I'm saying," Malcolm said, shaking his head. "All this couldn't have just happened. Someone orchestrated the whole thing, and they've done a damned good job screwing me up. Those TVs have got to be somewhere. I've sent Mitch and your security team out there to find them. We will get to the bottom of this mess."

"You sent my men out there?" Jason thought of the *Gauliacho* still out beyond the gates and cringed.

"I had no choice. I tried to call you, but you weren't answering your phone."

"We lost it on the mountain. We had our hands full."

Malcolm took a deep drink of his cup. "I get that. I'm sorry, man. Sorry about Mitch and Louis and everything else."

Jason nodded, then walked over to the sideboard and refilled his coffee. "We'll deal with them later. Right now, you're right. Our first priority should be finding that missing shipment. And you need to make damned sure there is nothing connecting you to that fire."

"I was here that night, trust me. Begging Celia not to leave me."

Jason paused. "I heard." Celia was the best thing that had ever happened to Malcolm. She grounded him in a way no one had ever done. "What happened?"

"She found out I asked you to go get Shay. She was furious."

"I would have gone after Shay anyway. I promised Dean."

"I know that. But she got wind that I asked the council for a marriage permit and freaked. It was stupid, and not one of my better moments."

"Yep. I'll agree with you on that one. Though in theory it was a good plan. We just didn't think it through real well."

Malcolm smiled. "That's an understatement."

"So where's she gone?"

"Who knows, but she'll come back. She has to. She is my only alibi."

Jason ran a hand across his face. "That sucks."

"In so many ways."

Jason had to agree. Without Celia here to hold him back, who knew what Malcolm might do. "But worse than that, as a pack we can't be dependent on only one Keeper. We need Celia here. What about Jaya? How's she taking this?"

"She's ready to string me up by the family jewels."

"I can imagine," Jason said dryly. "Celia is her only child."

"You know it. That old woman scares the shit out of me."

"Well, let's hope Celia doesn't stay gone for long."

"I hope not, though she was scary mad. That girl spits fire when she's angry."

Jason had to agree with him there.

"So, tell me," Malcolm said, looking at him over the rim of his cup. "How attached are you to Dean's girl?"

Suspicion prickled the hair on Jason's nape. "Very. Why?"

"I need something else for the town to focus on for just a little while and I think a wedding is just the trick."

Jason straightened. "No way."

"I know what you're thinking, but all we need is a little distraction."

"Shay is mine. I turned her. I...I want her. I've asked her to marry me."

Malcolm stared at him for a long moment before his lips widened into a large grin. "That good, eh?"

"Hands off."

"Hell, man, I don't have to actually marry her, though it would look damn good for me to be affiliated with Dean's daughter."

"Forget it."

Malcolm laughed. "I'm just pulling your leg. No, I meant you. I want *you* to marry her, just ask me to stand up for you. Show the town that we're together on this. I need her to be in my corner publicly until we find that shipment and settle this thing with Scott's house. Do you think she'll do it?"

"I don't know." Jason took a long swig of his coffee. "She was pretty shook up by all this. Dean died when she was real young. When she started going through the change, she had no idea what was happening to her. Why all these strange people were suddenly attacking her. She was out there alone and clueless."

Malcolm stilled. "How is she doing now? Did the transformation go well?"

"It wasn't easy. She was real spooked, as you can imagine."

"Tough break. What about the old man and Kate? How are they taking all this?"

"It was awkward at first, but I think they're okay with it. One thing is certain, they'd rather have her with me than with you."

Malcolm grinned. "I really don't know why they don't like me."

"Yeah, right."

"You and Dean were just as responsible for the toilet papering and egging as I was."

"Yep." Jason couldn't help the grin creeping onto his face.

"And you asked me to take over the pack."

"That's true, I did."

"And even when you came back…"

"Yeah, I know. I was in no position to take over, not after losing Maggie."

"You insisted I stay on as leader."

"I did, and up until now, I've never had reason to doubt you weren't right for the job."

"There's no reason to doubt it now."

"So, you're sure you're okay with me and Shay?"

"Trust me, Jason, in the past few days, I've had a lot more on my mind than Dean's girl or your love life. Especially with Celia gone."

They both were silent for a moment.

"She'll come back. She has to," Malcolm said.

"That's what I thought about Maggie." The words were out before Jason could stop them. Something dark fell over Malcolm's face. "I'm sorry," Jason said, backpedaling. "I guess I still haven't gotten over my own guilt for not going after her right away when she left here to go looking for Dean. She didn't stand a chance. But Celia's different. She's a Keeper. She can protect herself. But more than that, she is loyal to the pack.

She will come back, and when she does, I suggest you marry that girl before you lose her for good."

"You know it," Malcolm agreed. He set his cup down. "Listen, I know now is not the best time, but I have one more favor I need to ask of you."

Jason steeled himself. When Malcolm asked for a favor, it was usually not something Jason wanted to do. "What?"

"I know you just got back and you have Shay to get settled, but you are the best tracker we have. I need you to go back out there and help your men find that shipment."

"Malcolm, I haven't even made it home yet."

"I know. And normally I wouldn't ask, but will you do it?"

Jason thought of Shay and how much he wanted to take her back to his house and spend the day getting to *know* her better. How could he just leave her alone? He hadn't even had the chance to explain to her about Maggie, and he couldn't imagine she was going to take that well. But he also knew if he didn't help Malcolm find that shipment, Scott would have all the ammunition he needed to unleash a full-scale war against Malcolm and anyone who stood with him. It would be ugly. For all of them.

"Talk to Shay," Malcolm said. "Explain to her what's going on. She can even stay here with me if she wants. In fact, that might help the situation. We just need a little time to get the hotheads to calm down. By showing the two of you are strong in my camp, it will strengthen us against Scott and his minions. I can protect her here while you're gone. I swear I won't let anything happen to her."

"After what Mitch did, Shay would never stay here. But I don't think she should stay at Robert's either. I'll try to get her to stay at my house or Dean's. But, yes, have someone keep an eye on her. If Scott really is that unhinged, I don't want him anywhere near her." Jason set his cup down and they walked toward the door.

He wasn't sure if he was doing the right thing, but he knew Malcolm was right. He had to find that shipment before people realized it was missing. And before Scott could cause any more trouble. And somehow he had to tell Shay and her grandparents that he would be leaving, running away from his responsibilities to his mate. *Again.*

He would rather go back outside the gates and face a hundred demons than have to face the three of them right then.

Chapter 15

Shay stared at her grandmother in disbelief as she followed her through the doorway and into the kitchen. *Married?* Jason had been married? "He never said anything," she said, her voice breaking over the words.

"Maggie's disappearance was hard for all of us." Kate opened a canister and started filling the coffeepot with grounds.

Shay stared at the picture of the woman with the curling brown hair that she'd seen her grandmother looking at last night. *Maggie.* Her aunt. Her stomach clenched and she dropped into the nearby chair at the table.

"Those had been happy times around here," Kate said, following her gaze. "Your dad was leading The Colony after your grandfather stepped down. Jason was the Sheriff and his top advisor, but more than that, they

were good friends. The three of them had been inseparable. But then Dean fell in love with your mother, and
she got pregnant."

The rich scent of brewing coffee filled the kitchen.
Kate opened the fridge and took out a carton of eggs,
cheese and milk. Shay watched her while trying to absorb what she was saying, to picture what it must have
been like. For her grandmother, for all of them.

"Before Dean left to be with your mom, he and Jason
went to the council. They decided then that Jason, as
Maggie's husband and Dean's first in command, would
take over in Dean's place. They had a short period of
transition. Everything ran smoothly."

"So what happened?" Shay asked.

"Seven years later our daughter, Maggie, began to
believe that Dean was in trouble. She and Dean were
twins. She was always very connected to her brother.
Even when they were children…." She paused for a moment, her eyes closing as she succumbed to her memories. "Anyway, she was certain Dean needed her."

"He did," Shay muttered.

Kate began absently breaking eggs into a bowl.
"Maggie couldn't stop thinking about your dad. She
became obsessed with her need to find him."

Shay wrapped her arms around herself. She knew
what was coming, what her grandmother was going
to say. Kate stopped whipping the eggs and turned to
her, her eyes heavy with pain and rimmed with sadness. "Maggie begged Jason to go with her. But he said
he couldn't leave the pack. Malcolm was growing his
power base. He had fundamental disagreements with

the way the pack was being run. He wanted computers. He wanted internet and satellite. He wanted more of a connection with the outside world," she said, her mouth twisted with bitterness.

"You don't have a computer?" For the first time Shay realized not only was there not a computer, there wasn't a TV in the living room or a dishwasher in the kitchen. Everyday necessities she always took for granted were missing from this house. Was that the same for everyone? No, Jason had said that Scott wanted to take them away. That must mean some people had them.

"No, we don't," Kate said proudly. "And we don't want one. My husband always said it was better that way, stronger for the family unit. Both Dean and Jason had agreed with him and continued in that tradition while they were in charge. Why did we need to become embroiled with the problems of the outside world? Without technology we were a stronger community, we were able to focus on our family's needs, on ourselves and our neighbors."

Kate poured the eggs into the pan. "Of course, Malcolm didn't agree. He wanted to know everything, be on top of all of the latest and greatest technology, but even more than that, he wanted to profit from it."

"Profit?"

"We don't have a lot of money in our village. We've never needed it. We take care of our needs and we share with each other. That was never enough for Malcolm. Even as a young man, he always wanted more."

"It seems like he still thinks he can have whatever he wants," Shay muttered. "The audacity of that man, thinking he could send Jason to bring me back to marry him. A complete stranger. It's insane."

"That's Malcolm for you. I'm sure he thought his charm would sweep you off your feet the moment you met him."

"He's that egotistical, huh?"

"You got it." Kate smiled as she slid a plate full of scrambled eggs in front of her. "Coffee?"

"Yes, please." Shay added milk and sugar to her coffee. "Do you think Jason is going to be okay?" she asked as Kate sat across the table from her.

"Oh, yes. Jason knows how to take care of himself. You don't have to worry about him."

"So what happened, then, with Maggie?" Shay asked, though a part of her wasn't sure she wanted to know.

"Well, my daughter was always very headstrong. So against all our wishes and without telling any of us, she went after Dean on her own." Kate glanced once more at the picture on the sideboard of the beautiful girl with a shock of dark brown curls and a wide happy smile. "We never saw her again."

"I'm sorry," Shay muttered.

"Jason was furious when he discovered she was gone. He left immediately and went after her, but she'd already had a full day's head start. He never found her and when he arrived at the address Dean had given us, all of you were gone. He searched but never found any of you."

Shay tensed at her words. "That was the year my dad died. We'd moved several times."

Kate nodded, swiping at the corner of her eye.

"Dean's letters had stopped coming and then we knew we'd lost them both."

"What about my mom? Why didn't she write?"

"Harsh words had been said back then, before Dean had left. We never got the chance to put it right. Dean never came back to The Colony, not even for a visit after you were born. And how I wanted to see you." She reached across the table and took Shay's hand, giving it a squeeze. "But now Jason has brought you home to us."

"I had no idea I even had grandparents," Shay whispered. "No one ever told me."

"Of course you didn't, how could you? Now eat your eggs before they get cold, we have a busy day today."

Shay ate a forkful of eggs without really tasting them as she let everything she'd just learned sink in. Jason, who'd just asked her to marry him, had once been married to her aunt. That was definitely something he should have told her.

"So how did Malcolm become pack leader?" Shay asked after a few minutes.

Kate stood and refilled her cup. "Jason had been gone looking for Maggie and Dean for a very long time. And in his absence…"

"Malcolm took over."

"Yes. He instituted a lot of his changes and by the time Jason came back, many people didn't want to go back to the way things were. They were thrilled with their TVs and their internet."

"And I'm sure Malcolm made a fortune selling them."

"That goes without saying. People needed more

money to buy these modern contraptions. Suddenly there were a lot more things for sale, people began creating things, more stores and restaurants opened, more buildings and houses were being built. Our tiny little village had become a thriving colony. And Malcolm was the one everyone thanked for that."

"Then how does Scott hope to defeat him? And, no offense, but why would he want to?"

"Because Malcolm's power has gone straight to his head. We've all seen it. The council is concerned. There have been acts of violence. Nothing anyone could pin on Malcolm, he's too careful for that, but people who oppose him or his ideas, people who try to stand up and make changes, suddenly fall on hard times and become plagued with misfortune."

"And Scott?"

"While Jason was gone, Scott's house burned down. His daughter was hurt."

Shay's fork stopped midway to her mouth. "That's horrible. Is she going to be okay?"

"Yes, thank goodness. Malcolm is a terrible man, Shay. He needs to be stopped."

"Surely there must be proof?"

"How can there be? The sheriff is on his side, and most likely on his payroll."

"Then why would Jason work for Malcolm? He cares deeply about The Colony. I can't believe he'd willingly work for someone like that. It doesn't make sense."

"After Jason returned home without Maggie, he was a different man. A broken man. He didn't want the job as pack leader again, even if Malcolm would have given it back to him, which he wouldn't." She stood and picked up their empty plates, taking them to the sink.

Shay watched her for a moment, letting the words wash over her. She remembered that day when she'd thought Jason was going to die on the road beside the truck. He'd said it wasn't time for him to die, that he hadn't been tortured enough yet. She suspected she finally knew what he meant.

"He must have loved Maggie very much," she said quietly as she felt her heart splinter.

"Oh, yes. She was his whole world," Kate said, unaware of the pain she was inducing. "Much like he was hers. Afterward, Jason moped around his home doing nothing for almost two years. He'd given up everything. By the time he pulled out of it, he didn't know what to do with himself. The Sheriff's position had already been filled. He was a lost man, a shell of his former self."

"That sounds awful."

"It was. Malcolm came to him and offered him a position on his staff as head of security. Against our wishes, Jason took it. I won't say he's been happy, but he's kept himself busy. He takes his responsibilities very seriously."

Was that what she was, then, a responsibility? The food in her stomach was beginning to sour. She pushed the rest of her coffee away. "Jason lost everything because of his commitment to the pack. How could anyone call him a traitor? Has everyone forgotten? It's… it's criminal."

"I agree," Kate said, filling the sink with hot soapy water.

"What's going to happen to him now? What will Malcolm do to him?"

"I'm not sure. But he can't do anything without the council's approval, so try not to worry yourself too much."

"I suppose I should go get ready." Shay looked down at her sweats. "Do you have anything I can wear? My clothes are still in Jason's truck outside the gates and I'd like to be ready when Robert returns."

"I'm sure we can find something that will fit you."

Shay followed her grandmother into her bedroom.

Kate opened her closet door, looked Shay up and down, sizing her up, then pulled a long floral skirt and matching blouse out of her closet. "How's this? You're a bit smaller than me, but it should fit fine with a belt or a few safety pins. I wish I still had some of Maggie's things, you two are just about the same size."

Shay forced herself to smile. "These will be perfect, thank you." She took the clothes into the bathroom and turned on the shower. It wasn't until she was under the hot spray that she let the tears come and spill onto her cheeks. How could she have been so stupid? Of course Jason hadn't fallen madly in love with her after only a few days. His offer to marry her was only about protecting her, and about keeping her from Malcolm. He would never love her the way he did Maggie. Even if he could, he'd never let himself.

A broken man.

That was why it had been so easy for him to transform her and form their connection, to ask her to become his wife, because it hadn't been an emotional decision for him. He was doing what he always did—what was best for the pack. The admirable and responsible thing. She was such a fool.

Jason arrived back at the Mallorys' house just as Shay, Scott and his former in-laws were walking out the front door. "What's up?" he asked when he noticed the puffiness circling Shay's eyes. Had she been crying? His fists clenched and he had to take a deep breath to calm the surge of anger rushing through him.

"Jason," Shay said, relief easing the tension from her face as she walked toward him.

He pulled her into his arms, feeling immediately better as her softness melted into him. "You look sweet in your grandmother's dress," he whispered into her hair.

"We were just getting ready to go visit the council to explain what had happened on the mountain," she said.

He looked up at Robert and Scott, surprised that they'd acted so fast. "Thank you, but I've just explained everything to Malcolm. Shay and I will be talking to the council ourselves." He leaned down and gave Shay a quick kiss.

"What did Malcolm say?" she asked.

"He wanted to know what happened. No cause for concern. Everything is fine." He kept his tone casual, watching Scott closely for his reaction. But there was none. Not even a flicker crossed his eyes.

"That's surprising," Robert said.

"Well, since you're ready," Jason prompted. "Should we make our engagement official?"

Shay looked up at him and smiled, but it wasn't the

happy carefree smile that consumed her whole face and lit something warm within him. Instead, she didn't feel right; sadness seemed to be enveloping her. *What happened while I was gone?*

And then he knew. *Maggie.*

Surely Kate wouldn't have told her before he'd had the chance to tell her himself? *Of course she would.* The woman always had meddled too much. And she'd blamed him for Maggie's death.

"Is there a rush?" Shay asked, sounding suddenly hesitant.

He looked down into her faded blue-violet eyes and wished he'd had more time with her that morning. Time to make all the proper explanations, time to show her what they could have together if she gave him a chance. But he hadn't. And now he had to break the news to her here. In front of everyone.

"I… Well, yes. I have another job to do for Malcolm and I'm going to have to be gone for a few days. I'd like to talk to the council and see you settled before I go."

"You're going to continue to work for that man?" Kate asked, her tone hard and astonished.

Annoyed, Jason turned cold eyes on her. "Yes. I know you have your doubts about him, but Malcolm is a good man. I realize he can be hot-tempered, but he is passionate about the security and success of this pack. I trust him. I always have."

Kate stepped toward him, anger twisting her face. "A lot of us feel that the changes Scott wants to make and the ideas that he has are what this pack needs. Not more materialism. We're too in touch with the outside world. We're losing who *we* are. Our youth are getting antsy and want to leave. Instead of feeling like a haven, The Colony has begun to feel like a prison to them. And you, better than anyone, know how disastrous that will be for this pack."

She grabbed his arm, her bony fingers digging into his skin. "Malcolm has done that to us with his computers and his televisions. Sometimes too much information is not a good thing."

Stunned, Jason pulled out of her grasp. "Kate, I understand your concerns, but going back to being completely in the dark ages and oblivious of the outside world isn't the answer either."

"That isn't what we want," Scott added, approaching them and placing his hand on Kate's shoulder, offering her his support. "But neither do we believe that there should be a television in every home. Put one in the grand hall, in the neighborhood pubs and restaurants. Let technology bring us together, not isolate us."

"That's a grand pie-in-the-sky plan, but do you really think people will be open to giving up what they already have?"

Scott looked him square in the eye. "Yes, I do."

"And so do I," Robert said, stepping forward. "Had I known the debacle Malcolm would have caused this colony, I never would have stepped down in the first place."

"You stepped down for Dean. It was his time and you knew that."

"Perhaps. But I had no idea it meant so little to him, that he'd throw it all away." The bitterness in his tone surprised Jason. After all these years, he'd had no clue of the depth of Robert's anger. And Kate's, too?

He looked at his former in-laws, really looked at them and knew it was true. Jason knew bitterness, he knew disappointment and anger, but he never let it define who he was as a person or let it color his perceptions or paint his reality. That just felt like a betrayal to Dean and Maggie, and all they'd stood for.

Shay stiffened beside him and he pulled her closer. "Robert, trust me. This colony meant everything to Dean. It was his home, his family. He didn't make the decision to leave lightly, but Lily and Shay meant more. He couldn't live without them."

"You don't need to tell me how my son felt," Robert snapped.

Jason held up his hands in surrender. "I get that." He hadn't spent a lot of time around Robert and Kate during the past few years, but he never would have guessed the level of bitterness and hostility they carried within them. As he watched the emotions play across their faces—outrage and mistrust—he had to wonder if perhaps Malcolm was right. How far would Scott or even Robert and Kate go to return the pack to what they believed was its rightful state?

He hoped he wasn't about to make a mistake, but he had to know. He had to be sure. "I promised to help Malcolm find a lost shipment of televisions and computers. Apparently, his last shipment has gone missing. Do either of you know anything about that?"

He watched their faces closely as he said the words. The veering of their eyes, the subtle tightening of their lips, any sign of the truth. Genuine surprise widened Scott's eyes, while shock filled Robert's and Kate's faces.

"When everyone finds out that that bastard swindled their money…" Unable to finish her thought, Kate covered her mouth with a trembling hand and shook her head in disgust.

"You think Malcolm stole his own shipment?" Jason asked, clearly surprised.

"I don't believe there ever was a shipment," Robert said, his eyes sharp with anger, his jaw stiff and hard. He stepped even closer, until Jason could see the red veins in his eyes and the purple shadows beneath them. Robert lowered his voice. "I think if Malcolm could find a way to pin this theft on Scott, then he's well on his way to destroying his competition and solidifying his leadership."

"You believe that Malcolm stole from everyone just to maintain his pack leadership?"

"And destroy Scott's good name in the process? You damn well better believe it," Robert answered vehemently.

Stunned, Jason stepped back from him. "I'm sorry. I don't agree. I've been close to Malcolm all my life, and yes, he's ambitious, he's impetuous and driven, but he's not diabolical and he's not cruel."

"You've always had a blind spot where Malcolm was concerned," Kate muttered, her mouth twisted with disgust.

"We were best friends growing up, the four of us. Remember? You know him. You know the real Malcolm."

Kate's mouth hardened. "Oh, please. Even Maggie was beginning to have her doubts about him, and you know it."

Shay trembled in his arms. He looked down at her, certain now that Kate had told her about Maggie. He wished that she hadn't stolen that from him. But she always had been one to interfere, to think she knew better than anyone else.

Annoyance and frustration hardened his words. "Why would you say that, Kate?"

"You know it's true. You know she warned you about him. She told you he wanted your job. She begged you to watch your back."

"Maggie told you that?" Jason asked, clearly surprised Maggie would have gone that far.

A bleak shadow passed in front of Robert's eyes. "I've always wondered if she knew something the rest of us didn't. That if somehow her gift gave her knowledge about Malcolm that got her killed."

"You think Malcolm killed Maggie?" Jason asked, stunned with disbelief. How had Maggie's parents become so delusional?

"Maggie was strong and she was well trained, you know that. She never even made it to Dean's house. I don't believe the demons could have gotten to her that fast. In fact, I'm not sure I believe they got to her at all."

"Malcolm did not kill Maggie," Jason insisted, no longer wanting to continue this conversation. No longer wanting to be around them. "Malcolm loved Maggie. He always had."

"Yes, but she chose you, didn't she, Jason?" Kate

added bitterly. "And so did Dean. He chose you to run the pack, not Malcolm. You got everything he'd ever wanted, and still you couldn't see how badly he coveted what you had."

"Malcolm was right there with us. We were running things together. We were a family. All of us."

"And yet, in the end, it isn't you and Maggie leading our colony in harmony, it is Malcolm leading it with the almighty buck and an iron fist."

Jason was speechless. He had been completely clueless about what they'd been thinking for all these years. But on some level, hadn't he had some of these same thoughts himself? Thoughts he refused to let surface? To even acknowledge? The truth was, with Malcolm you never knew.

"It's true, Malcolm has made a lot of changes around here, but he has revitalized The Colony, too. He has made our lives easier in a lot of ways and, yes, some negative things have come with that, but we couldn't have kept things the way they were forever."

"Is that what you tell yourself to make your abandonment of your post all right?" Kate asked.

Surprised by her harsh words, Jason stared at her. Was she right? Even just a little?

Robert cleared his throat. "Jason, you need to consider something. If Scott didn't take that shipment, and I can assure you that Kate and I didn't have anything to do with it, then who do you suppose took it? Who in this colony could get anywhere near that warehouse of his? You handle his security—you tell us."

Robert had a point. And Jason didn't have an answer. But he sure did have a lot to think about.

"Where does Malcolm want you to go?" Shay asked hesitantly.

"I need to find that shipment before all hell breaks loose around here. And I need to start with Malcolm's warehouse."

"Where is it?"

"In the little town I told you about where Dean met your mom."

She stiffened as a shudder passed through her. "You need to go back out…there?"

"Yes." He turned her to face him, placing his hands on her shoulder. "I'm going to be okay. We both are. This is what I do. I handle security for Malcolm. I set up the detail on that warehouse. I will know if it was compromised. I go outside the gates all the time. Nothing is going to happen to me. And when I come back, we will have the biggest, brightest wedding you ever saw. In fact, Malcolm is going to throw it for us. Okay?"

He heard Kate gasp behind him, but he didn't know if it was because of the news of the wedding or Malcolm's involvement in it, and at that moment, he didn't care.

"I don't want my granddaughter anywhere near Malcolm," she insisted.

"Considering he's going to be my best man, that might be a little difficult."

"If you make it back from his next assignment." Kate's tone was harsh, but her words were worse. And as they sunk in, burrowing down into his subconscious, he couldn't help the nagging thought scratching at his brain. What if something happened to him and he didn't make it back?

Then Shay would be Malcolm's.

Chapter 16

"I'm taking Shay to Dean's." Jason was done listening to anything else Kate or any of the rest of them had to say.

"Shay, honey, you're more than welcome to stay here with us," Kate said, ignoring him completely.

"I know," Shay said. "And I appreciate that. But I'd really like to see where my dad lived."

"All right. I'll get the key." Kate turned and swiftly walked back into the house. Without saying another word, Robert and Scott walked toward Scott's truck, got in and drove away. Jason hoped he hadn't made a mistake telling them about the shipment, but he really believed from the surprised expressions on their faces that they knew nothing about it. But that didn't mean someone in their camp didn't.

"Would you like to come back to my house instead?" Jason pulled Shay close. Close enough to smell the lavender scent in her hair. He closed his eyes and breathed deep. "I'd love it if you'd stay there while I'm gone."

Now that she was safe within the walls of The Colony, he was sure he didn't have to worry about her, but he would feel better knowing she was in his house, waiting for him.

Shay pulled away from him, pushing down his arms. "I think it would be better if I was alone right now, Jason. I have a lot to sort out."

He stilled, trying to get a handle on her emotions and the best way to deal with them. "I don't want to leave you like this. You're upset and there are a lot of things we need to talk about."

She spun on him. Anger flashed in her blue eyes, turning them almost purple with her fury. "Right now, I really don't care what you want."

"Shay." He reached for her.

Tears brimmed, filling her eyes, making their color even more brilliant. "Why didn't you tell me about Maggie?"

Maggie. The woman he never wanted to talk about, let alone think about, and yet, somehow she always seemed to be there.

"Did you think I wouldn't find out?" Shay demanded. "Or had you hoped I wouldn't find out this soon?"

"I wanted to tell you myself, in my own way. But honestly, there wasn't much to tell. Maggie died years ago. She has nothing to do with us."

"How could she not have anything to do with us

when she's still alive and kicking right here?" She raised a trembling hand and rested it against his chest. "She's stopping you from moving on, from loving again. I know it. I can feel it. You can't hide that from me, Jason."

He shook his head in denial. "No—"

"Just tell me the truth. Is Maggie the real reason you wouldn't get close that morning in your truck, or was it your loyalty to Malcolm?"

Jason reached for her, wanting to show her how much she meant to him, hoping he could make her understand, make her believe that what he was saying was the truth. But she pulled away from him.

"You're wrong, Shay. Yes, I lost Maggie and at the time it felt like I'd lost my whole world. *She* was my world and I lost her because I put the well-being of the pack first. I have given the pack my life and I can't stop now. If I do, if I let this pack fail, then all the sacrifices I've made would have been for nothing. Her death would have been for nothing. Can't you see that?"

"What I see is that it is easier, safer, to focus on your job instead of your heart. Sorry, but I don't think you've dealt with your feelings for Maggie, and by running off and leaving now, you don't have to."

"There is nothing to deal with," he insisted. "What I once felt about Maggie has nothing to do with how I feel about you now. With you I have a chance at a new life, a new world. One I hope you will share with me."

"Then stay. Show me you mean what you say. Let go of your grief, of your feelings of responsibility to the pack, and start living for you. For us. Let Malcolm send someone else after the shipment."

"I can't. It's my job."

"To be at Malcolm's beck and call 24/7? We just got here."

"I know you don't understand. We don't operate like the outside world here. We don't work nine to five, five days a week. We just do what has to be done. It's hard to explain."

"Yes, and harder for an outsider to understand. But I can't marry someone who will always put the wishes of the pack leader first. Before us. Before me. I'm sorry."

A deep ripping ache settled inside him as her words sank in. She was right. He knew that; how many times had Maggie said the same thing? But it didn't make a difference. He couldn't turn his back on the pack. Not when they needed him. Not even for her.

"I'm sorry, too. But Malcolm was there for me when I needed him. I can't let him down. Not now. Not when he needs me, when the pack needs me so much. I can't turn my back on him. Just like I could never turn my back on you."

Her eyes softened and she took a step toward him. A step he wanted her to take so badly, but then Kate came back out with the key to Dean's house in her hand.

"Do you want me to take you?" Kate asked Shay, holding the key out to her.

Before Shay could answer, Jason stepped forward and took the key. "I'll do that."

Kate's lips thinned into a straight line of disapproval.

"It's all right. Thank you for the clothes." Shay took

Jason's hand and they walked toward one of Malcolm's trucks. Kate turned and walked back to the house, leaving them alone and giving Jason a very short time to try to change Shay's mind.

As soon as her grandmother walked away, Shay dropped Jason's hand. She hoped she'd made the right decision. She felt torn between wanting to be with him and not wanting to get any closer to him than she already was. She had to protect herself. She didn't know what she should do, and knew her options were limited. But one thing was certain; she and Jason did have a lot to talk about. She only hoped they could get things settled between them before he left, or she'd have a pretty miserable few days.

"Thanks for letting me do this for you." Jason's voice, like his gaze, was soft and yet it cut right through her. "I promised I'd deliver you safely to your father's house. I like to keep my word."

Shay nodded, afraid to speak over the lump in her throat, knowing if she wasn't careful it would crack and all her emotions would spill out—her anger over his leaving, her hurt that he hadn't told her about Maggie, her fear that he would never love her the way she needed or wanted to be loved. The way she suspected he had loved Maggie.

Jason opened the truck door for her, but before she could climb inside, the front door of the house opened and Buddy came flying out the door, almost plowing Kate down in his haste to get out of the house and back into the forest. "Come on, Buddy," Shay called.

"Malcolm lent me a truck," Jason said, opening the back door for Buddy.

"Nice of him." Shay tried to keep the bitterness out of her tone. It wasn't easy.

"He's just doing his job. Pack leader is an overwhelming responsibility."

"And apparently, one that is hard to let go of," she muttered.

He stiffened. She was being unreasonable, but she couldn't stop herself. He'd kept something critical from her. An ex-wife who happened to be her late aunt was not something she should have found out about from her grandmother.

They drove in silence following the curve of the lake. The water was beautiful, a deep bluish-green that reflected the majestic snow-peaked mountains in a stunning mirror image. As Shay took in the beauty, letting it wash over her, excitement began to grow and build within her. She tried to stop it, to not get her hopes up, but she couldn't. She was going to her new home. Her father's home.

With or without Jason, her new life was about to begin. She just wished he would be a part of it. She turned in her seat and looked at the strong profile of his jaw, the strength in his shoulders and hands. He was a man who took the world on his shoulders. She just hoped there would be room there for her, too.

"Dean's place is a little far from town, but it's right on the lake, which was his favorite place to be." He looked at her and smiled, causing her heart to ache. "Even though he was the pack leader, he never wanted anything fancy. It's one of the differences between his and Malcolm's way of doing things. Malcolm likes to live in style."

Shay bristled at his words, though she didn't know why. She had no reason to distrust or even dislike Malcolm; she'd never even met the man. So why did she? Was it her grandparents' mistrust?

Jason pulled the truck to a stop in front of a small cabin surrounded by towering pines. "This is it."

Shay stared at the rustic one-story log cabin with a long welcoming front porch running the length of the house. Two granny rockers sat on the porch, and a wind chime hung from the overhang.

"I love it. It's perfect."

Jason smiled again. "I knew you would."

His smile, the way his eyes met and held hers, thawed the chill she'd been feeling toward him ever since her grandmother had mentioned the name *Maggie*. Bittersweet warmth spread through her. She wanted to reach for him, to take his hand and hold it. But she didn't. She wouldn't. Not as long as he was leaving her here alone.

In one breath he'd asked her to marry him, and in the next he'd told her he was leaving her. Not a good way to show her he would always put her and their family first. As she opened the door, Buddy jumped into the front seat and raced across her lap, trampling her in his haste to get out the door. "Thanks, Buddy!"

He howled in return and ran circles around the truck, impatient for her to get out and get moving. She couldn't help smiling at the dog's enthusiasm. He lived in the moment. Always. Something she wished she could do right then, but she had to admit his excitement was catching. As they stepped up onto the porch, Jason took her by the shoulders and turned her to face him. "You can believe in me, Shay. You can believe in us. I'm not leaving you. I'm just doing a job. I will come back."

She gazed into his pale bluish-gray eyes and her heart ached. She wanted to believe him, but she couldn't. She'd lost everyone she'd ever loved and it was hard for her to believe she wouldn't lose him, too. Especially if he kept putting himself in danger. She needed to depend on him, to know he would always be there for her and just her, physically and mentally, with no ghosts hovering between them. "I wish I could."

He unlocked the front door. She walked past him into her father's home and felt an immediate punch to the chest. She inhaled a deep breath. The warm cabin had large planks of pine covering the floors, the walls, and even the ceiling; the entire room glowed with the rich, warm patina of wood.

"It's beautiful." And so much like her dad. If she squinted, she could easily imagine him sitting there in the leather chair by the window, reading the newspaper and drinking his coffee. She stepped onto a plush white area rug nestled in front of a mahogany-brown leather sofa. Twelve-foot ceilings and large picturesque windows framed the majestic mountain peaks and the glassy waters. "It's breathtaking."

Three deer stepped out of the trees and up to the water's edge, bending down to take a drink. "He must have hated leaving here."

Jason stepped up behind her and placed his hands

on her shoulders, then pulled her back into him. She rested there for a moment, watching the deer, feeling his warmth against her back and the safety of his arms as they wrapped around her. They offered comfort to an old sadness that still permeated her insides. Had things been different, she could have grown up here in this house, with her parents, safe and sound. But she hadn't.

"I wonder if he ever missed it. If he regretted leaving." Regretted having her?

"He had everything he wanted, everything he loved, right there with him." Jason turned her around to face him, keeping his arms locked around her. "Just as I do here. I will be back for you, Shay."

He leaned down and pressed his lips against hers. She wanted to pull away, to guard her heart against the onslaught of emotions pulsing through her—the want, the pain, the fear. But she couldn't. It was too late. The moment his lips touched hers she was lost and no matter how badly she wanted to squelch her love for him, to stop it from coursing through her, from growing stronger with each passing moment, she couldn't.

Her need for him was too vast—her need to see the spark in his eyes when he looked at her, to feel his longing in his touch, to hear the rich tone of his voice when he murmured her name. No matter how much she tried to forget, to push it away, she couldn't suppress her basic need to have him hold her as he was doing now.

She closed her eyes and let herself go, losing herself to his touch. In the slow gentle caress of his hands moving up and down her back. His lips pressed against hers, softly at first, then harder as his tongue swept inside her mouth, his desire devouring her as if he could pull all of her into him. As if he couldn't draw her close enough.

She knew how he felt, because she felt the same way. She returned his kiss with frantic urgency, as if with her kiss alone she could hold him there. But she couldn't. She knew that. She knew she'd have to let him go. Tears misted her eyes. She squeezed them shut and clung to his wide, strong shoulders, holding on for all she had.

"I love you, Shay," he whispered, and she wanted to believe him. Wished with everything she had that she could believe him. *But he was still leaving her.* He moved his confident and clever hands under her shirt, fingers kneading and pressing against her skin, igniting a sense of urgency within her.

It was all she could do to get out of her grandmother's clothes. Fabric tore as she fought buttons and the safety pin. Finally free, she pulled his shirt up over his head, her lips barely leaving his as his kisses consumed her. His tongue expertly moved over hers, filling her with a burning need that turned off her brain and turned on the rest of her.

Not wanting to stop for even a second, they dropped to the thick plush carpet, moving, dancing, pulsating to a rhythm that was all their own. She clung to his hard body hoping if she held on long enough, tight enough, then maybe he wouldn't go.

But even as his scent—woodsy and rich with the smell of the earth and water—reached inside her, she knew this moment wouldn't last. She inhaled it deep within her, sealing it within her memory, along with the taste of him and the feel of his hands on her skin.

He pulled her in tighter, positioning her beneath him, then thrust deep within her. Her body, familiar with his, moved on its own, matching his movements. She lost herself in the sensations as they washed over her—heat, passion, fire and an overwhelming hunger. She held him, screaming as her need clawed at her, tearing her apart and finally consuming her.

He stiffened, reaching his climax, clinging to her until finally they collapsed against one another, a mass of arms and legs and heat. And as her thoughts came back with her breath, she felt almost desperate to keep him there, because she knew if she let him go, she would never smell his scent again, never feel his touch.

He would be lost to her.

She didn't know how she knew that, except that she'd been around death long enough to taste its presence hovering in the air. And right now the room was thick with it.

"Don't leave me, Jason. I have a very bad feeling about your going. I can't explain…."

He held her tight, pulling her against him, nuzzling his lips against her neck, sending shivers racing down her spine.

"I know it sounds crazy. It is crazy. But it's all I can think about. If you go, if you leave me, you won't be back."

He pressed a kiss against her forehead, but he didn't say what she'd hoped to hear. What she needed to hear. She sighed.

"It will just be a couple of days. I promise. And I'm not leaving you alone. You have your grandparents to watch after you. And Scott. Visit them. Let them teach you about The Colony. Go shopping, fill this house with food and clothes and everything you need, and I'll be back before you have a chance to miss me."

"But I miss you already."

He laughed, and the warmth of it seeped through her. She was acting like a clingy female. She hated that, but she couldn't help it. She couldn't stop the fear blossoming within her. Especially when she thought of Scott. A shiver pulsed through her.

"What is it?"

"Scott," she admitted. "He scares me."

Jason sat up, leaning against the couch, pulling her up with him. "Why?"

She snuggled against him. "His aura is an ugly muddy dark red. Kind of like the *Abatus*. Though nothing moves within it, it's just a thick cloud that scares me."

Jason's pale eyes held hers steady. "You can still see auras?"

"Yes. Can't you?"

"No. Once we go through the change, we no longer hear brain activity or see colors. On wolves or men."

"But I still do. What does that mean?" She leaned her head against his chest, listening to the powerful beat of his heart.

"It means what I've always known about you, that you're special."

She twined her fingers in the soft hair on his chest and the trail that led down his stomach. "But what does that say about Scott?"

"That he definitely bears watching and shouldn't be trusted."

The sound of an approaching vehicle crunching gravel filled the room. "Damn," Jason said, jumping to his feet.

"Who could that be?" Shay muttered. Not wanting a repeat of that morning, she quickly redressed, pulling her grandmother's clothes back on, though the safety pin was hopelessly lost. Seconds later, there was a knock at the door.

Jason glanced out the front window. "Do me a favor and get the door," he said, pulling on his jeans. "I'll be back in a sec."

Surprised, Shay watched him disappear down the hall and into the back room. She hurried to the front door and pulled it open.

A man of medium height and build with wavy dark hair, brilliant green eyes and an easy smile stood in the doorway. "You must be Shay," he said, appreciation shining in his eyes. "I'm Malcolm. It's nice to finally meet you."

He held out his hand and Shay took it, thinking there wasn't anything scary about this man. No aura. Nothing to give credence to all the bad things she'd been hearing about him.

"Is he yours?" Malcolm asked, and tilted his head toward Buddy lying on the porch. "Beautiful dog."

Shay smiled. "Thank you. I suppose he's worn himself out exploring. Please, come in," she said, stepping back. As Malcolm walked into the house, Jason appeared from the back.

In that moment everything changed. Malcolm stiffened and suddenly there was tension in the air so palpable her nerves started jumping.

"I had hoped you'd left the truck here for Shay, that you were already searching for the missing shipment," Malcolm said, his voice low and dangerous, his nostrils flaring.

Jason leaned against the wall, calm, cool and confident. "I was getting ready to call you. Something's come up and I can't leave Shay alone right now."

Shay let out a small sound of surprise as relief tore through her, but the feeling of happiness was short-lived as Malcolm's anger became tangible.

"If you value your job, you will go where you are needed. And trust me, you are not needed here. Not now. I can look after Shay. That's why I'm here."

"Is that so?" Jason pushed off the wall and approached them. "Shay is my responsibility and you have plenty of men out there looking for that shipment right now."

"It's your job." Malcolm's jaw stiffened.

"Then you're right. I'm ready for a change. I'll return the truck and the keys this afternoon."

Malcolm stared at him, disbelief widening his eyes. Without saying another word, he turned and stormed out the door, slamming it so hard behind him the windows shook.

Shaken, Shay stared after him. "Wow."

"Yep," Jason said, letting loose a long sigh. "I was curious to see how he would react around you if he didn't know I was here."

"And?"

"And I didn't expect things to go the way they did."

"I can't let you quit your job for me."

"I didn't do it for you. I did it because Malcolm came here thinking I was gone, hoping to get you alone. He had no business doing that, no matter what his intentions were. He knew that. And instead of being reasonable when he discovered I was here, instead of being a friend and asking why I needed to stay here with you, he threatened my job. My job that I've performed for him without question or complaint for years. He is not the man I thought he was, the man he used to be." Jason sighed. "Maybe Kate was right and he never was."

"I'm sorry," Shay whispered.

"Don't be. I can't leave you. Not after what you said about Scott, not after what I've just seen. Malcolm's temper is out of control. I won't leave you here with the two of them and their war. I can't take that chance."

She walked into his arms and he held her tightly for a long moment. "Thank you," she whispered, then stepped up on her toes and kissed him.

As Jason held her, uneasiness consumed him. He'd never seen Malcolm behave like that before. Anger was one thing, but the man was over the edge. How far would he go to get what he wanted? Could he have stolen that shipment, or worse, burned down Scott's house?

"Are you all right?" Shay asked, looking up into his face, her palm resting on his chest. "You feel…disheartened."

"You have an uncanny ability to read my emotions."

"Maybe I just know you well." She smiled and leaned her head against his chest.

"I can't help thinking that if only I hadn't stayed gone for so long looking for Maggie, if I'd come back and at least tried to hang on to my responsibilities as pack leader…"

"I doubt Malcolm would have given them back to you."

"I could have stopped him. The council would have backed me. I shouldn't have let Malcolm stay in control once I'd come home. I gave up on living. I gave up on…everything." He placed a finger under her chin and lifted it until he could look into her beautiful blue eyes. "You gave that back to me. You've made me want to live again. I remember what it feels like to be alive. To be in love."

Tears swam in her eyes. Happy tears? He hoped so.

"So what do we do now?" she asked.

"We can't continue to let Malcolm play his games and after what you said about Scott's aura, he is no longer an option for pack leader."

"Why would anyone believe me?"

"Because Maggie knew things, too. And so did Dean. People trusted her, they trusted your dad and they will trust you, too."

"It should be you, Jason. You should step up."

"No, I had my time."

"But you would be perfect. You are honorable, and you have a deep concern for the pack as a whole."

"It should be you," he said softly. "It's the natural

progression of things. You are Dean's daughter, and you have a gift. A gift that can be very helpful to the pack."

Shock crossed her face and she stepped back from him. "Me? What do I know about running the pack? I haven't even seen the town yet. I don't know anything about The Colony, the way you live, your history or this so-called gift. No. It should be you."

"Well, in any case, whoever it will be, we have to go to the council. They need to know what's going on, they need to be the ones to deal with the proverbial shit hitting the fan." He winked at her then led her out the door.

The moment his feet hit the porch he knew it wouldn't be that easy, and that Malcolm was already a step ahead of them.

"Jason," Shay whispered, fear thick in her voice as she stared at the truck. The tires were flat.

All of them.

Obviously, Malcolm had lost it.

"What are we going to do now?" she whispered, looking around her.

She needn't have bothered. He knew who'd done it. He just hoped Malcolm was done with his childish pranks and was long gone.

"Walk," he said, and pulled a wicked-looking knife out of the sheath attached to his belt. He pointed at a small deer path leading into the forest. "And hope we're alone out here."

Chapter 17

"Where are we going?" Shay asked as she swatted away branches that kept snagging her skirt.

"Into town. It's about two miles from here. I would suggest we transform, but then you'd have nothing to wear once we got there."

Shay cringed at the thought. "That wouldn't be good." Though she had to admit she was tempted. She wanted to run again, to feel the earth beneath her and the freedom of running at full speed through the forest. As if he could read her thoughts, Buddy barked, running up ahead of them.

"I wouldn't mind," Jason said, giving her a lascivious smile, and then he winked at her.

As he did, her heart melted all over again. She hoped this feeling—this happiness bursting through her right now—never went away. But she knew better. Happiness like this was fragile and fleeting.

"I still can't believe Malcolm would stoop this low," Jason muttered, pulling back a large branch for her to pass. "Slashing tires is juvenile. What could he possibly hope to gain?"

Shay grabbed his arm, stopping him. "Did you hear that?"

He stilled, listening to the sounds around them. "What?"

"I don't know. I sensed something. Someone."

"Stay here, I'll go ahead and check." He stepped forward, disappearing around the bend and into the thicket of pine trees.

Shay wanted to say no, to stop him, but she did as he asked and stepped beneath a canopy of branches. After a moment, she heard a loud crash, then there was nothing but silence.

"Jason!" Shay ran after him, not stopping when the thick branches of evergreens clawed at her, tearing her clothes. That horrible sound replayed over and over in her mind as she rushed forward. Something ahead caught her eye. She hurried forward then skidded to a stop in front of a deep pit. The ground crumbled in front of her, pine needles slipping away beneath her feet. She teetered on the edge of a deep hole, pinwheeling her arms until she fell backward.

Terrified, she crawled forward and glanced down into the hole. Buddy barked from the bottom. Jason was lying next to him, his knife sticking into his leg, blood spreading across his pants and the ground beneath him.

"Oh, my God, Jason!" Sickness twisted through her as she crouched at the edge.

Lying on his back, Jason groaned while looking up at her. "It's a trap, Shay. Go. Get help. Hurry." His voice crackled with pain.

She looked around her but didn't see anyone. "I can't leave you here alone."

"You must." He groaned again, and she could hear the pain in his voice, feel it in the energy coming off of him. He was hurt badly.

"Who do I go to? Who can I trust?"

"Your grandparents. They're the only ones."

"How? I don't know where I am." Panic tightened around her, squeezing and stealing her breath as her gaze searched the green thicket. Was Malcolm hiding out there somewhere, watching her even now? Waiting for her to leave?

"Follow the sun," Jason said, his voice breaking.

"The sun?" Who was he kidding?

She looked up at the sky. She could do this. She had to do this. She stood. "All right, Jason. But don't you die on me. Promise me. Everyone always dies on me and I can't lose you, too."

"Don't worry. It's not time for me to die. I haven't done enough living yet."

Neither had she. Especially now that she knew what life could be like with him.

"I'll go, but you need to change. You need to heal, and you damn well better be up and around by the time I get back."

"You got it," he said, his voice barely audible.

"Watch him, Buddy," she said, then with fear blurring her vision, she ran hard and fast continuing down the deer path they'd been following, hoping there would be no more pits or nets falling from trees or anything else that would stop her. Because she wasn't looking and she wasn't thinking, she was only praying that she'd find him help on time.

After what seemed like forever, she burst out of the forest and into a clearing that ended at the edge of a cliff. There was no more going forward, only left or right. But the sun was straight ahead. She couldn't afford to get lost. She couldn't lose the time.

"Damn!" She peered down the side of the mountain into the green abyss. Not a sign of civilization in sight.

"What's wrong with you?" a voice asked from behind her.

Shay swung around as an older woman with long dark braids streaked with silver strands came walking around the bend, a large burlap bag slung over her shoulder.

"Oh, thank goodness," Shay said, rushing toward her.

"You look lost," the woman said, walking past her to a large rock outcropping on the edge of the cliff.

"Lost. Yes. You could say that. And—"

"Scared." The woman took off her bag, placed it on the ground, squatted over it and started rummaging inside.

"Yes, that, too. I'm so glad I found you. I've been frantic. I need help. I have to find the way to my grandparents'. Can you—"

The woman pulled a large reddish crystal out of her

bag, followed by a black and then a green one. She closed her eyes and started mumbling over them.

"Please," Shay said. "I need—"

The woman held up a hand stopping her, then continued chanting.

Shay swallowed a deep breath, trying to hold back the anxiety threatening to consume her. If she lost it, if she became a babbling idiot, she wouldn't be able to help Jason. She had to stay calm. Rational. Reasonable.

Oh, the hell with it.

She bent toward the woman, reaching for her, but before she could touch her shoulder, the woman stood and turned to her.

"How can Jaya help you?"

"My friend fell. He's hurt," Shay blurted, afraid the woman would stop her again.

"Then your instincts led you right, Shay Mallory."

They did? "How do you know who I am?"

The woman laughed, her deep voice rumbling through her chest. "Everyone knew you were coming. You're the only stranger we've had 'round these parts in years. Who else could you be?" She bent back over the rocks, her hands moving, hovering, palms down, almost touching the crystal surface as words, rich and guttural, rose from inside her.

Impatience reared its ugly head and had Shay bouncing up onto the balls of her feet. Was this woman going to help her or not?

"I'm sorry to interfere with—" Shay threw her arms out "—with whatever it is you're doing, but I need you to tell me how to find my grandparents' house."

The woman continued to ignore her, swaying back and forth, her eyes screwed shut.

Unable to wait any longer, Shay stepped forward and tapped her on the shoulder. "Please, if you could just let me use your cell phone so I can call—" She stopped, realizing she had no idea what their phone number was. Or if they even had a phone.

The woman's dark eyes shot open and pinned her with a steely glare. "Cell phone? You think I have one of those modern contraptions that spread radiation all over this beautiful green earth? Those people who use those things without thought to the delicate balance of nature are destroying this wonderful place we live in. You will never catch Jaya using one of those things." She closed her eyes and started swaying again.

Shay looked around her, searching for a truck or a car or even a motorcycle, anything this woman could have used to get way out here on this mountain.

"I walked," she said, staring at her through an eye opened just a crack. "The same way I do every day."

"I need help. Please. My friend—"

"I wouldn't lift a hair off my dog's head to help that Malcolm Daniels." She spat his name out of her mouth as if it burned her tongue. "Not after what he done to my Celia. I told my girl to stay away from him, that he was bad news. He let the power go to his head and he got lost, that one. But she has never listened to me, not since she was old enough to crawl. No matter how many times I warned her to stay away, she didn't. And now she got burned."

Leaving the crystals on the outcropping, the woman

picked up her bag and started to walk down the path, still mumbling about Celia and her heartbreak at the hands of Malcolm. Geez, did everyone hate that man?

"But it's not Malcolm who's hurt," Shay called, hurrying after her, surprised by the older woman's speed.

"Of course it's Malcolm. Celia left because you were coming. Because he insisted he was gonna marry you."

"But I'm not going to marry Malcolm. I'm with Jason. He's the one I'm going to marry."

"Jason?" The woman stopped and turned. Her eyes grew wide.

"Yes, Jason is the one who needs help."

"Oh, this is bad. Very bad indeed." She started walking back the way Shay had come. Back toward the trees and the deer path that led to the pit.

"Why?" Shay asked, confused and frustrated all at the same time. "I mean, *I* know why it's bad but why do *you* think it's bad?"

"Bad for Jason," the woman muttered, holding up a purple rock hanging from a long chain around her neck and kissing it.

"Very bad," Shay agreed. "He fell in a large hole in the ground and landed on his knife. He's hurt and bleeding right now. I need to get him help and I have no idea where I even am." She was beginning to shriek, her words echoing through the trees around her.

The woman stopped walking. "Well, why didn't you say that in the first place?"

Shay blew out a deep breath. "I can't imagine."

"Show me where he is."

"No offense, but he needs a doctor and someone who can get him out of that hole. I need to get to a phone."

"No. You need Jaya or your instincts wouldn't have brought you to me."

Shay sighed. "Fine. Follow me." She hurried back into the forest hoping she was doing the right thing. Because if she wasn't, if she was too late…

When they arrived back at the pit, Shay peered inside. Buddy stared up at her and whined. Her stomach dropped. "Jason's not there."

"Over here, child," Jaya said, her tone heavy.

Shay turned to find her leaning over a wolf's body lying beneath a tall Redwood. Her heart caught in her throat. "Is he—" She couldn't form the words, couldn't stop the fear reeling inside her, sending her staggering toward them.

Jaya didn't answer, just started running her hands over his body, her eyes closed, her lips moving in a low chant that Shay could barely hear. The woman pulled more crystals out of her burlap bag and placed them around Jason, resting the palm of her hands over each one as she repeated words over and over in a language Shay didn't recognize.

Shay dropped to the ground next to them and gingerly lifted the wolf's head onto her lap. He whimpered and Shay's heart broke at how weak it sounded. "Please, don't let him die."

"Here, put this on his wound." Jaya handed her an amber jar.

Shay twisted open the lid and found green paste inside. She stuck her finger into it and scooped out a thick glob that spread easily across the open wound on Jason's upper leg.

"His pulse is weak," Jaya said. "He's lost too much blood."

"We need to get him to a hospital," Shay insisted.

Jaya didn't acknowledge her words; instead she took the purple crystal from around her neck and placed it around Jason's, whispering more of her healing chants.

Shay rested her hand on his shoulder as tears welled in her eyes and fell onto her cheeks. "Don't die on me, Jason. You promised."

Footsteps approached on the path beside her. She turned, hoping help had finally come. Instead, Malcolm stood at the edge of the pit, his face a blank mask, blood smeared across the front of his shirt.

Jason's blood?

"If you want Jason to live, Shay, you will marry me right now."

"What?" Shay stared at him, disbelief muddling her mind as she tried to comprehend his meaning.

"After the ceremony, I will get him the help he needs."

"You did this to him?"

He shrugged, his eyes narrowing.

Fury surged through her, tightening her muscles and quickening her heart. "Jason believed in you. Stood up for you. He was your friend."

"As I am his. That is why I'm hoping you'll do the right thing for him, for the pack, for all of us and marry me."

Shay got to her feet, not wanting her tension and

anger to touch Jason. "You mean the right thing for you."

"I'm sorry it has come to this. I tried to send him away, to distract him, but he wouldn't do as he was told."

"He needs to get to the hospital now."

"Jaya," he said, looking past Shay and ignoring her pleas. "You will officiate the ceremony and bear witness of this marriage to the council."

"And if I don't?" Jaya said without leaving Jason's side. Without taking her hands off his shuddering body.

"You mean other than watching Jason die?" He shrugged his imperious shoulders.

Jaya's eyes narrowed into fine slits.

"Jason needs help. Let Jaya heal him," Shay demanded, even as panic and desperation clutched her by the shoulders. There was no use reasoning with the man. He was crazy, he was…unreachable.

"As soon as we get the marriage ceremony over with, Jaya can do what she does best and heal him. I'm confident she'll pull him through."

"And if she doesn't?" Shay countered.

"Then you'll at least know you did everything you could. Now get over here, old woman, and marry us or I'll end his suffering right now."

Nausea turned Shay's stomach as Jaya rose, leaving Jason and walking toward Malcolm. Shay followed, knowing he was telling the truth, certain that if she didn't do exactly what he wanted he would let Jason die, or worse, kill him in front of her. How could anyone have followed a man who looked like this? How could Jason have trusted him?

"All right, Malcolm," she said as she stopped in front of him. "I'll marry you."

In a hazy pain-induced blur, Jason watched Shay walk toward Malcolm. *No! Shay.* His words reverberated in his head as frustration grew within him. He saw Malcolm put his hand on her back. Claiming her.

Jason wanted to scream, would have screamed if he could have but the only sound he made was a pathetic whimper. The paste Shay had put on his wound was cooling the burning fire in his leg. But it wasn't enough. Helplessly he watched Shay agree to give herself to Malcolm. To voice his biggest fear. *I'll marry you.*

Once she married Malcolm, there would be nothing he could do to protect her from his every whim. To be with her. Fury and despair comingled and surged through him, fueling his adrenaline. Vicious snarls erupted from his throat. Desperately, he tried to get to his feet, but his leg wasn't strong enough to hold him and he collapsed back to the ground, his heart pounding painfully in his chest.

"Jason!" Shay cried, and tried to come back to him, but Malcolm pulled her away, whispering in her ear something he couldn't hear.

The acrid scent of her fear was so thick Jason could taste it in the air. He had to help her. He tried to move again, to crawl to her on his belly. He made it maybe a foot when his leg caught on a root rising out of the ground. He yelped as agony shot through him. The roaring of his blood though his veins and the pounding of his heart drowned out all sounds, even the frantic barking of Buddy still trapped in the pit.

Jason tried to move again, desperate to reach Shay, but the pain was so severe, blackness folded in on him. He fought it with what little strength he had left. He couldn't leave her now. Not like this. He'd promised. He said he'd protect her. He'd said he'd hold her in his arms each night, if only she'd marry him.

Marry *him*.

He tried once more to move, before the darkness claimed him and he saw no more.

Chapter 18

A numbing calm inched over Shay, seeping into her bones until she was so cold she could barely feel Malcolm's hand at her back, nor notice Jaya until she was standing in front of her.

"I do not abide by this, Malcolm. And neither will the council," Jaya said.

"Who will tell them? All they are going to find out is that you married us. Right here in the forest on her daddy's land. It's what Shay wanted, and we didn't want to wait another moment to be together."

"And what happens when the council sees what you've done to Jason?"

"What makes you think I did anything to Jason? He fell into a hunter's pit. Who knows how long that pit has been there? Hell, Shay's daddy probably built it.

No one has been on these lands since then, no reason for anyone to be."

Shay glanced back at Jason lying under the tree. He was no longer moving. She had to do something to help him.

Malcolm followed her gaze. "Let's get started, Jaya, before our friend bleeds out all over the place."

Shay couldn't let Jason die on her. Now that she'd found him, she couldn't lose him. But what could she do?

"Do you, Shay?"

Shay looked blankly at Jaya. What had she been saying? "I'm sorry?"

"Do you take Malcolm as your husband? To respect him always, as your leader, as your master?"

Revulsion stirred thick in her chest. *No!* She wanted to scream her denial. But she couldn't. Her mouth went dry as she tried to say the word Malcolm wanted to hear. But her tongue thickened and her throat closed up. All she managed to do was nod.

"What was that?" Malcolm asked.

"Yes," she whispered, and stole another quick glance at Jason.

The sooner they got this over with, the sooner Jaya could get back to him and they could get him to a hospital.

Malcolm's hand tightened on her back as he tried to draw her attention back to him. Shay stared straight ahead. She refused to look at him. He was beyond reprehensible. He was a beast.

"I now pronounce you husband and wife," Jaya said

the words but Shay barely heard them. Even as Malcolm tried to pull her to him, she turned, pushing him away. She had to get back to Jason, to get as far away from this animal as she could. But she couldn't. He wouldn't let her go.

She swatted at his hands, twisted and turned, trying to break free. "Let me go!"

She might be married to him, but that didn't mean she had to have anything to do with him. Before she could tell him so, Scott and two men appeared from out of nowhere.

"I'm afraid I can't let you do this."

Shay recognized him as one of the men from the cave.

Malcolm stepped in front of her. "What are you talking about, Mitch? And what are you doing here with him?" Malcolm gestured toward Scott.

"You have to help Jason," Shay said to her cousin. "He's hurt really bad."

"We will. But first, tell me what's happened here."

"My wife doesn't have to tell you anything," Malcolm said, stepping forward, chest out, shoulders back, fury glittering in his eyes.

"You're already married?" Scott's mouth hardened as he looked accusingly at her.

"I had no choice," she insisted. "And it doesn't matter. Jason is what matters. You have to help him," Shay pleaded when Scott still didn't move. She took a step back toward Jason. She had to get to him. Jaya was leaning over his body, her eyes closed, her lips moving.

"You're too late, Scott. It's over." Malcolm reached

back and grabbed her hand before she could get away, then started pulling her toward the path to her father's house. She tried to resist, but he yanked harder.

Before she could protest, Mitch and his friend stepped forward, blocking the path. "We can't let you leave."

Thank God. She tried once more to pull free from Malcolm's grasp.

"How do you plan on stopping us?" Malcolm sneered as his grip tightened, his mouth an ugly misshapen hole in his face.

Scott stilled, a calculating smile lifting the corners of his thin lips. And then they attacked, all three jumping on Malcolm at once. Finally free, Shay turned and ran back to Jason and Jaya. The shouts of more men arriving surprised her. Malcolm's or Scott's, she couldn't be sure.

"You need to go," Jaya whispered to her when she crouched next to them. "It's not safe. I've never seen so much bad energy in one place."

"Seen? Can you see the auras, too?"

Wonder widened Jaya's eyes. "You are a surprise, Miss Shay. Remember you have good instincts. Just like your daddy did. You can trust them. They come from down here." Jaya pointed at her stomach. "Never will they lead you wrong."

Shay put her hand on Jason's cheek, stroking the soft fur. "He looks worse."

"You can't help him here. Transform and run like the wind. Go get help. Tell them what happened," Jaya insisted. "I'll stay with him."

"I can't leave him," she insisted.

"Girl, you're married to Malcolm now. You have no choice. If you want to save this wolf then get out of here and get help. I can't do what I need to to save him here. I need him back at my house with my herbs and my crystals and, as sure as the moon rises, I can't get him there on my own."

Jaya's words dropped like a lead weight to the bottom of her stomach. *You're married to Malcolm now.* "All right. Tell me how to get to my grandparent's house."

"Follow the sun."

Shay stared at her, swallowing a groan. "Okay, when I get to the cliffs, right or left?"

"Left."

Suddenly a shot sounded. Surprised, Shay looked up and saw even more men than before fighting one another. Mitch fell to the ground bleeding.

"Go. Now," Jaya demanded. "They would rather see you dead than give the evil one more power."

Shay leaned down and pressed her lips against Jason's head. "Don't forget your promise. Don't die on me. I love you, dammit!"

She'd finally said it. She only hoped it wasn't too late. Choking back her tears, she started to stand. A shot cracked the air. Something whizzed by her. Hot pain seared her arm. She looked down. Blood seeped from a wound where the bullet had grazed her. She spun round. Jaya was lying on her back, blood spreading across her chest.

"No!" Shay dropped, crouching over her, pressing her hands against the wound in Jaya's chest, trying to stop the bleeding. The woman didn't move. "Jaya! Please, don't die. You can't die."

Tears flooded her eyes, blurring her vision, while she pressed as hard as she dared.

"Shay. Come on." She looked behind her and saw Malcolm reaching for her. His face pale as he stared at Jaya lying in the dirt.

She pulled back. "No!"

"That bullet was meant for you. You have to go. Now."

"I won't leave them." Tears poured down her cheeks. "I have to stop the bleeding." She pressed harder against the wound, blood seeping through her fingers.

"You have to, Shay."

"Help her," she demanded. "Jaya!" She shook the woman, but still she didn't move.

"She's dead, Shay. And you will be, too, if you don't move."

Dead.

"No." She started to sob, gulping big lungfuls of air.

Just then another man stepped out of the bushes, seemingly coming from nowhere. "Get him to Manny's," Malcolm said to him, then stepped forward, grabbed Shay by the middle, picked her up and carried her into the trees as his men and Scott's continued to fight behind them.

"Let me go!" She pounded him as he slung her over his shoulder, fists flailing against his back until she was crying so hard she no longer had the strength to fight him.

"I can't," he said. "They'll kill you."

"Why?"

"Because of me."

His words barely reached her. She closed her eyes and tried to block the images from her mind, of Jaya, her face turning pale as blood pooled on her chest. Jason lying next to her, barely moving, almost dead himself. The sickening thuds of men hitting and kicking one another. She couldn't think of it any longer. Instead she tried to think of the color of Jason's eyes when they were heavy and hooded with desire.

But even that hurt.

She didn't know how much time had passed before she resigned herself to the fact that they weren't going back. She couldn't get back to Jason. There was nothing she could do to fix this. Jaya was dead and Jason would probably die, too. Maybe even Buddy. Hot tears soaked the back of Malcolm's shirt as she bounced on his shoulder.

"You can set me down now," she said. "You're bruising my ribs."

He stopped. "Can I trust you not to run back there?"

She closed her eyes. "There's nothing I can do for them back there. Jaya died because of me. Because they were trying to kill me. I won't go back. But we have to find someone to help Jason. Please."

"One of my men is helping him." He set her on her feet, one hand steadying her. "Can you stand?"

She nodded. She could, but she didn't want to. She wanted to collapse right there under a tree, close her eyes and forget everything that had just happened. "How are they helping him? What will they do?" she whispered. "Will he be okay?" She couldn't think.

"I honestly don't know. I never expected…"

She looked up at him and was surprised to find his eyes swimming with sorrow and regret. But could she trust his emotions were real after everything he'd just done? Was he capable of true regret?

"We need to transform. Your arm is still bleeding. You need to heal and we have to get to my compound as soon as possible. It's the only place where you'll be safe. I'll make some calls and find out what happened to Jason. And to Jaya. Someone has to pay for her death."

"How did this happen? Why would anyone want to kill me?"

"Because you're my wife. You solidify my position. With you dead, they would have a better chance of taking over."

"You people are crazy."

"We weren't always." Regret once more crossed his face. "Jaya. Her daughter. They were very important to me. Now Jaya's gone and I don't know what we're going to do. I don't know how I'm going to tell Celia." He began unbuttoning his shirt.

Shay's eyes widened and she took a step back. "Wait," she muttered. She couldn't get naked in front of him. She wouldn't.

"Right," he said with what could have been a small smile, but wasn't. "I keep forgetting this is all new to you. I'll give you some privacy." He stepped through the bushes and behind a large tree.

She considered running, hightailing it back to Jason or trying to find help. But then she thought of Jaya lying on the ground, a bullet wound in her chest, and sadness, thick and heavy, fell over her, stealing her strength. There was nowhere she could go and she wouldn't get anyone else killed. All she could hope for was that Jason would get help. That Jason was still alive, and that Malcolm would take her to him. With reluctance she slipped out of her clothes and transformed.

A large black wolf stepped out from behind the tree and started running. She followed, running as fast as her legs would carry her. Free of her clothes, of her human skin, she realized she was also free from her emotions. The fear for Jason, the horror of Jaya's death was still there, but it was buried deep and no longer immobilizing.

She ran deeper into the forest, away from the scent of blood, from the sounds of anger and the footsteps of her pursuers. As they ran, she lost herself in the freedom and the sensations. She used her speed, her power to carry her away from the heady smell of death. Away from the fear. Except…she couldn't *feel* Jason.

The knowledge hit her fast and furious, blindsiding her. They'd been too late. The pain slicing through her was sharp and deep. She let out a long aching howl. She was alone now. Like she'd always been, like she was meant to always be.

They crossed a river, jumping over large boulders, moving silently through a grove of thick pines when the black wolf finally stopped before a large wooden gate. With his teeth, he pulled on a rope and the gate swung open. She followed him into a stone courtyard lined with trees and blooming flowers that surrounded a large pool and showcased a dark wood house framed by a towering wall of windows.

Shay glanced around the high-fenced compound as Malcolm changed, transforming back into a man. He stood before her naked. She dropped her head and looked away.

"I'll bring you a robe," he said, walking over to the gate. He locked it then disappeared into a small pool house.

Her gaze followed the perimeter of the fence, searching for another gate, another way out, but she saw nothing. Malcolm reappeared with a fluffy black robe in his hand. One that matched the one he was wearing. "Change back and put this on. We have a lot to talk about."

Jason woke to pain shooting through him. Someone was lifting him, carrying him, sending an excruciating throb reverberating through his body with each jarring step. He forced open his eyes, looking for Shay. Where was she? And then he remembered.

Malcolm.

His gaze fell on Jaya lying in the dirt, blood covering her chest. She had no heat signature. Not even the faintest sound of a beating heart or struggling breath reached him. Fear ripped through him. The Keeper of the Crystals, their healer, the one woman who kept the *Gauliacho* at bay, was dead. Without her to invigorate the crystals the demons would be able to breach the gates. Then all would be lost.

Despairing, a low keening howl erupted from his throat. Buddy started barking again. Pain arched through his leg. He cringed, whimpering as someone hefted him into the backseat of a truck. Before he could see who it was, or discover what they were going to do with him, darkness encroached and everything went black.

Malcolm was decent enough to turn his back while Shay transformed back into her human body. She quickly donned the robe, but it didn't matter, she saw the blood. It was all over her. Jason's blood? Jaya's? Or her own? It didn't matter. She started to shake as she stared at her hands, then the tears came once again.

"Shay," Malcolm said softly.

She ignored him and rubbed her hands back and forth across her robe. She had to get it off.

"Come on." He put his arm around her shoulders, but she jerked violently away.

"Don't touch me," she said through gritted teeth.

"I'm just going to show you to your room so you can get cleaned up. Okay?"

"No, it's not okay. Thanks to you, *nothing* is okay."

He nodded, acknowledging her words, then turned and walked toward the house. Reluctantly she followed him through the back door and into a large great room filled with multiple leather sofas, a giant-screen TV and a pool table. Bar stools lined a large granite counter that separated the room from a kitchen filled with top-of-the-line stainless-steel appliances and a hanging rack of gorgeous copper pans.

She followed Malcolm across the slate tile floor until they reached the towering front entryway. He continued down a hallway of plush carpet to the first bedroom on the right.

"Feel free to shower. I will leave some clothes for you outside your door." He left, shutting the door behind him.

Grateful to be alone, she walked into the large spacious bathroom, locked the door behind her and turned on the shower. Dropping the robe, she stood under the hot spray, letting it wash over her, washing away the dirt and the blood and the soreness, but it couldn't wash away the image of Jaya lying there, staring up into the sky, or of Jason bleeding all over the ground next to her. Her stomach clenched, turning and twisting. She bent over, collapsing to the floor, and succumbed to her tears.

They continued to come in heart-wrenching sobs until there was nothing left and she felt exhausted and hollow. She climbed out of the granite shower and wrapped herself in a deep brown plush towel. Jason was right; Malcolm did like the finer things. The thought of Jason brought fresh tears to her eyes. She still couldn't feel his presence anywhere. She blinked back the tears. She had to stop crying. If he truly was gone now, then she was stuck here in The Colony without him. She had to make the best of it. For him. For her dad. For everything they'd both sacrificed. *For her.*

Even if she had to stay married to Malcolm, she wouldn't live here with him. She would move into her father's house and get to know her grandparents, and try to find where she fit in this community. And she'd do it alone. Just like she always had. Just like she always would. She walked out of the bathroom and saw a pair of women's white sweats on the bed. "So much for leaving them outside the door," she muttered.

As she put them on, she couldn't help wondering

whose they were. The missing Celia whose heart Malcolm had broken? She felt sorry for the poor woman. She'd lost the man she loved, her home and now her mother. But how could she have loved Malcolm in the first place? Better yet, how could Jason have trusted him? Have called him a friend? The man was a pig.

On top of the dresser sat a silver tea service with a steeping pot of Earl Grey tea, cream, sugar and two cookies next to a porcelain teacup. The spicy aroma of the tea filled the room and called to her. She poured it into the cup, but set it back down before she took a drink.

She didn't want it. She didn't want anything from that man.

She sat on the bed and lay back for a moment, staring at the ceiling, wondering what she should do next. She looked around the room for a phone, but realized it wouldn't matter if there were one. She didn't know her grandparents' number. There was no one she knew here whom she could call.

She rolled up into a ball on the bed, hugging her knees, replaying every moment of the day in her mind. Her eyes drifted closed and she let them. She wanted to lose herself in sleep. To stop thinking and disappear.

But she couldn't.

She sat up. She had to be strong; she had to find a way out of this house and into town. She had to find Buddy. And most of all, she wouldn't let Malcolm get away with what he'd done. Not to Jaya, to Jason or to her. Someone in town would be able to help her find her grandparents or this council. She found a pair of flip-flops in the closet, slipped them on then opened the door as quietly as she could and peered out. She saw no one.

She walked down the hallway toward the front door. Again, no one was in the great room or the kitchen. Where was Malcolm? Maybe he was taking a shower. This might be the only chance she had to get away from him. She slid out the front door and hurried toward the front gate.

And heard raised voices.

Keeping to the side of the house, she crept forward until she could see around back. Malcolm was sitting at a table by the pool with another man. A man she recognized as the second man from the cave.

"Your marriage is no longer valid, Malcolm. It no longer matters. Everyone who witnessed it is dead. But what's worse, Jaya is dead."

Malcolm ran a hand down his face. "I know."

"Where is Celia?"

"No one knows."

"We have to get her back here. Jaya never finished energizing the crystals. If Celia doesn't get back here to finish the job, the barriers are going to fall."

Malcolm stood up and leaned over the table, both hands braced on the glass. "Don't you think I know that?" he hissed.

"You know her better than anyone—where would she go?"

"Hell, I don't know, Louis. She was furious at me. You know how she gets. She is more hot-tempered than I am."

"What the hell was Jaya doing there in the first place?"

"I don't know." Malcolm straightened and collapsed back into his chair. "I will find Celia. I promise. I'll fix this."

"You're going to leave? Now?"

"Do I have any choice? Who else am I going to send? There is no one. Jason is—"

His words cut off. It was just as well. Shay didn't think she could hear any more. She wrapped her hands around her middle and did everything she could to keep the anguished sob inside her.

"Jason is still hanging on," Louis said.

Shay gulped a surprised breath.

"Right after you left I loaded him into my truck and took him to Manny's. I checked on him before I came here. It's dicey. At this point, he could go either way, but right now he's still alive."

Shay gasped a breath as her heart heaved in her chest.

"Thank the gods for that," Malcolm said and actually sounded sincere.

"What the hell happened, Malcolm? He wasn't supposed to get hurt. No one was. And what about Mitch? What could Scott have possibly promised him to betray us like that?"

"I have no idea. But Scott would never have been there if Mitch hadn't clued him in to our plans."

"I hated to bail on you like that but I had to stay hidden, I couldn't let on that I was there and once I saw them attack you, I called for reinforcements."

"I get that. I do," Malcolm said. "I don't know how everything got so out of control."

"That's the understatement of the year."

"I'm just glad you were able to save Jason. Now, listen, I'll find Celia. I'll make this right."

"You know Scott will take over while you're gone."

"I guess I'll have to deal with him when I get back, but I have to go. I caused this mess, I have to try to fix it."

"Celia won't be too happy to see you, especially once she hears about her mom and the role you played in her death. Are you sure you'll be able to get her to come back?"

"Celia might hate me, but she loves this colony. She won't let everyone die."

"I hope you're right about that."

"Me, too."

"So, how's Dean's girl?"

"Shaken. Badly. I've given her a sedative. Hopefully she'll sleep for a few hours and we'll be able to talk before I go without all the tears and hysterics."

"What are you going to do with her while you're gone?"

Shay thought of the hot tea and was thankful she hadn't touched it. Not wanting to hear any more, she retraced her steps back to the front of the house and to the front gate and slipped through. She had to get to town and find this Manny before Malcolm discovered she was gone. Right now there was only one thing that mattered to her.

Jason was alive.

Chapter 19

Shay kept to the woods as much as possible, afraid to step onto the road and have one of Malcolm's men find her. She thought of Jason and mentally reached for him, trying to let her instincts guide her. Wasn't that what Jaya had told her? To trust her gut? She stopped next to a tree, placed her hand against the bark to steady herself and closed her eyes.

She focused on Jason's pale blue-gray eyes and the intense way he looked at her—no, looked *into* her. As if he really saw her. Which now she was sure that he did. Her lips curved up into a slight smile as she thought of him, and she almost felt him, a tentative pressure deep inside her. It was his warmth, but it was weak. Very weak.

"I'm coming, Jason. Hold on," she whispered, hoping he could sense her, too.

She continued to walk, thinking about the rich tone
of his voice, his soft touch and easy smile. She loved
the way he grinned and winked at her. He must have
known when he did that, no matter how scared or upset
she was, her heart would soften toward him and she'd
be lost. She couldn't help it, any more than she could
stop herself from loving him.

She wished she had something of his to hold in her
hand, but she had nothing but the taste of his kiss on
her mouth and his earthy scent filling her mind. She
continued forward, reaching for him, for their tentative connection. She must believe in it, like Jaya said.
Feel it. Trust in it completely. Only then would she be
able to find him.

She continued through the forest following that connection for longer than she'd hoped, but soon she heard
something ahead of her. She slowed, keeping to the
trees, when she came across two boys fishing in the
river.

"Hello," she said, stepping forward out of the thicket.
"Can you help me?"

Surprised, they turned and looked at her, their ado-
lescent faces breaking into toothy smiles.

Twenty minutes later she was standing in a general
store telling her grandparents everything.

"Malcolm did that?" Kate asked, disbelieving.

"And Scott, too. There were a lot of men and they
had guns. I didn't see who fired the shot that hit us." She
looked down at her arm, now scabbed over and almost
healed. The same bullet that had hit her had killed Jaya.

"What are we going to do?" Kate asked her husband,

her eyes filled with fear. "They almost killed Shay, Robert. And they killed Jaya. Jaya!" She emphasized, horror filling her voice.

Robert put his arms around her shoulders and hugged her to him. "We'll figure it out," he said. "Shay, we need you to come to the council and tell them everything you just told us."

"I can't. I have to go to Jason. I've already spent too much time here."

"This is critical, Shay. You don't understand the implications of what Jaya's death means for The Colony."

"You're right, and that's why it doesn't matter if I'm there. You can tell them everything I just told you. And honestly, I don't care about your rules or your laws—all I care about is Jason. And right now, he needs me."

"We'll take you to him," Kate said, when Robert opened his mouth to protest more.

"Thank you," Shay said. "I know I don't have any right to ask, but after you talk to the council, if you could please—" Her voice broke over the lump in her throat. "If you could please check on my dog. I think he's still down in that…that pit." Fresh tears filled her eyes as she thought of Buddy alone and scared down in that hole. She didn't even know if he'd been hurt. What if those men…?

Kate pulled her into her arms. "Oh, sweetie, don't you worry about a thing. You go to Jason. We'll take care of Buddy. We'll take care of everything."

"Thank you," Shay whispered, trying to speak through a throat tight with emotion. The moment her grandmother wrapped her in her arms, the shell that she'd erected around herself crumbled and hot tears pricked her eyes. It was such a relief to be able to share her pain, to have someone care and finally help. To have family.

Five minutes later, her grandparents dropped her off at a small white clapboard house two blocks down from the general store. A posted sign out front read Manuel, Healer.

She said goodbye to her grandparents and hurried through the gate in the small white-picket fence and ran up the gravel walk and up the steps to the front porch. The sign on the front door read Please Come In. She opened the door to the tinkling of bells and stepped into to a small waiting room. Two people sat in chairs along the wall, not speaking but looking at her with open curiosity. Shay looked around for a receptionist or anyone to help. She closed the door behind her and stepped into the room when a small man with long black, hair tied back with a leather strap, and deeply lined weathered skin hurried toward her.

"You must be Shay," he said the moment he saw her.

"Yes." She was somewhat surprised, though she didn't know why, not after everything that had happened to her today.

"We've been waiting for you."

We? Wariness instantly clouded her mind and she took a step back. Was Malcolm there? Had he discovered she'd left his house and come looking for her?

"Come," he said, gesturing her forward. "Jason needs you."

At the mention of Jason's name, relief crashed over her, washing away all her misgivings. "How is he?"

"He'll be better with you here to help him. You have strong energy surrounding you. Come. He's been calling for you in his sleep."

Shay followed him into a back room and saw Jason lying on a small bed, a tall white candle burning by his head, the rich dark scent of incense filling the room. She rushed to his side and quickly took up his hand. His skin was pale and dark circles rimmed his eyes. His hand was cold to her touch. She placed it between both of hers and rubbed, trying to warm him.

He turned his head and cracked open his eyes. A small smile lifted his lips. "You came."

She smiled back at him. "As soon as I could."

"You all right?"

She sat in a chair by his bed. "I am now."

His eyes drifted closed. Fear tightened her grip on his hand as she listened to him pull in a ragged, weak breath.

She sat with him all day and all through the night, refusing to leave his side while he slept and struggled to hang on.

Manuel gave her several smooth stones and instructed her on how to put them on Jason's pulse points, the words to say and how to open herself up to the Universal energy. She did as he instructed, wanting to do anything she could to help, though she didn't understand how it worked and wasn't sure she believed it would... until she felt a sensation of warmth entering her hands. As she placed them on Jason, focusing on her strength as Manuel had told her to, a tingling sensation swept up her arms and onto her scalp.

Maybe it would work. "You can do this, Jason. Be strong. Focus on us, on our love and on your promise to hold me in your arms until I fall asleep every night. I'm holding you to that."

He didn't stir as she spoke to him, telling him how much she loved and needed him. She just prayed that somehow he could hear her and understand. That he knew. She continued for as long as she could, murmuring over the stones, conducting her energy and pushing her strength toward him until, exhausted, she laid her head against his cool hand, closed her eyes and fell asleep.

The next morning, Shay woke to Jason stroking her hair. She lifted her head and found him smiling at her.

"Good morning," he said.

She grinned, wide and foolishly, loving the color that had returned to his face. "It sure is. You're looking better. Much better."

"Yeah?"

"And your energy levels feel high, too."

"You can feel my energy?" he asked.

"I can," she said, somewhat surprised, yet pleased.

"Cool. What else can you feel?" He waggled his eyebrows at her.

Just seeing the sparkle in his eyes sent warmth surging through her and practically had her melting into a relieved puddle on the floor. Tears threatened, but she held them back. She was done crying. "I almost lost you," she whispered, afraid to say it aloud.

"I'm not going anywhere," he said. "I promised you, didn't I?"

For a moment they just stared at each other. "How much do you remember?" she asked.

"I'm not sure. I... How's Jaya?"

She hesitated. "She didn't make it."

Jason sucked in a deep breath in a whistling hiss. Before she could say anything else, she heard the bell ringing in the front room and Manuel demanding that someone leave his house. Seconds later the door burst open and Malcolm entered. Shay stood and placed her hand protectively on Jason's shoulder. "You can leave. I'm not going with you."

"I know," Malcolm said. "I didn't come here for you. I came to apologize to you both."

"We don't want to hear it," she said.

"And to tell you I'm leaving," he added.

"Just like that?" Jason said. "After everything you've done, do you really think an apology is enough?"

"No," Malcolm admitted. He looked terrible, like his face had fallen, sinking as his muscles went slack.

"What about the shipment?" Jason asked. "Are you just going to run off and leave everyone high and dry?"

"There was no missing shipment," Malcolm admitted. "It was a ploy, a distraction, something to get you out of town so I could work on your girl here."

"What were you hoping to accomplish?" Shay asked, stunned by the lengths this man had gone to get to her.

Her grandparents had tried to warn her about Malcolm, but she hadn't listened.

"To win you over to my side. Get you to understand what was at stake and why it was so important that you at least give the impression that we were together. That you were aligned with me."

"And for that, you had to send Jason away?"

"Yes. He is in love with you. If he told the council his intentions to marry you, the game would have been up."

"And Mitch on the mountain?" Jason asked, his eyes flashing with anger. "What was that about?"

"I have no idea. Louis said he'd left Mitch alone for a few minutes when he heard the shot. He couldn't believe what had happened. Apparently, Mitch had been working for Scott for a while, undermining my operations, doing everything he could to sabotage me. I've been going crazy trying to figure out why everything has been going wrong. Parts from my shipments have disappeared. I've had funds misappropriated. Every move I've made has been met with a countermove. Now I know why."

He rubbed his hand across his face and then looked at Shay almost apologetically. "You, Shay, were my last hope. Scott knew that. I think Mitch was trying to kill you that morning on the mountain. Maybe even you, too, Jason. If neither of you made it back to The Colony, everyone would have blamed the *Gauliacho*. No one would have ever known what he'd done."

Shay shuddered.

"What's going to happen to them now?" Jason asked.

"I'm not sure how much can be proved. Mitch is dead."

"How?"

"Shot in the battle yesterday."

Shay remembered seeing him fall to the ground. She collapsed back into the chair next to Jason's bed.

"The sheriff is rounding up Scott and his men and mine. They're testing our guns, trying to determine which ones have been fired. They'll figure out who shot Mitch and Jaya."

"You think Scott was the one who tried to kill me?" Shay asked as disbelief coursed through her.

"We're not sure yet if it was Scott or one of his men who fired the shot."

"What about the sheriff? Doesn't he work for you? How can this investigation be trusted?" Shay demanded, not wanting to believe her cousin would go that far to get rid of her.

"Cal works for The Colony, not me."

"But he came and took Jason yesterday morning."

"He does favors for me because he's a friend. But he wasn't there when Jaya got shot. I believe when he finishes his investigation, he will discover that Scott killed Mitch to keep him from confessing the magnitude of what he's done. If he had, Scott would never have been able to stay in The Colony."

"Do you think they'll figure it all out?" Shay asked. She didn't know why she believed a word he was saying. She knew she shouldn't, not after everything he had done, but there was a clarity of tone in his voice. She could hear his honesty ringing through in his words.

"I'm not sure," he admitted. "Right now, they're making a lot of arrests and gathering testimony. It could take a while to get to the bottom of it. If they ever do. It's becoming apparent that Scott was the one who burned his own house down and planted evidence to try to pin it on me."

"With his daughter inside?" Jason asked, shock raising his voice.

"People are speculating that he didn't know she was there. That her getting burned because of his vendetta is what drove him over the edge and made him come after us like he did."

Jason's eyes narrowed. "What drove you to do the insane things you did?"

"Listen, Jason, I never meant for you to get hurt. You were just supposed to fall into that pit and hang out there for a while. That's all."

"But I did get hurt and Jaya is dead, putting us all at risk."

"I know that. I pulled you out of the pit, I had Louis bring you here."

"After you insisted we marry," Shay said.

"True," he agreed. "But I tried to do everything I could to salvage a situation that went horribly wrong. And that's why I'm here. The pack is coming apart. I need to do what I can to fix it."

"What more could you possibly do?" Jason asked, sarcasm heavy in his tone.

Malcolm smiled. "You look like you're going to make it. You need to step up. Both of you."

"Geez, thanks for your concern."

"Listen, I'll be the first to admit I'm a bastard, but that doesn't mean I wanted anything bad to happen to you."

"What about your marriage to my girl?" Jason asked through a tight jaw.

"What marriage? It never happened." Malcolm turned toward the door.

"Where are you going?" Jason demanded, his tone filled with disbelief.

"I need to find Celia. I drove her away and now, because of my actions, her mother is dead. If we don't get her back here, we won't have anyone to rejuvenate the crystals and protect The Colony from the *Gauliacho*."

Shay shuddered at the mention of the black shadows and their insidious whispers.

"I'm going to bring her home."

"You expect us to trust you can do that after all you've done?"

"No, I don't, but it doesn't matter. I have to make things right. You, Shay, the old woman, my men, none of this was ever supposed to happen. People weren't supposed to die. I don't know how it all went wrong."

"It went wrong because you let the power go to your head. You became greedy."

"Maybe. But it's over now. Besides, you're in no condition to go after her yourself. For once, you're going to have to sit here and trust me to get it right."

"I did trust you."

"Not enough to go after Maggie. You had to do that yourself. Now it's my turn." Malcolm turned to go.

"Wait," Jason said, his sharp tone cutting the air.

Malcolm turned back to him as Jason held out his wrist to Shay. "Please?"

Shay began untying the knots that fastened the bracelet Shay had never seen him without. She realized as she looked at it again that the green, black and red stones intertwined within the black cord matched the crystals she had seen in Jaya's bag.

"Jaya gave this to me to wear on my travels. It's made from the same crystals surrounding The Colony. She regenerated it when she was healing me. It will offer you protection from the *Gauliacho* for three days."

As Shay undid the final knot and removed the bracelet from Jason's wrist, the stones pricked her palm, sending an uncomfortable sensation creeping along her skin. She handed it to Malcolm as quickly as she could, not wanting to touch it a moment longer. As she did, as her hand brushed his. She could see the darkness hovering within him, but she also saw a shimmer of light buried down deep. Perhaps a remnant from his childhood before he'd succumbed to his lust for greed and power? Was that the part of him that Jason remembered? She didn't know him well enough to say for sure.

"And take this. For Celia." Jason lifted the chain with Jaya's purple stone from around his neck.

Malcolm looked grim as he took it. "Thanks."

Shay glanced out the window as she heard the sound of a car pulling up out front. "It's my grandfather, along with four other men."

Malcolm stiffened. "They're coming for me."

"Go out the back," Shay said. "We'll tell them we didn't see you."

Jason looked up at her, surprise filling his face as Malcolm left.

She shrugged. "He's still lost, but perhaps if Celia forgives him she can help him find his heart."

"And if she can't? If she turns him away?"

"I guess I'm a hopeless romantic and want to believe she won't."

He smiled and reached for her hand. "That's why I love you."

"Do you really think he'll be able to find her?" she asked, incredibly thankful that it was Malcolm leaving The Colony and not Jason.

"We better hope that he does. For all our sakes."

Seconds later, her grandfather and four other men squeezed into the room. "Shay," her grandfather acknowledged, then turned to Jason. "Jason. It's good to see you're looking better than I expected."

"Thank you." He looked at Shay, that spark she loved so much filling his eyes. "I had a lot of help."

Shay stood still by Jason's side as the four older men took her measure. The council. These men had the power to alter her life. She should have been intimidated by their intense stares, but she wasn't. She clutched Jason's hand, took a deep breath and then told the men everything.

Including her marriage to Malcolm.

Luckily, it didn't matter. The marriage wasn't legal. It was performed under duress and the only witness was dead. Her grandfather, Robert, would file the papers immediately to legally annul the proceedings so no one could ever come forward and claim that she and Jason could not be married. "Nothing is standing in your way now. Nor, for that matter, is there any reason to rush a wedding. Take your time. Get to know each other. Make sure you are both certain you are ready for a lifetime commitment."

Her grandfather's words resonated within her, and as she looked at Jason, the same worry and trepidation she'd felt yesterday morning in her grandfather's house, after having learned about Maggie, came rushing back. He was right. There was nothing threatening them, no reason to rush. To not be absolutely certain. For the first time since Jason had fallen into that hole, she felt an overwhelming sense of sadness. She'd been so happy he was alive, she'd forgotten all her reservations about him, about *them*.

"Also, Shay, we think you might be the best candidate to lead the pack. At least temporarily. Consider it a sort of probation."

"What?" Shay asked, his words pulling her up from her dour thoughts. "But I don't know anything about your community. How could I possibly run it?"

"You will learn," Robert said. "You have your father's gift of being able to see people's true intentions. That will help you more than the day-to-day knowledge of life here in the village. You will learn that soon enough."

"Jason should lead the pack. He has the experience. He has the trust of the people. But more than that, he cares deeply about this pack. If this pack is going to heal and be successful, you need Jason at the helm."

"Jason put Malcolm in charge to begin with. His

judgment is suspect," Robert said, his lips thinning into a hard line.

"Perhaps, but you said I have the gift of being able to see people's true intentions, and what I see is a pack that needs healing. You have your own issues with Jason, Robert, but they don't have anything to do with his commitment to the people here."

"You're damn right I do," he said, his cheeks reddening. "My daughter is dead because of him. I will not allow this pack to be placed in his inept hands."

"Well, once Jason is my husband, I don't believe you'll have much choice."

Sputtering with indignation, her grandfather turned and walked out of the room. Part of her wanted to follow him, to make things right. He was her family, her *only* family. But if Jason was going to be her husband, she needed him to respect that. Although a part of her was afraid her grandfather never would.

An awkward silence filled the small space after her grandfather left. Shay wanted to say something, anything, to try to make it right. But what?

"Is that your intention? Are you going to marry?" one of the council members asked.

Shay turned to Jason and saw the doubt there, lingering. She pushed out a deep breath, but before she could answer, she heard Manny coming down the hall.

"Not only does our girl Shay have the gift of sight," Manuel said, squeezing into the small room behind them, "she also has a gift with the crystals. With proper training she will be a great healer."

"Can she rejuvenate the boundary stones?" One of the council members stepped forward to ask.

"That is yet to be seen." Manuel took a silk cloth and used it to pick up a large black oblong crystal off a shelf, and held it out to her. "Place your hand over the crystal and tell me what you feel."

As everyone watched with expectant eyes, Shay took a deep breath and reluctantly touched the crystal. The same uncomfortable sensation she'd felt with the bracelet hit her, a prickling feeling that burned her palm. She snatched her hand away.

"I'm sorry, but it's very uncomfortable."

Manuel shook his head with regret. "It's all right. This crystal is formed from dark energy. Very few of us who are gifted with being able to manipulate the stones to heal can tolerate their touch." He turned to the council members. "No. She won't be able help us."

"Celia is gone," the council member said, shaking his head. "There is no one else in The Colony who can rejuvenate them."

"Malcolm has gone after her," Jason told them.

Surprise filled all their faces. "After everything that has happened, you want us to put our faith in Malcolm?" one of them demanded.

"Do we have any choice?"

"Yes, we'll send someone of our own after Celia. We can't depend on Malcolm to do what's best for the pack any longer. For all we know, he's left so he doesn't have to face his judgment for all the damage he's caused."

Jason nodded with understanding. "Perhaps. How much time do we have?"

"Fourteen days at the most."

"Fourteen days until what?" Shay asked.

"Until the *Gauliacho* breech the perimeter," Jason said, squeezing her hand, but it didn't help relieve the absolute certainty that once more her world was about to fall apart.

"I'll go after him," Jason said quietly. "I'll make sure he brings her back."

Astonished, Shay turned to him. He was going to leave her again? "But you can't," she muttered, her voice barely louder than a whisper.

"I'm the best one. Not only am I the most familiar with the outside, but I know how Malcolm thinks. We don't have time for mistakes or mishaps."

Shay heard his words, but they didn't matter. They weren't true. He wasn't leaving to save the pack. He was running away from her. Because her grandfather was right, his duty to her was over. He was no longer obligated to her to keep her safe. And that was what was driving him, what had always driven him, and without it, he didn't know what to do. Didn't know what he wanted. Certainly not to marry her. And as the truth sunk in with ice-crystal clarity, her heart shattered.

"Am I up to it, Manny?" Jason asked the healer.

Manny looked at him thoughtfully, rubbing his chin. Then he just nodded. "I see this is something you have to do. But keep it simple. Don't overdo it."

Not trusting herself to speak, and unable to stay a moment longer, Shay turned and walked out of the room.

Chapter 20

Jason watched her go. He was an idiot. He knew that. But he had to save the pack. With Manny's help, he got out of bed. "I don't have a vehicle," he rasped as his stitches pulled in his thigh.

"Take mine." Manny dug a set of keys out of his pocket.

"I'll leave it by the gate where I left my truck."

Manny nodded grimly. "I won't try to stop you. But I will tell you you're pushing it."

"Thanks. I'll be careful." Jason walked toward the door as doubt pulled at him, twisting and turning. By the time he climbed into Manny's small four-door, he was out of breath and sapped of energy. What was he doing? He didn't have an answer. He just drove forward down the road as fast as he dared, heading south. With any luck, Malcolm's head start wasn't as big as he feared and he'd catch up to him sooner rather than later. An hour later, driving faster than was wise, he rounded a bend and saw Malcolm in front of him. He flashed his lights, and soon Malcolm was pulling onto the side of the road.

"Jason, what are you doing here?" Malcolm asked, disbelief thick in his voice as Jason opened the passenger door and climbed in.

"I'm coming with you to bring back Celia."

"What help are you going to be? You can barely stand up. And look at you, you're the shade of goat's milk and let me tell you, it ain't a pretty sight."

"Thanks for your concern, especially considering how I got here, but I'm fine," Jason said drily.

"You'll only slow me down."

"I'll be healed by the time we find her. Now where are we headed?"

"*We're* not headed anywhere. I'm doing this alone. Celia is my responsibility. My mistake."

"You can't do it alone. And we can't take the chance. If you fail…"

"I won't fail. Go home to Shay."

"Shay is fine."

"Is she? Not if she's figured out why you're really here."

"She knows why."

"Then she knows you're still not over Maggie?" Malcolm's gaze locked onto Jason's.

"Maggie has nothing to do with this."

"That's why you're running away from the first woman you've loved in years. Sitting in my truck, slowing me down when you can barely stand, let alone fight a demon. You are no use to me and you know that."

"I'm not running away from anything."

"And yet here you are, willing to risk going beyond the gates when you can barely walk just so you don't have to face your true feelings about this woman."

"The pack is my responsibility. It's my fault you're in charge."

"Yes. Yes," Malcolm mocked. "It's all your fault. It must be great to be you. Get over yourself."

Jason closed his eyes. "I'm over Maggie. I have been for a long time. She…she was leaving me."

"I know," Malcolm said softly.

Jason wasn't expecting that.

"It's why I offered to go with her to find Dean."

Jason turned to him, wondering if Kate's allegations were true. "Because you wanted her for yourself?"

"Because I knew she would go without telling you. She was stubborn that way."

Jason sighed. "Yes, she was. She wanted time alone. Without me. It got her killed."

"Her choice. Not your baggage to carry."

"When I couldn't find her, I was sure she was still alive out there, that she'd found Dean and she just didn't want to come back to me."

"But she wasn't."

"She wasn't," he agreed.

"You need to go back, Jason. The truth is you are in love with Shay and it is scaring the shit out of you. Shay is not Maggie. You no longer need to live up to Maggie's or her parents' expectations. You no longer need to hide behind the 'shining armor' you're carrying. Admit it, it's gotten too heavy. Now you can go back and you and Shay can lead the pack together. The way it should be. You have a chance to make things right this time. Shay has given that to you. You'd be a fool not to take it. Stop running and hiding and go home."

"You think that's what I've been doing?"

"Guilt is an ugly motivator. But the truth is Shay wants to marry you. She doesn't have to. No one is forcing her. She wants to be with you."

"This has nothing to do with Maggie or Shay," Jason said, though his bravado was gone as Malcolm's words slammed into his gut with the force of a Louisville Slugger. "We have to find Celia."

"You're a coward," Malcolm said, his green eyes hardening. "Face it."

"Maggie died trying to get away from me."

"She died trying to find herself. It's time you let her go. You're on your own now, brother. Responsible only for yourself and all your dumbass decisions, and you damn well know it. Now if you don't mind?" Malcolm reached past him and pushed open the door.

Jason got out of the truck and stood there long after Malcolm had driven away.

Shay stormed through her dad's house, looking in closets, the pantry, searching for anything to do that would quell the nervous energy flooding through her system. If she stopped for even a minute, her thoughts would go back to Jason and the last time they were together right here, in this living room. On this floor.

When she'd been happy.

When she'd still believed they had a future together.

Now she knew better.

Disgusted, she left the room, the house, and went to the shed out back. Inside was an array of gardening tools hanging on the wall. She picked up a hatchet and a shovel, walked out of the shed and kept on walking. "Come on, Buddy," she called. She would find that pit, and she would fill it, even if it took her a week. If it hadn't been for that pit... She stopped herself midthought. The problem wasn't the pit. It was Jason. She'd told the council they were getting married, she'd told her grandfather that they were getting married despite Robert's feelings about it, and Jason had run. He would rather face down a demon than stay and say he wanted to marry her. She was an idiot.

She berated herself as she trudged through the bushes. It didn't take her long to find the spot. To see the blood. She tried not to look at it and instead set down the tools and started dragging branches and bushes, anything she could find that was already lying on the ground, and threw them into the pit, trying to get rid of it once and for all. It and all the horrible memories that came with it.

After a while, she had to walk farther and farther to find loose debris, until finally, with the pit half-full, she just picked up the shovel and started to dig. Digging until she was so exhausted she couldn't think about Jason or the way he'd left her. She collapsed next to a tree, tears filling her eyes as she wondered what she would say to him when he finally came back. *If* he came back. *If* she wanted him back.

Buddy whimpered and sat next to her, dropping his head in her lap. She stroked his soft fur and leaned her head back against the tree, closed her eyes and thought about absolutely nothing. She didn't know how long she sat like that—listening to the birds, feeling the cool breeze on her cheeks and smelling the heady scent of pine—when she heard the snap of a twig. And felt something…ominous; a pervasive dark energy that crept under her skin.

She opened her eyes and found Scott towering above her. A thick cloud of angry red surrounded him. Her heart dropped to her stomach and she choked on a deep watery gasp.

"What are you doing here?" she said, her voice sounding surprisingly strong.

"I've lost everything and everyone because of you," he said, his tone hard and sharp as the obsidian glittering in his eyes.

"No," she said, pushing to her feet, one hand stretched out against the tree for balance.

"You did this to me." He stepped toward her.

Buddy started barking and snapping at him.

"Call off your beast," he demanded.

Fear for her dog, for herself, closed in on her, focusing her senses, narrowing her vision so all she saw was him, all she heard was the heaviness in his step, the rasping of his breath. An acrid smell of anger rose off him. No, that wasn't quite right. Not anger. *Revenge.* It was all he thought about. All he wanted.

"What are you going to do?" she asked.

"What should have been done before you stepped

foot into the Colony. If Mitch hadn't missed." He grabbed her arms and yanked her off her feet as if she weighed nothing. Buddy went crazy, lunging at him, attacking his arms, and still he held on tighter. He was a rock. A monster.

In a quick, fluid movement, he thrust her toward the edge of the pit. She teetered backward, her feet hovering on the edge as she pinwheeled her arms. She looked behind her down at the debris below, still so far.... She couldn't stop herself. She was toppling...falling.

It was a hard landing. Branches broke beneath her, cushioning her fall and yet digging into her, bruising her at the same time. And then Buddy was flying into the pit. She rolled out of the way as, yelping, he fell next to her.

"Buddy," she whispered, and tried to gain her balance on the shifting dirt and branches. He lifted his head and whined. Thank goodness, he was fine. They both were. But then she heard movement above. She looked up and saw Scott standing above them on the edge of the pit holding a large boulder above his head.

"No, please!" she cried, lifting her arms to cover her head as she prepared for the blow.

Jason had just reached Dean's house when he heard Buddy barking. He knew Buddy's barks well enough by now to know that something was wrong. Panicking, he hurried as fast as his legs would take him through the woods. He knew as he'd stood out on that empty road that his life was no longer on the outside. His life was here. With Shay. If she'd still have him. He was ready to take the chance, to open himself up to her, to trust her with his future. So where was she?

He heard Buddy yelp. Dammit! Why had he left her alone? Because Malcolm was right—he was a yellow-bellied coward, through and through. Not anymore. As he ran he pulled off his shirt, his pants, his shoes and transformed just as he heard Shay scream.

As his true self, he flew through the forest, running down the path, and then he saw Scott standing above the pit, a rock in his hands high above his head.

Without warning, Jason jumped, knocking Scott backward to the ground. He jumped on top of the man, clamped his jaws around the soft skin of Scott's throat and ripped.

Chapter 21

"I love your home," Shay whispered as they watched the sun rise from a blanket on a small beach behind his house. The lake's water lapped the shore and a soft breeze fanned her cheek.

"I hope you'll consider it your home, too," Jason said, then leaned down and kissed her lips gently.

Her heart started beating faster and she knew there would be no holding back, no more trying to protect herself from him. She was wide-open and ready to give him all she had to give. No matter what it would cost her. "I was so afraid you were going to leave and never come back."

"I ran and I'm sorry. But I needed to do that. I needed to see that this is where I belong. With you is where I want to be. If you'll still have me, I'm not going anywhere. You have given me my life back, but more than that, you've given me the courage I needed to face my life again. To stop running and hiding."

Propping herself up on her elbow, she leaned her head on her hand and smiled down at him. "You mean no more going out of the gates."

"I'm staying right here and running The Colony with you."

She smiled. "I always thought I wanted a love like my parents had, one that would shape the foundation of my life where nothing else mattered, nothing but being with each other."

He pulled her down to him and kissed her deeply, making her momentarily forget her train of thought.

"We can have that. We will have that," he said.

"Yes, but now I know I want so much more than that. I want to be part of your life and your community. With my parents it was them against the world, but with us, we are part of *this* world. We can make a difference for so many people. It's a lot to take in."

"You are going to be a great pack leader."

She smiled. "Only because I am going to have a great teacher and partner." She kissed him tenderly on the lips, melting as his warm hands slipped under her shirt and started their clever caresses that stole her breath.

"What about your grandparents?"

"I hoped when I got here that I was finding my family."

"I'm sorry."

"You are my family now."

"They might come around one day."

"Kate will," Shay said confidently. "But I'm not so sure about Robert."

"He might once you ask him to walk you down the aisle."

Her heart warmed at the thought.

"Things are going to be a lot different around here," he murmured, kissing her again. "We're going to have to begin some serious training on how to fight the *Abatu,* security will have to be tripled."

"Hmm, but you are still recovering, so you're going to have to get used to giving orders instead of jumping in to do everything yourself." She pulled his hand back to her breast.

He smiled, renewing his efforts. "True. But with my own personal healer, I'm feeling better already. In fact, let me show you just how good I feel."

He rolled her under him, pinning her to the soft ground and kissing her until she couldn't think, couldn't argue, could only feel the desire heating her blood and making her squirm.

"I hope you're not going to stop there," she murmured when he finally let up.

"Not on your life."

He was nuzzling her neck, sending fire shooting through her when Buddy came running up and jumped on top of them, a loud whine coming from behind the pinecone that was lodged in his mouth.

"Buddy," Shay groaned, thinking the dog had to have the worst timing in the world.

Jason laughed. "Drop it, boy."

Buddy did. Jason picked up the pinecone and chucked it as far as he could into the woods.

"You realize you're only encouraging him. He's

going to come running back and want you to throw it again. Then what are you going to do?"

"Take you to my bed."

She laughed as he picked her up and carried her into his house. Her house. *Their house.*

Where she would never be alone again.

Epilogue

With the moon floating high in the sky, Shay and Jason ran into the night, circling the lake, following the perimeter of The Colony's boundaries. As they ran by houses nestled in the woods, Shay took a moment to listen, to get a sense of the people inside. People she would soon be responsible for. Before long, she lost herself in the magic of The Colony, a place where she could be free to embrace her new life. Joy overwhelmed her and for the first time ever, she felt completely happy.

There would be no more running from house to house, town to town, never knowing what she was running from. She no longer feared being alone or never having a family of her own. Jason had given her that. She chased after him, reveling in the freedom coursing through her veins, in the forest's scents so much more vibrant filling her wolf's nose, in the stretching and pulling of her muscles as she sped across the ground, her nails digging into the earth.

As they raced one another, straddling the edge between danger and safety, up the towering rock cliffs, past the crystals she could see glowing in the moonlight, an unsettling sensation washed over her, seeping into her bones, making her fur bristle and her tail fan.

She stopped on a large rock outcropping, peering over the edge into the night, her night vision taking in details her human eyes never could—the heat signatures of the small animals flitting through the woods and the larger ones of those that stalked them.

Jason stood on the rock next to her, staring off in the distance, his nose raised high in the air as he smelled the acrid metallic scent reaching them from far away. Shay whined softly, and pushed against him, feeling his warmth. And then she heard it, far off in the distance, the reason for her anxiety, the reason for the knots tying themselves into tight bundles in the pit of her stomach. The threat. The black shadow eclipsing her happiness. The insidious whispers floating on the night air.

Abomination.

Abomination.

Abomination.

* * * * *

Don't miss
SLEEPING WITH A WOLF,
in stores winter 2014!

Discover more romance at

www.millsandboon.co.uk

- ❤ WIN great prizes in our exclusive competitions
- ❤ BUY new titles before they hit the shops
- ❤ BROWSE new books and REVIEW your favourites
- ❤ SAVE on new books with the Mills & Boon® Bookclub™
- ❤ DISCOVER new authors

PLUS, to chat about your favourite reads, get the latest news and find special offers:

- 🛇 Find us on facebook.com/millsandboon
- 🐦 Follow us on twitter.com/millsandboonuk
- ❤ Sign up to our newsletter at millsandboon.co.uk

_WEB